Step Toward You

Liz Ashlee

Step Toward You
Copyright © 2018 Liz Ashlee
All rights reserved.

ISBN: (ebook): 978-1-945910-50-0
(print) 978-1-945910-84-5

Inkspell Publishing
5764 Woodbine Ave.
Pinckney, MI 48169

Edited By Rie Langdon
Cover art By Najla Qamber

DEDICATION

For my dad, who has always been my number one fan and supporter, even though he's never, *ever* allowed to read my writing.

LIZ ASHLEE

CHAPTER ONE

Silas

One: We admitted we were powerless over alcohol—that our lives had become unmanageable.

The alcohol is the first thing I smell. It always is. It's also the first thing I think about when I wake up, and the only thing on my mind for the rest of the day.

Beer is always my drink of choice when I'm alone, but when someone's near, it's always vodka. Clear, no smell, no one ever guesses it's on me. Tonight, though, I didn't go with either of those. I wanted whiskey. I wanted the burn of it as it rushed down my throat, infecting me. I wanted to forget yelling at my mom, how I'd called her something nasty and regrettable—and how it hadn't felt nasty at the time and I didn't regret it.

Two: Came to believe that a Power greater than ourselves could restore us to sanity.

The coppery taste in my mouth and the blood making it impossible to see are clear signs that this isn't just another morning after a binge. No, it's still night.

Three: Made a decision to turn our will and our lives over to the care of God as we understood Him.

1

A smattering of memories overtakes me. Drinking at the bar—the bartender cutting me off. Stumbling to the nearby liquor store and buying the bottle of whiskey from the wary-looking guy who probably considered calling the cops, but didn't. Then driving, then flying, then darkness. Now this.

Blood, alcohol, numbness, upside-down in the seat of my car.

Four: Made a searching and fearless moral inventory of ourselves.

There was another car.

Five: Admitted to God, to ourselves, and to another human being the exact nature of our wrongs.

I hit somebody.

Six: Were entirely ready to have God remove all these defects of character.

I hit somebody and I want another drink. I want to move, even though I know I'm bleeding, and I want to find the whiskey. I want to drown in it.

Seven: Humbly asked Him to remove our shortcomings.

Eight: Made a list of all persons we had harmed, and became willing to make amends to them all.

How many people were there in the car? *God, don't let them be dead.* What if there were kids? What if it was a family? What if it was old people? What if…

Nine: Made direct amends to such people wherever possible, except when to do so would injure them or others.

If I'm not dead, then they can't be dead. I should have died.

Ten: Continued to take personal inventory and when we were wrong, promptly admitted it.

I don't even know what I said to my mom, and it probably doesn't even matter because there's no way it outweighs all of the other shit I've done. I do remember telling my dad to fuck off, and giving him the finger, but he can take it. My mom—she can't, and she doesn't deserve to.

Eleven: Sought through prayer and meditation to improve our conscious contact with God as we understood Him, praying only for knowledge of His will for us and the power to carry that out.

If I hurt anyone, I want to die. I *hope* I die. It'll be the only way I'll stop drinking, because I don't have the strength to change.

Twelve: Having had a spiritual awakening as the result of these steps, we tried to carry this message to alcoholics, and to practice these principles in all our affairs.

Sirens, lights.

I'm not going to die.

Goddamn it.

***

Present Day

"What are you doin' sleeping out here?"

I jolt awake, ready for the fight I've learned to expect. One hand automatically braces to protect myself, the other one removes the knife from my pocket—a knife I never had the luxury of having before and would be arrested for having now. It's the most security I've had in two and a half years.

But I don't need to protect myself from my dad. No, he's not a threat—*I'm* a threat to *him*. So what's stopping me from turning the knife on myself? I wish I knew.

All of a sudden, one of the chains on my parents' porch swing breaks free and my ass crashes to the ground. The wooden seat cracks beneath me. Shit, I better not have any splinters in my ass. Even if I deserve them—which I do—there's not a soul out there who deserves the lowly job of removing them.

"Damn it," I grumble, kicking at the wood.

Dad holds out a hand to help me up, fear and worry in his eyes. Of the two, it's the worry I don't like.

I stare at his hand, the gesture so foreign that my head starts to spin. When was the last time someone tried to help me out? Everyone's been so devout in knocking me down, forcing me to stay, pushing me farther into the ground. No one's wanted to try to pull me back up. Not even Dad.

Between me and my younger brother, Brandon, it's always been clear he's the favorite. I'm just the screw-up son my dad has to claim because of blood. Since I was born, I've probably aged him by thirty years, most of which has happened over the last three years. The gray revolting against his brown hair, the bags beneath his eyes, the frown lines etched into his forehead—it's all from me.

I stand on my own, refusing his help, then pat the wood chips off my frayed, holey jeans. Dad drops his hand and I don't miss his disappointment. I can't even win for losing. The man should be glad I didn't take his hand. The less contact, the less likely I am to spread the poison I seem to carry.

"You don't like your room?" he asks.

I shrug. I like it fine. Or I used to like it fine. It's still the way it was when I was sent off. My mom kept it clean, but nothing's moved. Some sort of shrine for if I ever decided to come home—maybe it's her way of willing everything to return to normal. I want to be grateful for the comfortable mattress, the door that locks, the window that opens, the bathroom down the hall where I can go without being watched, but I can't. Walls are too confining.

"Well, you'd better tell your mom that," he says. He tilts his chin up at the house. It's an olive-colored two-story with a wraparound porch and a giant back yard, perfect for a perfect family that doesn't include me. We moved to Collette, a small, coastal town void of the tourist industry, when I was three. I'd like to say it's home, but it's never been home. The people here hate me just as much as I hate me.

"Your mom's making pancakes in there," he adds.

I run my hand through my hair. It's too long and

shaggy. I haven't had much time to cut it—or wash it, for that matter. I don't think I want to. It keeps people at a distance. "Not hungry."

"They're not for you," he tells me.

I raise an eyebrow. Then who the hell are they for?

He shakes his head. His disappointed look is really starting to piss me off. Wordlessly, he opens the door and motions for me to go in.

I glance down at the porch swing. I'll make sure I build a new one before I disappear, when my parole is up. It's the least she deserves.

"Don't worry about it," Dad says. He takes the opportunity to steal my knife away while I'm distracted, and I doubt I'll ever get it back. "It's old, anyway."

Instead of answering, I head on inside.

Pictures line the walls, capturing memories that are lost to me. In most of them, I see another man growing up. Looking at them is confusing, like looking through a kaleidoscope and not knowing what I'm looking at. It's the same for everything else in this house. The couch, the fridge, the damn silverware—I can't get my head wrapped around any of it.

My mom's humming to herself and flipping pancakes. There's more batter and a bowl of blueberries dusted with sugar on the counter beside her. This sight is one from a kaleidoscope, too—a look back at every Sunday morning before I was sent off. Except now I'm out, I'm here, and it's a *Tuesday*. I hate all the changes and I hate everything that *hasn't* changed.

I just hate life, end of story.

"Your swing's out of commission, Karen."

"What?" Mom spins around, her eyes wide. Once her gaze settles on me, her eyes close and she lets out a breath. "There you are. Where were you last night?"

"I needed some air. Slept outside," I mumble.

She nods as if my answer makes all the sense in the world. She smiles brightly at me, but it doesn't fool me in the least. Since I've come back, she's been worrying and over-calculating everything. "I'm glad you didn't wander off too far, then."

I don't have a response, so I clench my jaw and look down at my bare feet. This isn't how my life is supposed to be. Sure, I was living in a crappy motel, then eventually on the streets, until my parents saw me working construction on the side of the road and practically forced me to stay here, but at least I wasn't bothering anyone. I was just a random guy no one paid attention to or cared about. Then my parents came along and whisked me away. They see it as some sort of bridge toward fixing our relationship, and fixing me. They don't understand how the hurt will be worse if I stay.

"Do you have any plans for this morning?" she asks, changing the subject.

I look at her sideways. Do I have any plans? Is she serious right now? *Sure, Ma, I'm going to go to the corner market and shoot the breeze with the guys.*

"I don't think he does," Dad says, sounding overly calm in his gotta-keep-shit-from-hitting-the-fan voice. I've come to know this tone well. He steps around me and gets down a coffee mug and a travel mug from a cabinet.

"Right," Mom agrees. She plops a pancake on a plate, then another. "Well, Silas, I was hoping you'd do me a favor. Your father has to get to work and I have to get to the bookstore early to open. Do you think you could take this over to the neighbors?"

Yeah, the neighbors really want to open up their door to find my ugly mug staring back at them. They've probably have seen my *real* mug shot in the newspapers. Everyone wants to start their day with a criminal knocking on their door. Sure, right.

I'm about to say no, but Mom looks up the ceiling and lets out a soft, anxiety-filled breath. "I'd really appreciate it."

"Sure," I say.

At least I'll be knocking on their door as a criminal who can't say no to his mom.

***

Knock on door. Don't make eye contact. Hand over plate. Leave immediately.

My fist has barely hit the door of the yellow ranch house when my gaze is drawn to my disfigured knuckles. I suck in a deep breath. I don't belong in this neighborhood, not with a fighter's hands. I've seen myself, I know what I look like—the mangy, homeless man who wandered in off the streets, which is basically exactly what I am.

Last I remember, there was an elderly lady who lived here. She claimed I was "terrorizing her". Okay, so I was. She was a straight-up bitch who used to always call the cops if my parents had a party for a special occasion and she liked to threaten to shoot our dog. I always figured running my bike through her yard or throwing eggs at her house was payback. Once, I even broke into her shed and fucked a girl there.

Shit, I had a destiny to be a jackass from the beginning. No wonder I turned out the way I am.

No one answers the door and I sigh. Thank the fucking lord. There's no way in hell I'm going to deal with that old bat without getting sent back to jail. I set the plate of pancakes on the table beside the door and start to turn away. Pancakes delivered, job done.

My foot hits the second step as the door swings open. Great, now my task list is thrown off. Door's been knocked on, plate's been delivered. I *am* in the middle of leaving. But what was the third thing?

I turn around and immediately remember: don't make eye contact.

Too late.

Staring back at me is a set of blue eyes that have to match the color of the ice inside my soul. I've never seen ones so bright or as beautiful—ones that make me want to sail away in them. They're kind, too.

Over the past few years I've seen some eyes holding so much rage and regret and resentment that they're black, no matter what their color is. The first time I saw myself in the mirror when I got out of jail, I saw it in my own, and I've seen it ever since, except the rage, regret, and resentment is morphing into nothing. Just hardened emptiness.

These sweet, pretty eyes are tear-filled, though, and for the first time since I got back, I want to fight something other than myself. I want to fight for the sweet spirit I know has to hide behind those eyes.

"Hello?"

They belong to a girl who barely makes it to my shoulders. Something about her makes my chest tighten. Normally, I go for the tall ones—where their legs go on for miles and you barely have to glance down to see their ass sway. But there's something delicate about this one that reminds of a bird who needs a nest for protection. Her long, black hair is falling over her shoulder, tied in a ponytail, and she's wearing a T-shirt that could swallow her whole, with equally huge sweats on. One pant leg is cut at the knee.

I narrow my eyes, an intentionally hostile maneuver. This girl's left me dumbstruck, which pisses me off. Scares me, too. I don't need a chick in my life who will expect more than a night's worth of my time. I don't need one who's gonna want to change me or fix me or do whatever the fuck it is girls like to do when they see a "bad boy". I can't be changed, and I'm a hell of a lot worse than a fucking *bad boy*. The devil's got his teeth sunk in me.

She does something I don't expect. She narrows her eyes right back. But on a nice face like hers, I doubt this is a side most see. This is a spark that rarely gets ignited. I'll bet the only reason for it now is the exhaustion causing her eyelids to droop and her face to turn the color of a beach's dried sand.

Someone lets out a broken scream instead the house. Panic and terror seize her expression and then she's running, leaving me standing on the porch steps like an idiot.

Should I investigate the scream or to pretend I was never here? The first option will shatter every step I've taken to protect people from me, while the second…yeah, definitely not the one my mom will be proud of.

I let out a disgruntled sigh and chase after her. Even though the house is yellow, it's in no way cheery. Outside, the grass is too tall and the plants are dead, or close to it. The inside is no better: it's dark, gloomy, and empty. Too much like my jail cell.

I follow hushed words and pain-filled cries until I'm at the end of a hall, where I can hear more clearly.

"—told you to wait," the girl says.

"I thought I could make it," answers a woman's fatigued voice.

I step into the bathroom and find the girl leaning over a frail woman who's so thin that the indentations of her bones are visible. She has the same eyes as the girl, who I'm guessing is her daughter, but this woman's beauty is lost. Instead, she is skeletal and ghostly.

She's curled up on the floor, blood dripping from her elbows. The daughter is struggling to help her up, but the woman isn't doing much to make it easier. I'm not sure she can. Not with a body that looks like it's about to snap in half.

"Here," I grumble and step past the daughter. "Let me help."

The girl doesn't argue, but looks at me like I'm some sort of hero. How did we go from glaring at each other to this? I can barely handle taking care of myself, let alone another person. I don't have the capacity to care anymore. I'm the opposite of a hero.

I take the mother in my arms and cradle her against my

chest. She weakly holds out her bleeding arm and if I had half the mind, I'd tell her not to bother. She smiles up at me warmly, not the least bit worried about how there's some strange guy holding her.

Her bones pop and crackle and I slacken my arms, trying to offer as much support as I can without crushing her. She sinks in to my body with a winded breath that squeaks free of her lungs. Her daughter's not the bird: she is, and her wings are broken, in need of mending. I was never the one scooping up baby birds and putting them back in their nests—that was Brandon. Before today, I couldn't have cared less about saving things. I've always been a Darwin type of guy.

"Where to?" I ask, my voice sounding like sandpaper.

The daughter points to the open door across the hall. I carry her mother into the room. It's on the small side, with shades drawn and the walls painted a deep maroon, making the place even darker. Nothing matches—the drapes are yellow, the bedspread is green, the lampshades are brown with white feathers. There's a stack of books on a nightstand beside the bed. On the other side of the bed, where another nightstand should be, is medical equipment.

I set her down on the bed and she sinks into the mattress, still holding up her arm. I just now notice she's wearing a pair of blue pajama pants with penguins all over them. The daughter's dressed for the day, but her mom's ready to spend the rest of the day in bed. I reckon her day begins and ends with bathroom breaks and food.

"You can set your arm down, Mama," the daughter says, rushing over to the dresser and grabbing a lunch bag. She sets it on the bed and unzips it, then pulls out some disinfectant, gauze, and tape.

"I don't want you to have to clean these sheets again," the mother tells her genuinely. "I'm such an inconvenience."

"No, you're not," the daughter says in a soft but firm voice. "It's okay. Now give me your arm so I can clean it.

It'll sting."

"Everything hurts now, sweetie. So much that nothing hurts." She lets her daughter take her arm.

The woman doesn't even flinch as her daughter dabs the antiseptic, then wraps the bandage around it. All the while, I stand in the doorway watching. I can't take my eyes off the scene. The pretty daughter with the eyes, which—if they had hands—could reach inside my heart and squeeze it. The woman who's so sick that I can't help wondering why someone like me is never the one in bed dying. What higher power gives me, a killer, the right to live, but sends a mother to her grave?

"Who are you, handsome?" the mother asks, a flirty air to her voice. Something about it makes me like her a little.

The daughter's hands still. "That's Silas, Mama."

Her mother's mouth opens and forms a little O. Only it's not the usual shock-and-fear face I get. This one's different. There's a hint of a smile there. Huh. Weird. It's also strange that this girl, who I'm pretty sure I've never met before, knows my name, even though I don't know hers.

"He was bringing over food from Mrs. Manning," she explains further.

The mother's grin grows. "Ah, I see. Always tryin' to fatten us up and now they're sending over their son so we can have dinner *and* a show."

The daughter's electric gaze flickers to meet mine and then away just as quickly. A blush creeps up her cheeks. "Mama."

"What? We both know you do enough, Rooney. Besides, you don't exactly know your way around the kitchen."

Rooney. It's a strange name, but it fits her. It almost fits her too well, if you ask me. I don't like the way just thinking the name makes my chest start to tighten.

"That's not what I was—" Rooney begins, but must have thought better of arguing. Instead, she smiles back, drawing my attention to full, strawberry-colored lips. "I get it from you, though. I remember a lot of toast that you covered in cinnamon to hide the burnt parts."

"And you always ate it with a smile, my sweet girl." She runs her thumb along Rooney's cheekbone and then tucks the girl's hair behind her ears. "You keep that with you."

Rooney's smile vanishes and she closes her eyes tightly. "I'm gonna walk Silas out," she says, and turns toward me. When she opens her eyes, the tears are back in them.

Shit.

"Thank you, Silas," her mom calls as we walk back out into the hallway. "Stop by again if you get the chance."

I follow Rooney out to the front porch. The entire time she stares at her feet, using the backs of her hands to swat at her tears. By the time we make it outside, I'm back to my usual state of pissed off. Why is Rooney her taking care of her mama all alone? Isn't there someone here to help her? She needs more than a neighbor bringing her food. She needs someone to do everything she can't, physically and mentally. I sure as hell can't be that for her, but there's got to be someone out there who can.

She faces me but her gaze won't meet mine, which I'm glad for. This way, I don't have to get caught up in her eyes again.

"I really appreciate what you did," she says in a soft, Southern lilt.

I don't respond "anytime" because I wouldn't mean it—I'm not about to making helping a habit. Especially since something feels like it was just stolen from me and I'm not sure what. I give her a stiff nod and grip the back of my neck until my jagged nails draw blood.

"Mama…she's sick…"

"Look," I say, tightly. I don't need to hear it. I don't *want* to. This girl has a power over me, which is something I haven't allowed before. All because of those tears. Her eyes. That face. It's freaking me the fuck out and I can't deal with it. "Mom just asked me to drop off food."

Her back straightens and those blue eyes turn fiery as she sets her gaze on me. "All right. I understand. I'm sorry we inconvenienced you. Have a nice day."

I stare after her as she storms back inside. Another bridge burned. Good. One less I have to traverse.

Suddenly she turns around, her hand gripping the door. "You know what, I've heard stories about you—where you've been. But I wasn't going to judge you because people make mistakes. That's somethin' my mama's instilled in me since the beginning. Except you…" More tears fall, but this time she doesn't wipe them away. She lets crash to the floor. "You just proved that some people don't understand how to *not* make mistakes."

I stand there, staring at the door long after she's slammed it. I'm surprised and in awe of this girl for not taking my shit. But it's not enough to keep me from feeling relieved. At least someone sees I'm no good.

CHAPTER TWO

Rooney

I pace the kitchen, muttering to myself as I try to talk myself down after meeting Silas. I can't go back in to Mama this way. If I'm worked up, she'll be, too.

Besides, she'd probably use how much Silas affected me as a lead-in for one of her lessons in second chances. Because she was loose in her day and doesn't know who my father is, Mama believes that everyone has it in them to pull their life together. I disagree; I don't think Silas will. Maybe he did something kind, but that doesn't mean he's a kind person.

I stop and stand tall. I won't let Silas ruin my remaining time with Mama. As it is, the doctors say I may only have two months at most left with her. I plan to make those two months memorable, all the time praying for more, but expecting less. The adult part of me can see she's in pain and how when she does eventually leave me, she'll be released of it. The other part is selfish and childish, because I know when she's gone, I'll never see her again. I'll have to live the rest of my life without my mama—my best friend—there with me.

My tears turn from angry to sad. All I've been doing for the past few months is crying. You'd think I would have run out of tears by now, or come to terms with things, but I haven't. I'm still in the same place I was when I first found out, and I don't see it changing.

I just have to keep reminding myself she's still here. Weaker, maybe, but at least she still has her spirit about her. Silas might have ruined my day, but it was worth getting to watch her smile at him. Whereas I've always been the quiet, loner type, Mama's always been wildly outgoing. Having someone other than me to talk to has to have made her happy.

I remember the pancakes and head back to the front door. I peek through the peephole to make sure Silas' gone. He is. The pancakes are still where he left them. A good thing, because I'm pretty sure I'd cut off my own leg to get some of Mrs. Manning's pancakes. They're delicious. I step outside and grab them.

She's been making us meals since Mama became bed-bound. I've never been more grateful for anything in my life, because Mama was telling the truth. I can't cook. The only thing I can really make is cereal, which isn't enough to keep her healthy. Even if I wasn't dating Brandon, Mrs. Manning would still have done this to help us out.

"Are you feeling up to eating, Mama?" I call out as I peel the plastic wrap from the paper plate.

"No, sweetie," she calls back in a faint voice. She starts coughing and my heart begins to break. *It's only her usual cough.* "Maybe some milk?"

"Okay," I say.

I fix myself up a plate of pancakes and put the rest in the fridge. Maybe she'll eat later. I pour us both a glass of milk and head to Mama's room. She's lying in bed, staring blankly at the ceiling.

Lately I've caught her doing this a lot, seeing something I can't seem to see. I wonder if she's thinking about what's to come. I want to ask her if she's scared, maybe even if she's ready, but I'm afraid to. We both know she's not going to get better, but talking about it...talking about it is the most difficult battle I've ever faced.

She sits up to take the glass, which is enough to make her wince. I sit down on the bed next to her and lean back against the headboard. I cross my legs and set the milk in the hole between my thighs, and the plate over top. I take a bite and smile around the mouthful. "These pancakes are the Holy Grail of pancakes."

"I'll make sure to eat some later, then," she laughs. She takes another drink and then lies back again. I cringe at the sound of her spine popping. I really need to get to the store and buy some of those vitamins the doctor was talking about last visit. I figure I'll go when while the home health nurse is here tomorrow.

Mama closes her eyes and lets out a breath through her nose. When she opens her eyes again, they're clear of whatever pain that horrible popping noise put her through.

"So," she begins and I know she's about to bring up our visitor. "That was the infamous Silas Manning?"

I nod. *Infamous* is right. Not to mention the town's most hated. Whatever happened with Silas occurred before we moved here. Brandon won't talk about it and I've never had the nerve to ask. All I know is there was an accident and people died and Silas was sent to jail. I'm not sure how much evidence there needed to be as to why I shouldn't have someone like Silas in my life right now. Or ever.

"Well, don't write him off too soon, sweets," Mama tells me. "Did you notice how attractive he was?"

I did. Which was something I really, really didn't like. Looking at him made my stomach do funny things and my cheeks heat up. There was something absolutely beautiful about him, but that beauty was hardened by his stiff, unapproachable demeanor. His eyes were a deep, rich caramel color, but they were also emotionless. His jawline was perfect in every way, crafted like a thing of the gods. There was a small dimple in his chin, which is something I usually find a little creepy, but after seeing it on his face, I have to say I've changed my mind. He also had blondish-brown hair falling in waves to his shoulders and I couldn't help wondering if it would feel as soft as it looked.

The worst part was how, before he showed his true colors, I was checking out his body as he carried Mama. He was tall, not that I have a really good description of tall in my vocabulary considering *everything* to me is tall. Not an ounce of him was fat, either. He was complete muscle, from his rippling arms to his backside. Lord, even his butt was perfect.

Oh no, not good.

"Mama, I'm dating Brandon."

"I don't see how that plays into this conversation," she says.

I sputter out a few syllables which don't make sense. "He's his brother."

"Yes, but that doesn't mean you can't take a peek at Silas. And we both know Brandon is a bit of a bore."

"Brandon's fine." I like Brandon exactly because he's a bore, not that I'd admit it to Mama.. In my chaotic life, I crave stability and Brandon fulfills that need. He's sweet, kind, and wonderful.

Mama waves a tired hand at me. "All right, I get it. No talking about the boyfriend's hot older brother. That one seemed a bit too...*off* for you, anyway."

I can tell she needs a nap if she's giving up on me this easy. "You want to go to sleep, Mama?"

She nods her head. "If you don't mind. Lie with me for a bit?"

I set my plate and drink aside, hers too, and then snuggle down into the bed with her. I lie facing her, while she remains on her back. Eventually her breathing begins to even and I curl closer to her. "I love you," I whisper.

When she falls asleep, I'm terrified she won't wake up and every time she wakes up, I'm terrified she'll have to spend another day like this.

***

I settle down into my bed for the night and set the baby monitor on the mattress beside me. Mama doesn't know I bought these—she'd probably freak if she knew, say how I spend too much of my time worrying about her. But this is the only way I can sleep. Without it, I'm usually up half the night, straining my ears to hear all the small sounds she makes. Her wheezing breaths, the words she mumbles in her sleep. It's also wakes me up when she calls out my name or when she's crying out in pain.

My phone rings and I automatically know it's Brandon, which is something else to like about him: he's punctual. Every night he calls me at nine on the dot. He's away at college right now, taking summer classes so he can co-op in the fall. I miss him a lot. Having him to talk to at night makes me feel like I have something normal to grasp. No matter how bad the day is, at least I have his calls to look forward to.

"Hey," I say, snuggling deeper into my covers.

"Hey," he says back and I can hear the smile in his voice. Brandon always just been a smiley guy. Even when I told him about Mama, he had a sympathetic smile on his face. "I miss you."

"I miss you, too."

"How are things?"

"The same," I murmur, closing my eyes. I always hold back my tears because I want these phone calls to be happy. "How're you?"

I decide not tell him about Silas. I'm afraid it might ruin the conversation. I'm not sure what I'd really have to say about Silas if we did talk about him. *Your hot brother is a jerk who doesn't care about my dying mother.*

"Good," Brandon answers. "Bored. I don't know why I didn't choose to take these damn classes online. Then I could be home with you. Bad enough I'm gone for the fall semester, too."

I agree wholeheartedly. We've only been dating for a little over a year, since Brandon came home for spring break after we'd just moved in next door. I was a senior in high school then and he was a freshman in college.

"But you'll be back here soon," I remind him. "Mid-summer break, remember?"

He chuckles. "And after-summer, nearly-fall break, too. At least we have something to look forward to—something good, you know."

"I can't wait."

"I can't, either. I'm sorry, but someone from class is sending me a video chat invitation. Somehow I've become the unofficial tutor."

"Lucky you, molding minds and all," I joke, but it comes across as false.

"I hate having get off here, but guilt will get the best of me if I don't answer."

"Okay. Same time tomorrow?"

"Same time tomorrow," he repeats. "Love you."

"Love you, too. Bye."

"Bye."

The phone clicks off and a sense of loss overtakes me. I try to stifle it down because it's wrong to feel like you've lost someone when they're still alive and breathing—you're taking them for granted. I reach over and click the baby monitor off and then I head back to Mom's bedroom. I slip back into the spot beside her.

The truth is, the only thing I really look forward to is having another day with Mama.

CHAPTER THREE

Silas

"You going out for a run?" Dad asks me.

I glance up at him as I lace my *running* shoes. No shit, Dad, I'm going fishing. I ignore him and continue tying up my laces, then I stand and start untangling some ear buds. This is Brandon's iPod, so hopefully his music's good. Mine was dead after all these years.

"Don't you have an AA meeting tonight?"

I grit my teeth because it's not his business. At twenty-three, I'm perfectly capable of dealing with my own shit. I can take care of myself behind bars and on the streets, so I can handle myself here. "Tomorrow."

He nods, backing away, obviously sensing my hostility. "Just wonderin'. I've got my NA meeting so I thought we could drive together, but if you're going tomorrow..."

He trails off and I just stare at him. We're not going to be addict buddies. I'm not going to go with him to the rehab center so he can attend his Narcotics Anonymous meetings while I attend my Alcoholics Anonymous meetings. I'm not in the mood for that bonding shit. At least his addiction didn't end in death.

"Have a good run," he says and goes into the kitchen. He's a teacher, so doesn't work during the summer. Yesterday must've been his last day.

I head outside, turn on the playlist I made, and start down our road, past my neighbors' house and away from town.

Even when I didn't have place to stay, I still made sure to get in my daily run. It's not until my lungs start to burn, my head starts to lighten, and my legs turn to mush that I finally reach a point where I feel like I'm alive. Pain makes me feel whole. What sort of a sick shit am I? The only time I feel good about myself is when I feel like I can't go on any farther—a personal punishment for robbing people of their lives.

I don't pay attention to where my legs are taking me. The music pounds in ears, turned up so loud that a passerby could make out the words to the songs. My footsteps form a cadence with the rhythm as my heart starts to beat double-time.

Finally, I can't go any farther and I come to a halt. I lurch forward, hands on my knees, and I feel like I'm about to throw up. I gasp for air and as I jerk up in the motion, I freeze.

There are crosses on the bend in front of me. Each is painted white, with flowers on the ground below them, as well as all sorts of other things. A bicycle figurine, a stuffed frog, a pair of worn sneakers with hand-drawn pictures on them. Picture frames.

Shit. Shit. Shit. Fuck.

I start pacing, my finger nails digging into my skull. Holy hell. How did I wind up here? Why? I can't do this. I can't be here. I can't…

I throw up.

Everything pours out of me and I wish all my memories and thoughts and my whole self would pour out, right along with it. I want to disappear. Why the hell did someone think putting me on this earth was an okay idea? I shouldn't even be alive. There's no point in creating lives if they're just gonna be taken. It's the same for the life who does the taking. Cut out the middleman. Do your own bidding.

A car's tires squeal by and I jump back, memories of that godawful night flashing through my brain. What little memories I have. There's more blank holes than anything. Squealing tires, screaming, flashing lights, death. Then, nothing, before I was put behind bars.

"Die, motherfucker!" someone screams as the car passes.

My nostrils flare and I grab blindly for something to throw. I come up with a rock and I hurl it at the car's back window. "I wish I fucking could!" I scream back. And then I'm falling to my knees, crying for the first time since I was a kid.

I did this. This is all on me. These crosses...they're my fault.

I need a drink.

CHAPTER FOUR

Rooney

Sometimes, I hate going home. Knowing what is waiting for me there nearly paralyzes me. Home means facing all of the things I'll lose along with Mama—the shoulder I cry on, the person I banter with, the mama I still let hold me.

In some ways, I've already lost most of that.

I can't bring myself to talk to her about the important stuff anymore. I can talk to her about Brandon or about crappy traffic or about the weather, but I can't talk to her about my fears and her health and what comes *after*. God, I don't even know what sort of funeral she wants, or where she wants to be buried. *If* she wants to buried. I'm in this eternal nightmare of conversations I can't seem to have, and don't want to have.

I drive to a small grocery store in the next town over, just to get farther away from home. Saving as much money as I can is top priority and Mama's medicine is cheapest here.

I left after I gave Rita, the home-health nurse, my weekly update about Mama. While I'm gone, she bathes

Mama, does a general health assessment, offers Mama all sorts of services we can't afford, works with her on physical and occupational therapy skills, which she isn't able to use, and gives her a few tips about keeping up a healthier lifestyle.

If only those tips had been there before the cancer infiltrated Mama's body.

I slide out of the junky car and stuff my keys into my purse, then grab a cart from one of the returns and set my purse in it. The grocery store is small, but its collection is eclectic, with a pretty good selection.

I pull out my list and begin making my way through the store. I spend special time in the vitamin aisle, picking out every single one the doctor and Rita recommended. I'll stuff as many pills down Mama's throat as I need to, to make sure her final days are comfortable. I also pick up a few easy-to-make food items, silently thanking Mrs. Manning once again for being so kind and making us meals. There's no way I'd have the time—even if I could cook—to make us food.

After I finish getting everything I need, I double-check my list, then I crumple it up. I decide to reward myself with a visit to a section of the store with homegrown goodies I like to peruse but can't afford.

When I turn down the aisle, my blood immediately turns cold.

Silas.

What are the chances I'd come across him in a store outside of Collette, that no one else happens to be in, just a day after I first meet him? Evidently, one-hundred percent.

His teeth are gritted and he's staring through the refrigerator doors at the beer. His neck and shoulders are tense, the prominent vein just below his jaw ticking away. His fists are clenched at his sides and I'm not sure if he's about to attack the beer, or take it. His shirt is drenched in sweat and sweat beadlets are dripping down his temple.

His long hair is pulled back into a bun, showing off ears, which are surprisingly pointy. There's a pretty hefty scar heading from the just below his ear and down his neck.

I'm gawking. I know I am. Even if he was mean yesterday, there's something about him I can't look away from. Probably the disastrous beauty he possesses.

I start to back up, but my cart gives me away by squeaking loudly.

Silas jumps and his body tenses *even more* as his glare finds me. All the blood is drained from his face as he watches me with anger. But it's mixed with something else. Embarrassment?

His nostrils flare and he spins and walks in the opposite direction of me.

My own anger begins to spark as I stare at the spot where he was just standing. If anyone deserves to be mad, it's me. Not him. So why aren't I? Why am I standing here, staring the spot where he just was, wondering what's going on in that beautiful, disastrous head of his?

***

I make it home before Rita leaves, and she spends the last ten minutes talking to me. She goes over everything new, making sure I understand it all. Then, in a grave voice, she tells me something I can't wrap my mind around.

"So she's only got a month?" I repeat.

Rita nods her head. When she realized it was just me and Mama, she began treating me with a lot of care. Whenever we sit down for these talks, she always holds my hands and looks like she's fighting back tears of her own. Maybe she goes home to a nice, clean life, but every day she has to deal with other peoples' messy, broken ones. I don't know how she does it.

"I thought we had…I thought…" I choke off into a sob. I tear a hand from Rita's and clamp it over my mouth.

"I know," Rita says sympathetically. "There's never enough time with the people we love."

I look around the house. It looks exactly as I feel: dusty, dark, with random crap lying everywhere and anywhere. I haven't been able to keep up with cleaning over the last few months, so I've let it go to waste. Mama's never been one for order, but she'd hate to see this now. I'll have to clean it soon. At least then, her dream will be restored...

"Rooney," Rita commands softly, forcing me to look back at her. "You still have time. She's a fighter and she's fighting. We put time limits on bodies, not on spirits. You might have less or you might have more. Nothing's changed. You just need to keep doing what you're doing."

"Thank you," I whisper.

Rita pulls me into a hug. We sit like that for a while as I continue to sob.

Eventually my tears dry up and I'm able to pull myself together. I thank her again and walk her out. She gives me one final hug and heads out to her car, back to whatever life she has outside of her purple scrubs. Maybe I'll have to send her a card, to show her my appreciation. I'll bet she holds people all day long, but in the end there's no one to hug and tell her it'll be all right.

I quietly make my way down the hall to Mama's bedroom. She's always exhausted, but even more so after Rita's visits. I expect her to be asleep, but she's staring up at the ceiling again, only this time there are tears in her eyes. My own eyes get watery and I suddenly feel like a little girl, wanting to run into her room during a thunderstorm. I want her to hold me and tell me it'll all be all right.

But she can't hold me, and she can't tell me it'll be all right.

"Oh, hey, honey," she says, trying to compose herself. When she sees I'm crying too, she shakes her head, her chin quivering as her face contorts with another wave of sobs. She brings a shaking hand up, but clearly the movement is too much for her. Her hand instantly drops back down to where it was. "Come here."

I do as she says and take the spot I slept in last night. I can't find the words to speak. They're stuck in some deep recess, which I'm afraid to try to find, for fear it'll break open and my heart will fall out, all mangled and bruised.

"I'm not ready." She closes her eyes tightly. "I'm not ready to leave you yet, so I'm not going to. You're stuck with me until I can't take it any longer, okay?"

"Okay," I murmur.

She opens her eyes, and gone are her prior emotions. A small smile plays on her dried lips. "I'm surprised they're even ready for me up there. Don't they need more preparation than this for a hell raiser like me?"

I can't hold back a giggle.

CHAPTER FIVE

Silas

I clench my sobriety chip in my hand as I take a seat at the back of the room in the rehab center. Yesterday, I almost lost the battle. If Rooney hadn't miraculously appeared at the same grocery store, there would've been nothing to stop me.

The first time I took a drink I was thirteen, and from then on, alcohol just felt necessary to my living. I liked the taste of it, the way it made me feel, how when I drank, I felt lighter.

I wasn't even a mean drunk. I've always been the stoic one, the one more likely to brood in the background than crack a smile, but when I drank, I wasn't that way. I suddenly got a sense of humor about me. I was the life of the party.

That only stayed cool until I was eighteen—when I started taking chances when I fucked chicks, drinking anything and everything in my sight, even if it was eight in the morning, and pissing off everyone who cared about me. Then, when I was twenty... I reached my breaking point.

The crash is the sin I'm supposed to hand over to God while I'm at these meetings. I'm supposed to atone for what I've done and start owning up to my mistakes, all while promising never to take a drink again.

I couldn't rein myself in yesterday and it drives me fucking nuts—it took some girl I don't even care about to realize what I wanted—*needed*—to do was fucking wrong. I should have been able to pull myself together on my own. What's the point of being out of jail and having this stupid chip, if I can't do that?

I've been coming to these meetings since I was released, per my probation orders. I used to have to attend meetings like these when I was in prison, and everyone's basically in the same place at those. At these meetings, everyone's at a different stage in their alcoholism. Some of them have realized the path they were taking and have managed to get off real quick. Others, like me, didn't.

An elderly man takes the seat next to me, even though there are at least ten empty chairs. I clench my jaw and move a seat over. Like hell I'm sitting with him. I recognize this guy—he's basically the alcoholic right-hand man to our group leader, Jordania. He's her AA class favorite, who makes a point to meet everyone and strike a bond with them over life's shitstorm. I guess it's my turn, but he's gonna have to fight if he thinks I'm going to hold hands and sing "Kumbaya".

Jordania takes her spot at the podium. We begin the meetings as we normally do, with the reading of the Twelve Steps. After about a month's worth of meetings, I had them memorized. Even got them tattooed on my back for safekeeping.

Once Jordania is done reading the Steps, she gives a quick talk about finding your sobriety again if you lose it. As if it's something simple. But I'll give it to her—I needed to hear that speech tonight. We'll all continue to need it for the rest of our lives. Eventually, she opens the floor for us to talk.

She goes through about thirteen of us, two of whom refuse, one being me, before she lands on the old guy next to me. He stands up, his bones cracking, and takes the aisle to the podium. Looking at him, you can tell he's spent a lifetime drinking.

"Can I, uh, have a chair?" he asks Jordania.

She nods and grabs him one. He immediately plops down in it like he couldn't have stood a minute longer. He pulls the microphone down to his level and leans in, elbows on his knees. "Most of you know me, but the name's Bob, and I'm an alcoholic."

It happens just like in the movies, everyone says, "Hi, Bob." Only some are more enthusiastic about it than others.

Bob glances around the room, his gaze landing on each of us. "I'm sure you all can tell I'm not your average member. I'm seventy-two. Age don't stop the urge. It saddens me and makes me happy that some of youse are younger. Glad to see you're fixin' your lives now, rather than later. Took me until about ten years ago before I finally dried up and got myself in order. My daughter came to find me, showed me pictures of my grandkids, and told me if I changed my ways, I could be in their lives. She forgave me for everything I did, and I decided enough was enough—I got to changin' my life. Since then, I've gotten to know my daughter and my grandkids—one of my sons, too. But the other son, he can remember the man I used to be so he stays clear of me. Those kids—if I'd have realized sooner that loving them was worth fighting the addiction, then I might've been in their lives longer."

He clears his throat. "I was a good dad. Attended every school function, always told them I loved them, praised them when they needed it, knocked them down when they needed that, too. But then I'd get to drinkin', and that's when I'd become a nasty son-of-a-bitch. I used to get so drunk, so belligerent, I'd beat my wife. When my son was about seven, I started taking my hand to him, then my other son and my daughter. It was a sad cycle, and I made my children grow up too fast because of it. They didn't deserve my behavior—they didn't deserve the father I was giving them."

He breaks off, and I see tears start to form. The man's over seventy and he's probably told this story thousands of times, but here he is still getting choked up over it. I can understand it, though. When I'm his age, I'll probably be the same way, if not worse. Hopefully, I'll be dead by then.

"One night, I beat my baby girl so bad she had to go to the hospital. Of course, I went on to do the only thing I knew how to do: I went to the bar. Drank myself unconscious. The next day, when I finally stumbled home to apologize—to say I'd never hurt them again when I knew full well I would—my wife and kids were gone. That was the tipping point. Didn't see them again and I punished myself every day for letting them go, until my daughter tracked me down and pushed her way into my heart. That's my story."

His story ends just as fast as everyone else's does, traveling along the same path: we take a drink, we let the drink control us, we do something horrible while we're drunk, we drink some more until someday, we finally change—wanted or not.

He stumbles down the aisle and takes the seat he was in before. His shoulders are slouched and he's wiping at tears, and I only glower at him. He's who I'm going to be someday, only I won't have a family. Not even any friends. It'll just be me and no one to disappoint.

Jordania takes his spot at the mic and says, "That's all we have time for. If you would like to join in for a prayer, it'll be led by Greggory up here on the stage. Everyone else, feel free to grab coffee and cookies."

I stand up and stretch, ready to go home. First, I have to get her to sign a paper for my probation officer, saying I was here. I'm only allowed to miss four meetings, and I have to provide a valid excuse when I do, like I'm still in school or something.

Jordania smiles at me, already taking out her pen. "You gonna speak next week?"

"Sure," I answer.

She purses her lips. "Hmm, sure you will."

I only stare back at her blandly. If I don't want to talk, I won't. She can give me that fucking I-know-more-than-you-do look every week, but she doesn't know a damn thing.

"Silas."

Shit. Jordania's still got my paper and I can't leave without it, so Bob's taking the chance to become my new bestie. I turn and glare at him.

He comes to a stop beside me. "Should really invest in a cane. These hips," he grumbles.

Jordania smiles brightly at Bob. Not a happy comment, Jordania.

"Am I your next victim?" I ask Bob, point-blank.

Jordania makes a choking sound, but Bob works to contain a smile. Huh, interesting.

"I don't think victim is the right word, especially here," Bob counters. "But sure, you're my next victim. Figure the best thing I can do is try to help out my kind. There's a few things you can learn about wastin' your life away, kid—and not just on the drink."

"I don't need your help," I mutter.

He shrugs. "Maybe, maybe not. But I've already got your number, so we'll see about that."

I glare at Jordania. "You gave him my number? Ever heard of confidentiality?"

She smiles again. Stupid fucking fake smile.

"See you next week," Bob says.

Like hell he will. I don't need bonding or a friendship to make the alcoholic journey easier. It shouldn't be easy. I *want* to suffer through it.

***

By the time I make it home, I'm ready to claim my new spot in the hammock on the back porch, and sleep until there's no sleep left in me. I grew used to having the stars above me from my time out on the streets, so it's feeling safe to me that's new. It's also the part I hate, because I'll never be safe. No one ever is.

The walk from AA took about an hour, but it's better than riding in a car. I refuse to get into a car unless I have absolutely no other option.

I drop the cigarette I'm smoking to the ground and grind it into the sidewalk with my foot. Mom would freak if she knew I'd taken up smoking. At least I'm not addicted to *that*.

I stuff my pack and my lighter deeper into my pocket to hide it. Stupid fucking AA meetings, always stressing me out.

The first-floor lights are on in my house. I don't feel like dealing with them tonight. I haven't exactly been the chattiest or the friendliest, but I couldn't give a fuck. They're the ones who wanted me, and I'm giving them me. This way, when it comes time for me to leave, they'll realize they were better off without me.

I unlock the door and step inside. "Silas, is that you? Are you back?"

If it is me, then where the hell else would I be? I can't telepathically unlock the door from the rehab center. I don't answer her, but instead amble my way into the kitchen.

My steps falter. Rooney's sitting at the island. I hate how she affects me—I'm physically stumbling at the sight of her. But she's so damn pretty. Too damn good, too. Her back is straight, her hands gripping the counter. God, even a girl this good can see the evil in me. She sees the truth.

She stiffly turns around in her seat, aiming those baby blues at me. Even if they're filled with dislike and disgust, and maybe a bit of fear, her eyes are fucking gorgeous. The breath-stealing kind of gorgeous.

I let my gaze wander down from her eyes and it can't help but land on her tits. I'm not even looking at her to ogle her, to make her uncomfortable. I'm looking at her because her tits her are perfect. Just when I thought this girl couldn't be any more of a dream, she goes and wears a tight-ass tank top, which makes me realize she's some sort of creature sent down from heaven to torture me.

They're even the perfect size. A size that would fit perfectly in my hand—my mouth. Shit, I can imagine flicking my tongue across her nipples as she bites back moans. I wonder what color those nipples are? Holy hell, I'm getting hard just imagining it.

When was the last time I thought about giving a girl pleasure, rather than a girl giving *me* pleasure? I don't even know when I last kissed a girl, let alone met her needs. It's always been about the release: the fuck or the blow, and then I'm gone.

Mom clears her throat and my body snaps to attention. Shit. I trudge over to the refrigerator and grab a piece of pizza to heat up. I came in here to let Mom know I'm home, and pizza, that's a deviation—something for me to do while I collect myself.

I close my eyes tightly and try to calm my body down. Good tits should not turn me on this much. I need to get laid. Preferably by someone with even better tits, to wipe Rooney's from my mind. Are there tits more perfect than hers? I somehow doubt it.

As much as it kills me to admit it, this deviation isn't about anything other than staying near her.

"I'm packaging up some things for Rooney. Would you mind helping her carry it over to her house?" Mom asks me as she places muffins into a basket.

I grit my teeth. What the hell is it with my mother and feeding her? Why doesn't she just make them move in with us while she's at it?

"I can carry it," Rooney says quietly. "I'll be fine."

"It's a lot," Mom answers in a voice that implies she's not going to take no for an answer. From either of us. "He'll help you."

I glance back to see Mom staring at me with a question in her eyes. Rooney's gaze is fixed on the green marble of our countertops. Because they're so interesting. I snap my attention back to the pizza as I remove the plastic wrap and place it in the microwave. I start the timer.

The one good thing I'll admit about coming home is the food. Homeless shelters and handouts are nothing compared to a home-cooked meal, or takeout.

I hear Mom go back to fumbling with her muffins. "You said your mama likes these?" she asks.

"She loves them," Rooney answers, her voice wavering. "They're her favorite. They're about the only thing I can get her to eat anymore…" Her voice trails off as her tone turns sad.

I was a fucking jackass to treat her the way I did. Maybe I need her to dislike me, but she doesn't need one more thing against her.

"What did the doctors say?" Mom asks.

I can't help turning around. Rooney's gaze has lifted from the countertop and is now on me. Mom's looking away, probably trying to make Rooney comfortable, but Rooney's going to be uncomfortable, no matter what. She needs someone to look at her—to be a part of this horrible situation with her. She has to feel so fucking alone.

She blinks rapidly. I don't know what to do, other than stare blankly back at her.

Those tears make the pit of my stomach ache in ways it's never ached. She's beautiful and perfect, but I recognize the brokenness inside of her. Outside of my guilt, I'm not sure I've ever felt much of anything. But now, there's a girl who's making me feel shit, and I'm at a complete loss. The only way I know how to react is by *not* reacting.

"They're only giving her a month," she says in a carefully even voice. But the tears raining from her long, soft eyelashes give her away. "I'm losing her."

The microwave beeps behind me and while I go completely still, Rooney jumps about a mile. Her attention goes right back to the countertop. Good, that's where it belongs.

So why do I want it back?

I take the pizza cut and toss it into the trash can while Mom's not looking. Any hunger I might've had is gone.

"You know you're welcome over here whenever you need a breather, or if you need to talk, okay? Travis and I both love you, and we'll do anything to make this easier."

My parents love her? What? Am I missing something, or isn't she *only* our neighbor?

Mom lays a fabric napkin over the muffins. She then pulls out enough meals and sweets to last Rooney and her mama a lifetime. She motions for me to come over and grab some. I take the majority of them, leaving Rooney with the job of carrying the basket. She gives Mom a hug, murmurs a thank you, and follows me outside.

"You don't have to do this," she whispers so softly my ears strain to hear her.

I stop and glance over my shoulder. She's trailing behind me and comes to an immediate halt, just short of running into my back. She looks up at with eyes so wide and innocent that my fingers itch to drop all of this food and run across her cheekbones—to try to understand the essence which makes her seem so...*good.*

What made her born like this, while I was born a killer? What made me deserve to be bad from the get-go, and her deserve to be good? Whatever it is, I want to breathe it in and hope it spreads.

I know that's impossible. There's nothing left to make good inside me. My insides are black, charred bits of a ruined soul. If I ever had one.

"I have to," I tell her in just as quiet of a voice.

She hugs the basket to her chest, the question in her eyes before she even asks, "Why?"

CHAPTER SIX

Rooney

"Step Ten. Continued to take personal inventory and when we were wrong, promptly admitted it," Silas answers after a long gap of silence. His fingers curl around the Tupperware containers he's holding. His jaw clenches, and his eyes flash with an intensity different from anything else I've seen from him.

Sure, before, I could tell he was checking me out, and there was an intensity in his eyes which was blatant lust, but this intensity I can't describe. It's almost like he's grasping desperately at something he can't seem to reach. I wish he could. I think he needs it.

"I wronged you, Rooney."

His saying my name makes my heart trip. His voice isn't allowed to have that power. I need to hate him for the way he treated me, so I can my protect myself. I don't need any more damage than I've already taken. The armor around my heart is about as thin the plastic wrap on these muffins.

I don't know what else to do but follow him. I sift his words over in my head. The only way he's wronged me is by being so heartless, but it feels like there's more to it than that, as if I'm not the only one he's trying to apologize to. For someone who works so hard to stay distant, maybe he's the opposite of distant, which is why he's trying so badly to hide away.

There's a pretty big gap between our houses, with trees separating them. You can tell the definite line between their house and ours, because all of a sudden the grass becomes higher, with gangly weeds poking their heads out. Since Mama started getting really bad, I stopped cutting the grass. Mr. Manning was doing it there, for a while, but then his schedule got busy. I need to take the time when Rita's here next time to do it.

We get to my front door, I reach out for the knob and turn it.

"You didn't lock it?" Silas demands in an almost accusing voice.

I startle. I wasn't expecting to him to say anything else. I swallow the thick lump in my throat and stare down at the knob. "The lock's broken. I haven't had the time…"

Silas lets out a breath and I don't have to turn around to see his disapproval. I can feel it coming off him like a tsunami. So now he cares? Mama would likely tell me to get used to it.

Mama.

Fear pricks and I open the door and run in. I go straight to the monitor I left sitting on our kitchen table. I turn it on and bring it up to my ear. I immediately hear Mama's labored breaths. *She's okay.* Leaving her for that short time scared me. Brandon sent me a text asking if we could cancel our phone call tonight so he could study. I told him I was okay with it, even though I wasn't.

When Mrs. Manning called me and asked me to come over to pick up the food, I suspected maybe Brandon had asked her to make sure I was okay, but then I saw all the food and realized it wasn't last-minute—Brandon hadn't asked her to. Mama had been in a deep sleep when I left, so I hoped leaving her would be okay. Thank God it was.

Silas gave me a look that actually seems worried. "She okay?"

I let out a relieved breath.

He inclines his head in the direction of the counters. "Where can I put these?"

"Anywhere's fine," I answer. "I'll sort through it later."

He sets the food on the counter space, and I put the muffins beside the microwave. I lean back against the counter and stare up at him. He stares back at me, brows furrowed. All the tension in the world is in his movements as he rakes a hand through his long hair. His mouth opens like he's about to say something but then he clamps it shut, shaking his head. Without another word, he turns away and walks back through my house to the front door.

As it closes shut with a surprisingly soft click, I sink to floor and wrap my arms around my legs. I set my forehead on my knees and realize that even though there was mostly silence between Silas and me, it was a type of silence I forgot could exist, because this silence...the silence of being alone, is the only one I know now. As much as I've wished Silas Manning would've never shown up on my doorstep, now I'm wishing he'd come back.

I've come to be afraid of nearly everything about life, and being alone is undoubtedly one of those things.

***

Mama's strong enough the next day to get to the couch. It's good to release her of her prison whenever we can.

Today is going to be a good day. I can feel it. Mama's even up to eating one of Mrs. Manning's muffins.

I usually judge our days in good and bad. The bad days are always hopeless, when I have no choice but to face reality, but good days are where I can live, enjoy my time with my mama, and tuck away memories of her that I know I'll need someday.

I bring her in a muffin and Mama's shaking hand takes it. She's been intently looking out the bay window. I'm not going to ask why. The last time Mama did something like this, it turned out it was just her mind playing tricks on her by making her believe a deer was in our front yard.

I head into the kitchen to get myself a muffin. When I walk back out, Mama's barely eaten any of hers because she's too distracted. Her gaze flickers up to me and then back outside.

"Honey, is that who I think it is out there mowing our yard?"

"What?" Sure enough, I hear the faint sound of a mower. I walk up to window and have to blink a few times to make sure I'm not somehow partaking in Mama's delusions.

Silas' on his dad's riding lawnmower, clear out by the road, mowing our lawn. Shirtless. Even from here, I can tell his physical perfection doesn't stop at his face. I can't help pressing closer against the door, like a dog looking for her master. All I want is to see more of him. Maybe all of him.

"I guess it is," Mama muses. "Why don't you offer him some water?"

"Mama...I can't."

"Water is not an invitation into your bed." She chuckles, the sound raspy, and I face her because I love it when she laughs. I know she's about to say something I'll need to store away, because it'll be something purely Mama. "Although that's not always the truth. There were a few man-candies I let into my bed for that, or less."

I bite my lip to hold back my smile.

"Take him some water? Please?"

"Only for you."

She goes back to watching and I quickly pour a glass of water. With Mama's back turned to me, I make sure my clothes are straightened. I don't want a repeat of him checking me out. It made me feel good, too good, and I can't let it happen again. The only person who has the right to look at me like that is Brandon.

Brandon isn't ever here to look at you, though, a small voice whispers in the back of my mind. *Brandon has never looked at you the way Silas does.*

As I'm walking out, Mama calls, "Make sure you're in my line of sight. This is my favorite type of daytime television."

I can't help but laugh. I shut the door behind me and head for Silas. He's driving in the opposite direction. I grip the water with both hands, my eyes wandering down his backside. It's strong, tan. Muscles rippling as he clenches the wheel. I never thought I'd find a back sexy, but his is. The slight curvature of his neck, the angle of his shoulder blades, his narrow hips, they're all things I could drink in. I bring him water, but really I'm the thirsty one—thirsty for him

No, bad. Very bad. *God, Rooney.*

There's some sort of script tattoo covering his entire back, but I can't make it out from here. All of a sudden those muscles pulse and shift as he turns the mower and heads straight for me. My hands begin to shake, water sloshing over the rim of the glass.

Get it together. I'm sure Mama's thoroughly enjoying this.

His hair is pulled back beneath a baseball cap and I can tell exactly when he notices me, because the brim jerks. So does the lawn mower. He gets it set back on its path and then continues driving until he stops just in front of me. He turns it off and cautiously slides out of the seat.

My heartbeat slams in my ears at the sight of him. From far away I thought he was drool worthy, but from here? Oh. Oh my. His abs are chiseled in such a way that even people who work out for hours every day couldn't accomplish. Each ripple is pulled tight, creating a small valley my hands yearn to explore. My head may be telling me to get it together, but my hands evidently have a mind of their own.

Over his left rib cage is another tattoo with more script I can't read, but it's written in a way like someone scribbled it angrily over his skin. There's a small trail of blond hair running from his bellybutton and disappearing down into his black basketball shorts, with that v-shaped indention in his pelvis disappearing there, too.

He takes off his cap and runs his arm over his forehead to wipe off the sweat. In the process, his pec jumps. Oh my God. Literally, God. He has to be one. Scratch that, with the attitude he's shown me up until yesterday, he was probably made in the image of one.

"I brought you water," I stutter.

His hand freezes and he glances down at the water, like it's some sort of explosive that he needs to be wary of. "Why?"

"Mama asked me to." Does there need to be a reason? Can't I just do something nice for him? Why do I sound so unconfident, like I'm lying?

"She did?" he asks, eyebrows raised.

"Yes," I say more strongly.

That seems to be enough for him to realize that should he take the water, it won't spontaneously combust. He brings the glass up his lips and downs half of it in one gulp, his throat working as he does. He levels his head and wipes his lips with the back of his hand. All I can do is watch with rapt attention, unable to look away.

"How is she?" he asks, sounding like he might actually care to know.

"Good today. Great." I turn slightly and point back to the window. I'm sure when I get back she'll want to dissect everything which happened from the minute I stepped out the door to when I walked back inside. "She's watching us. Wave."

I do, but he doesn't. I drop my hand and nervously tuck it at my side, when I turn back to him, he's closer and staring down at me. He looks puzzled, if not lost. He brings his free hand up to my cheek and rests it there. The callouses on his hand scratch at my skin, but it's not a bad kind of scratch. It's real. "I'm going to ruin you, Rooney. I can feel it."

My breath catches under his intense, too-aware gaze as his words sink in. A purely masculine scent overwhelms my senses, smelling of cigarette smoke and sweat and I can't seem to get my brain to start working. I'm not sure what he means because we're nothing to each other. Maybe this is the fourth time we've interacted in the span of four days, but I'm pretty sure if he was to walk away, he'd forget me just as quickly as we entered each other's lives. I'm not sure Silas keeps much of anything with him except for his anger and misery.

I cover his hand with mine and try to see straight through his eyes to whatever it is he's trying to tell me. "We all get ruined, someway, somehow," I whisper, thinking about Mama. She's ruined, but she's not broken. She's stronger because of her ruin. And so is my love for her. Maybe I'm stronger, too.

His jaw pops and he drops his hand, stepping away. He hands me the water and looks away, down at the ground. "You'd don't understand."

"I do understand," I whisper back. "I understand that you always walk away. That you're about to right now."

A faint smile touches his lips which seems so *sad* it's worse than any jaw pop or frown or glare. The smile is there and gone before I can memorize or enjoy it, it's replaced by a hard, thin line. "You're right."

He turns around and walks back to his mower, starts it up, and continues on. He doesn't look back

I turn around dejectedly and head back for my house. The man's a mystery I don't need to be cracking, but I want to, because he still has the chance to be alive. He should be cherishing that.

I put on my fake face for Mama, because today is going to be a good day. and I prepare myself for her interrogation.

"I'm back, Mama," I say in a peppy voice as I shut the door behind me. "I hope you enjoyed today's episode of—"

Mama's clutching at her chest as she gasps for air, her once pretty face turning a pale shade of blue.

The first thing I do is scream.

CHAPTER SEVEN

Silas

I hate hospitals.

I have since I was a kid, and my appendix burst. I was so freaked out, Mom and Brandon stayed with me. I hated the people who roamed the halls, the white walls, the fluorescent lights, the bad food. The hospital is a lot like clowns are for some people—you don't see them a whole hell of a lot, but when you do, your nightmare awakens again. Every time I've been sent to one since then, nothing good has come of it.

After the accident, I woke up in a small room, without any windows and handcuffs shackling me to the bed. A policeman stood by the door. For a second, I didn't know why I was there, what had happened. Then the dam broke and everything flooded in. My memories proved, without an ounce of doubt, that I deserved to be hospitalized. Truly, I deserved to be dead—but a few months later I got a three-year sentence, which ultimately turned into two, with good behavior.

I wasn't even in for a month before they were shipping me off to the hospital, after some guy rammed a knife into my back.

I don't know what had possessed me to come here with Rooney. After she'd walked off, I turned the mower off to collect myself. Then, I'd heard her start screaming. I'd stumbled off the lawn mower and smacked my leg so hard, I was surprised I was able to run as fast I had. Adrenaline, maybe.

When I'd gotten there, I could tell her mama was bad off. She didn't look like she could breathe, and every time she'd try, panic would flare in her eyes. I'd called for an ambulance.

By the time they'd gotten her there, her mama had stopped breathing, and I'd had to pry Rooney off her for them to be able to take her away. Right then, I'd felt a fierce need to protect Rooney from whatever she was about to face. She'd clung to me in a way no one else ever has. When the EMT had asked Rooney if she was going with them to the hospital, Rooney had tugged me with her, and hadn't let go, since.

I got into a fucking moving vehicle for her, and came to a fucking hospital. Now I know I *really* need to stay away from this one. She's dangerous to me, which makes me a whole hell of a lot more dangerous to her.

Her small hand is wrapped around mine as she watches the doors of the TCU. My foot bounces uncontrollably as I try to work out my nervous energy. I bring my free hand up and grip the back of my neck as tight as I can, squeezing my eyes closed at the same time.

Mostly, I hate this hospital because *she's* here somewhere.

"Thank you for coming with me," Rooney says.

Outside of her scream, I've noticed she rarely talks above a whisper. Somehow, the whispering is louder than any yell could be.

I don't have an answer for her. It's not like I really had a choice in coming. The steel grip of hers wasn't gonna let go of me even if I wanted her to, and while part of me was screaming over the contact, the other part was quieter than it's ever been.

This is still Step Ten, too. If I can help her, I need to. Who knows, maybe one of the pieces in me needing redemption will gain it. Just a piece of me, not all of me.

A nurse walks out through the double doors and Rooney sits up straight. I can feel all of her fear and hopefulness. Her hand squeezes mine surprisingly tight.

"Decker?" the nurse calls.

I don't even know Rooney's last name. Evidently, it's not Decker. She sinks back down into her seat, those tears I've come to despise forming in her eyes. I hate seein' her cry. I don't know why, but each tear feels like a punch to the gut.

"I'm not ready," she says so softly I barely hear her.

Every time I shut my eyes, I see the two people I killed, the one I *didn't* but would've been better off if I had...I see their families. I see those crosses—even before I saw them, I imagined what they might look like. I see my parents' faces at my trial. I remember how this is all my fault, yet I'm the one who lived. "No one's ever ready."

She looks up at me, tears springing loose, and I realize I'd said the wrong damn thing. I should've wrapped an arm around her or told her everything would be okay. But it won't fucking be okay. Nothing's ever okay. Life sucks until you die. I'm not going to sugarcoat things with Rooney. Just because she has a pretty face and a kind disposition doesn't mean she doesn't deserve the truth. Lies will only make the next month, and the space after, even more difficult.

The wrong damn thing happens to be the right fucking thing, in this case. I may be the worst kind of guy, but at least I'm honest.

A nurse walks in and I'm too lost in Rooney and my thoughts to pay attention until Rooney suddenly sits up at the name "Oliver."

I glance up at the nurse and go still. She's glaring at me

so strongly, I'm surprised I don't burst into flames. Jackie Walker, one of *their* friends.

I remember her because she sneaked into my room one night while I was here and started yelling at me, not hearing me as I begged her to find a way to let me die. By the time the policeman, who was taking a restroom break, showed up, she was hysterical. Someone from HR even came and threatened to fire her if she didn't calm down.

We treat ALL patients, the HR representative had hissed as they walked out, thinking that I couldn't hear them, *including the ones who we don't believe need to be saved.* I don't blame Jackie for her reaction. She'd had to see the evidence of my destruction in her friend every day since the accident, because of her job.

"Will you come with me?" Rooney asks.

My hand suddenly feels cold and empty and I break away from Jackie's hatred to see Rooney's hand is missing from mine. Without holding it, I realize just how anchored to the world her touch had been making me feel.

Her hand slips back into mine and I realize I've never held someone's hand before. She gives it a squeeze as she stands, pleading with her eyes for me to follow suit. I stare back at her and then make the first decision I've made in a long time that is as much selfish as it is selfless. Wordlessly, I stand up. Rooney lets out a breath, relief washing over her face.

"Family only," Jackie practically snarls. Her gaze falls down to the shirt the EMT had given me. She glares.

Yeah, I get the irony. I'm the one who kills people and I'm wearing a shirt claiming I save them.

I clench my teeth. Jackie has the right to be a bitch toward me, but to Rooney? No. Jackie doesn't know anything about Rooney, aside from how her mama's dying. That should be enough to make her back off.

I narrow my eyes. "What makes you think I'm not?"

Jackie makes another angry noise. So much for the Hippocratic Oath, or whatever.

I'm about to tear into her, give her another reason to hate me, when Rooney steps in front of me.

"Let us back to see my mama," she commands, warning in her overly calm, even voice.

Jackie's eyes go wide and she steps back, obviously realizing now is not the time to bring up old grudges. The way Rooney's looking at Jackie, Rooney could take her, and Jackie knows it.

We follow behind Jackie. I know from experience, it's only one or two nurses to each patient, and no one can get in to see the patient without being called. They were able to get Rooney's mama stabilized on the ride over to the emergency room, but because of her condition, they'd sent her off to testing and then up to the TCU.

Jackie tells us the room number and then turns off into a nurses' station. Rooney's mama's room is at the very end of one of the halls, and her door is wide open.

I'm so out of place and tense, like some bear trying to pretend he's a human. Someone else should be here with Rooney. Someone who'll say the right shit and be able to touch her without worrying about hurting her, or getting hurt. She needs someone strong, stable, who can act as a pillar for her to lean against, not like me, an alcoholic with a past, who can't even manage to hold himself up.

We step into the room and Rooney lets out a small gasp. I'm sure she's probably seen her mom in a hospital bed before, but every time probably feels new. Scarier. Her mama's asleep, chest rising and falling in staggering breaths, so pale she nearly matches the white sheets of the bed. She looks even frailer and tinier than she had when I carried her a few days ago. Her heart monitor shows her all-too-slow heartbeats. I can't imagine Rooney dealing with this all by herself.

There are two men standing beside the bed, one dressed the same as Jackie. The other is clearly the doctor. "Hello there, Rooney," the doctor says with a sympathetic smile.

"Hi, Dr. Demarco," Rooney says, mustering up a smile.

"Who's this?"

"My, um—" Rooney glances at me with a confused look. "This is Silas."

"And you're okay with Silas being here?"

Rooney takes a step closer to me. "Yes," she says.

Dr. Demarco nods. He's got to be my father's age, but his hair's grayer and his arms could probably crack a nut—or a neck. "All right, Rooney. We've talked a lot about how in stage four, the cancer metastasizes. Spreads into other organs within the body. Well, it looks like the cancer has begun taking its toll on her lungs."

Stage four? It's in her lungs? I don't know what to think, or how to react. Especially when Rooney's body suddenly molds into my side, as if she can't hold herself up.

"Her lungs?" she repeats, choking on the words.

I don't know what to do, so I settle on placing a hand on the small of her back, my fingertips just barely grazing her body. She needs this and I'll give it to her. If I do one good thing in my life, I'll let it be this.

"Rooney, your mother's health is deteriorating, and what happened today was an effect of that. The cancer moving to her lungs will not shorten her life expectancy." He says this slowly and Rooney's eyes go so wide with hope, it makes a thin crack in the stone casing around my heart.

"I still have my month?"

"As long as she remains stable, yes."

Rooney nods, but then her expression falls. "This wasn't because I...because I moved her, was it?"

"No," Dr. Demarco says. "Keeping her stable means keeping her comfortable, but it also means keeping her happy. Her body's already worn down, and as much as you can't make things better, you also can't make things any worse. Your mother would rather live her last weeks happy, rather than in a bed waiting for her death." He offers Rooney a kind look. "You're doing a wonderful job with her. Don't let this change that. Now, we're keeping her here overnight for observation. We don't see your mama waking up tonight, so if I were you, I'd go home and get some rest before she comes home tomorrow. Thomas, here, will keep a close eye on her."

Dr. Demarco squeezes Rooney's shoulder and then leaves the room. Thomas starts messing with a laptop on a portable station.

"Can we stay for a little while?" Rooney asks me.

I can see the fear in her eyes. She thinks I'll say no. A part of me thinks I might say no, too. If it was any other person, I might. But this girl has made an impression on me since the moment I first laid eyes on her, and it's an impression I can't seem to shake. I said I'd wronged her, but I think I've actually wronged myself. I'm letting myself tangle with something I'm not capable of handling.

"We can," I answer, my voice so gruff I barely recognize it.

She starts crying again, but I think it's more out of relief. "We have a month."

The sound of her voice, the way she curls into my side like I'm more than I am, it makes me greedy and before I can stop myself, my palm presses harder against her back.

***

Dad picks Rooney and me up, and drives us back to his house. He said Mom wants Rooney to come home to our house first, so she doesn't have to be alone.

During the silent drive home, I rewrite the Twelve Steps in my head so they're about Rooney instead of alcohol. I'm not addicted to her, but I know what it's like to have something in your grasp that has control over you, something you begin to need as much as you want, and how it can eventually turn to addiction.

The first Steps I formulate deal with distancing myself

from her, but the last ones deal with staying as close to her as I can. That's a problem, because the way I see it, both of those options can hurt her.

I'll never forgive myself if I'm not here for her if her mama falls again, if they have to go to the emergency room, or if Rooney just feels like she's about to lose it, and there's no one there to take care of her. And not just by bringing her food, but by giving her some sort of foundation so when she falls, she has somewhere to land. I don't know a thing about foundations, but I know a whole heck of a lot about falling. That's more than she's got.

The car comes to a stop in our driveway and I immediately get out. I rest my arms above my opened door and lay my head against my forearms. All this thinking has made my head hurt, and the car ride has only worsened it. For the time being, I think I'll keep to walking most places. I ride in cars when I have to, but it freaks me the fuck out. Stresses me. Doing it twice in one night has me wanting to take a drink.

"Are you okay?"

Rooney's hand presses against my shoulder and I jolt, her touch something like fire licking ice. No one usually dares to touch me, not even Mom, mostly because I'd never let them and they know it. But I can't seem to stop Rooney. Her touch is so soft and caring and completely unlike anything I've experienced in the last few years. She's the good in this world I always seem to forget.

I lift my head and see her looking at me with concerned eyes, her own face tilted upward toward mine. She's too close, so close I can smell strawberries. I swallow and back away from her before I do something stupid like touch her again. "Headache."

"Oh," she says. "I'm sorry if I—"

"Not your fault," I cut in, my voice taking a tone I don't intend. Keeping her at a distance while keeping her close, plus the car ride, is too much.

She drops her gaze and tucks her hair behind her ear. I

hear her mumble another unnecessary apology before she fast walks to catch up to Dad. I'm such an asshole. Shit, I don't know how to do this. How to be a friend to someone, how to be *nice*. I can be blunt, brutal, uncaring, dismissive, but nice? I'm not sure if that's possible. This redemption thing might be a learning process.

I shut my door and head up after them.

I stand in the corner of the kitchen while my parents talk to Rooney. She just ignores me. I need to figure out a way to apologize. Step Ten is stuck on repeat.

Mom asks Rooney for an update on her mama and Rooney gives it, her voice choking on the words *four* and *metastasized*. The way she tells the two of them, almost like she's reading a script, makes me think she rehearsed the speech in her head, during the drive. When she's finished, there are more tears in her eyes, but she fights them back, biting her lip. Staying strong.

Her gaze flickers up to meet mine then, and I raise the drink I have in my hand to acknowledge how well she did, but she looks away too quickly. My parents both try to comfort her, but the more they try, the more Rooney starts to looked panicked. They don't seem to notice, though, Mom absently rubbing Rooney's knee and Dad's eyebrows furrowing.

The phone starts ringing and Mom turns her attention to me. "Can you get that?"

Can I answer the fucking phone? My head starts pounding even harder. It had better be some telemarketer I'm free to hang up on. I grab the phone from its cradle beside the microwave and say, "Yeah?"

There's a pause on the other end of the line. "Silas?"

It's Brandon. Shit. I am not in the mood for family catch-up time. Wherever the hell he is—I haven't even thought to ask—he can stay there. Most people idolize their big brothers and I think Brandon did, but I idolized him even more. He's always been the opposite of me and for as much as I've cheered him on, I've been jealous of him.

"You there?"

"Yeah," I answer.

"I can't believe…fuck, it's good to hear your voice," he says, sounding completely honest. I don't get how my family doesn't hate me. It pisses me off, because they should. I changed their way of life when I screwed up. Mom's bookstore started doing less business, Dad became a point of controversy at the school, and I know Brandon's reputation got tarnished. I put this family through hell and they still treat me like they always have.

"Listen, I've been meaning to call you since you got…home, but I've been busy with school. We'll have to catch up when life calms. I'm callin' about Billie. How is she? How's my girl doing?"

I guess Billie is Rooney's mom's name, but what does he mean by *his* girl? Did he get into some sort of cougar shit while I was away? "Your girl?"

Right as I say it, Rooney's eyes snap to mine, her pretty mouth falls open, and I get it. My simple headache ramps up to a pounding migraine.

My brother's voice as he answers, "Rooney," almost physically hurts.

I have to clamp my mouth shut as I hand the phone to her. Here I am talking about redemption and not wanting her to be alone and wanting her to have someone to lean on—and she has my fucking brother? Where the fuck has he been through all this? He should be here, taking care of her. She's the type of girl you jump off a cliff for, if you have to. She's sunny and bright and fucking perfect, and he's somewhere else while she cries and slowly loses her mother.

The phone is barely in her hand before I'm walking away.

"There you go again," she says, low enough I can't help but wonder if her voice has somehow crept inside my subconscious.

CHAPTER EIGHT

Rooney

Even though I keep listening for Mama, expecting to hear her—and then devastation washes over me when I don't—there's just silence. It's even more terrifying than when she's crying out in pain.

Oh God, is this how it's going to be when she's gone? Am I going to be listening for her and missing her and expecting her to alive when I know she's not? I can't imagine being in this house without her, not after we'd stayed up long nights, dreaming up a home almost exactly like this one. When we came across it, she kissed the side of my head excitedly and said this house was a piece of cherry pie God was giving us. I jokingly told her it was more like *lemon* pie.

Back then, she laughed more than she slept. She enjoyed dancing to old rock music. She'd sing at the top of her lungs to wake me up in the mornings. She went out with friends, made plans, and *lived*.

Her life right now isn't living, and I know I'm being selfish to want her to stay here with me. Wherever she's going, she'll be happier and healthier, but we won't be together. I'll be alone in this little yellow house, missing her, because I'll have just lost a piece of my heart, which is something I'll never be ready for. I'll always need Mama, even when I'm old and gray. I don't know if I can go without telling her I love her at least twenty times a day, warm hugs and stupid banter only we would find funny. There are parts of her I've already lost—my mama isn't this mama—but she's still my mama, and no girl should lose their mama when she still needs her. And I still need Mama. I always will.

My chest tightens and I feel like I'm under water, too far from the surface.. A panic attack. I looked them up online and read how it's best to either ride it out, or distract myself. I've been having a lot of them since Mama got diagnosed with ovarian cancer. Since I was told this was a war she couldn't win, no matter how many battles she fought.

I roll over, hoping something will be outside my window to distract me. Surprisingly, there's someone sitting in the dark, beneath a tree, in the Mannings' backyard. It has to be Silas. I hope it is, because the next thing I know, I'm putting on a hoodie and trudging outside in my bare feet.

After the phone call from Brandon, Silas disappeared. I know it was wrong to not tell him about Brandon and me, but I never really had the chance. I'm sure he also thinks Brandon will get the wrong impression, but Brandon won't—he's trusting. He also probably thinks Brandon's told me things, but Brandon's only ever been vague Silas needs to realize how the important part isn't what I know, it's that I'm still here.

I'm not sure why I even want to be Silas' friend. It's not like I think he'd make a good one. Maybe it's because the first impression I got of him was how carefully he lifted my Mama into his arms, like a beautiful piece of mosaic art, and I've been holding that impression close to my heart—trying to find the same man in the hardened exterior he shows.

Those moments when he slips up are when I want him to let me into his life, like today in the hospital. Then, of course, he went back to being the *other* guy, and ruined it.

He's on the ground with his back against the tree. One of his legs is bent, his elbow on his kneecap and his hand pressed into his forehead. The other hand is holding a cigarette between two fingers. He's shirtless again, wearing only a pair of loose-fitting sweats. Coming over here doesn't seem like such a good idea now. Especially because my stomach is doing flips. No man should look this good.

All of his muscles tense when he hears my footsteps. He glances up at me with his usual hardened look. "What are you doin' over here?"

"Couldn't sleep," I admit as I sit beside him.

He brings the cigarette up to his lips and takes a long drag. He blows the smoke up toward the sky, his eyes tracking the cloud until it finally blends into the air. "You shouldn't be here."

"That's for me to decide," I say, bringing my legs up to my chest. I rest my cheek on my knees and give him a pointed look. "I can be anywhere I want, with *anyone*."

I can see an argument spark, but instead he winces and presses his thumb against his temple.

"Shit," he breathes.

"What's wrong?" I ask. I'm still wired tight after finding Mama. Everything seems like the end of the world.

He shakes his head, not answering me.

"What's wrong?" I repeat.

He squeezes his eyes shut and taps his head with a finger. "Migraine."

Mama flashes in my mind. Headaches and migraines are another reason to miss her. I drop my legs and cross them, then pat my thigh. "Lie down."

All the pain littering his face disappears as confusion arises. "What?"

"My mama's always rubbed my head when I get

migraines—she says it'll either relieve you of your pain or make you fall asleep, but regardless, the migraine's gone. Let me try to do you."

His lips fall apart and his eyebrows knit together. His eyes darken in the same way they did in his mama's kitchen—like he's seeing something worth lusting over. Like he wants me.

All of a sudden, it clicks what I said and my heart rate kicks up a dozen notches as I try to fight off embarrassment.

"I meant let me make you feel better. Crap, let me—"

A chuckle comes from him, causing everything but the pounding of my heart to wash away. It's a rough chuckle, like it's fighting to spring free of all the dust that has settled over it. His chuckle makes me feel proud, because I know it's not something many have been lucky enough to hear. It's as rare as it is beautiful.

I can't help feeling greedy—I want more. I want a smirk, a smile, a laugh.

"No matter what you say, it's gonna come out as something I can't have, so you might as well stop," he says in a low voice that sends a shiver down my spine.

Luckily, he doesn't see, because he's shifting and then lying down on my lap, resting his head on my thigh. He's so close and it makes me lightheaded. He smells too good and he looks too good and, if I'm being honest, the weight of his head on my leg feels pretty good, too.

The fluttering in my stomach immediately stops when it becomes clear how—despite all of his bad qualities—I might be attracted to Silas Manning. I can't be, though. I'm dating his brother. Plus, Silas' too much for me to handle right now.

I love Brandon and I need the security he provides. I can count on Brandon. He won't walk away whenever he can't handle something.

"Do your worst," Silas says, his voice sounding tired, like he's lost a fight.

Regardless of my attraction to Silas, it would be nice to have whatever he'll give me. Brandon is a few hours away, and I need someone who's *here*.

I drop my hands to his head and move his hair away. I don't need to, I just want to know what it feels like. It's exactly like I imagined, soft and thick, without any tangles. I wonder if it's always been this length—if this Silas looks like the same Silas from before he went to prison. I'd never paid close enough attention to him in pictures, because he felt like a stranger to the Mannings. The only reason I recognized him was because he has the same nose and eyes as Brandon, but Brandon's stockier, and closer to my height.

It might be a little strange if I keep stroking his hair. I brush the rest of it away and then begin rubbing small circles into his temples, every once in a while letting a finger brush over his eyelids or his forehead. I can feel the heavy thrum of his headache in his pulse against my thumb. It has to hurt bad. He's not a talker, so all those thoughts he keeps rooted inside have to be exhausting.

The more I rub, the more his muscles relax and the tense scrunch of his face fades, until he looks like he's a million miles away, almost asleep.

"What causes your migraines?" he asks, his lips barely moving.

I lean my head back against the tree as I continue. I can't keep watching him. "Anxiety. I'm a worrier."

"Don't see how you couldn't be, given your situation."

I nod, a little glad to have his consolation. "What about you? Your migraines?"

The pulse against my thumb speeds up and I can tell it's a question he doesn't like. I'm about to recall my question when he lets out a shaky breath.

"Everything," he answers vaguely, but it's still an answer.

We remain quiet for a while, chirping crickets the only thing keeping us from complete silence. My gaze falls to the tattoo on his ribs. I can now read it now. There are three names there: Maggie Jonas, Melanie Parker, and Victor Daniels. When I glance back at Silas' face, he's staring up at me. I'm surprised to find his expression is guarded instead of angry or blank.

"Step Eight," he says. "Made a list of all persons we had harmed."

I will myself to nod and not ask questions. I doubt he's ever opened up like this to anyone else and I can't see him giving me any more, no matter how much I want him to.

"I don't want you to be on this list." His eyes squeeze tightly closed and he brings a hand up to rake it over his face. "And I'm fucking terrified that you will be."

"Why?" I ask. Rather, I almost beg.

He doesn't answer and I half-expect him to leave, but this time, it's like he's purposefully forcing himself not to. He rolls over, so his cheek is on my thigh, and his hand wraps around my bare ankle.

"I ruin everything," he says so low and so sad, I'm reminded of how there are millions of ways the way of the world can hurt you.

***

Mama falls asleep during the fifteen-minute car ride home. She made me aware, multiple times, of how the nurses were very disruptive during the night. Plus, she spent most of the day acting all antsy about getting home, and she's probably worn herself out. When I got there, she'd already made the nurses dress her so she'd be ready when she was discharged.

I pull into our driveway and I'm surprised to see Silas on our porch with a tool chest and the door wide open. He's fixing the lock. I swear, he's the most confusing man to ever exist. He talks about ruining me, but all I've seen is him fixing.

He turns around at the sound of my car. There's no

way to be stealthy in this thing—there's something squeaking underneath the hood I don't have the money to fix. Shoulders hunched, Silas stares at where the noise is coming from. He must think there's nothing about Mama's and my life that isn't in disrepair. He shakes his head as he walks toward us.

"Mama?" I murmur, facing her. I rub her arm as gently as I can. Her poor body is like one giant bruise from all the poking and prodding she's had since this whole thing began. "Mama, wake up. We're home."

She stirs and her eyes blink open exhaustedly. She says something that comes out garbled, a smile touching her lips. I wish I could go back to the days of bad grades and middle-school dramas, because back then I didn't know what the end of the world felt like. How it is when you can't speak, for fear you might start crying, or how your heart seems to be living in your stomach, or how, with every breath, you realize it could be the last.

Silas opens her door and Mama's head swings clumsily to the side. She speaks again and Silas gives me a confused look, hoping I'll decipher it.

"She's really worn out," I explain. I get out and round the car to do whatever I can to help. By the time I get there, I realize it doesn't take much to lift Mama anymore. I used to be so jealous of her because she was so beautiful—curvy, her boobs bigger than mine, and a butt guys my own age always seemed to drool over. Now, she's not even an echo of that.

I quickly get into the back seat and pull out the wheelchair. I was never happier than when a man at one of the medical aid shops referred me to a thrift store when I didn't have enough money to pay for a wheelchair. At the thrift store, they gave it to me for free, so long as I promised to return it when I no longer need it. I burst out in tears in the middle of the store, and the lady pulled me into a hug.

"Walk," Mama mumbles, and I know enough of her

personality to know exactly what she's thinking.

Silas slips her into the seat of the wheelchair and once she's seated comfortably, I start pushing her up the driveway. "You're tired, and the last thing I need is you falling in the driveway and getting hurt. Do you want to go back to the hospital?" I ask.

"I'm not your child," she answers, her voice clear now.

Of course it is.

Silas chuckles from behind me and my cheeks heat up. I can't believe he came over to help us. I figured we're friends after last night, or something like it, but I didn't think that he would do this. I didn't think he would be here for me. Us.

"You're my mama," I tell her. "And I'll do anything for you." To make you comfortable. To keep you safe, so I have you longer.

She glances over her shoulder at me and I can see my thoughts reflected in her eyes. She's always been this way—five steps ahead in deciphering the way I'm thinking or feeling. I don't know how many times she's had to sit me down and explain my life to me because I was too clueless to do so myself. But I guess sometimes it's easier to face the stuff happening to other people, than it is ourselves.

Silas runs ahead of us and goes to open the door wider.

"Don't think you got out of talking about yesterday because the big C reared its ugly head," Mama warns.

"*Mama,*" I intone, knowing full well that if Silas were any closer, he'd hear us.

Her shoulders shrug. "You're not going to have me in my old age, so I figure it's best to get the saying-things-loudly part out of the way."

I shake my head. Only Mama would use her illness as a card for getting away with whatever she wants.

She can throw me everything she's got for this next month and I'll take it all.

Silas comes back toward us, stopping at the top of the

steps. He glances down at Mama's feet, then back up at us, not bothering to communicate his question. What's sad is I'm getting used to this from him—I'm getting good at reading him. Well, minus the weird things he says. Those never fail to catch me off guard.

"Do you think you can make it up those few steps, Mama?" I ask as I round the wheel chair, so I can see her as I talk to her.

Suddenly, her ambition to walk doesn't seem so great. She casts a nervous looks down at the stairs, then she glances up at Silas. A flirty, fun smile transforms her face, but I can tell it's fake. Admitting your dependence when you've been independent for so long has to be hard.

"Well," she says, "why would I walk when such a strong man can carry me inside?"

Something sparks in Silas' eyes—but it quickly dies away. Was it some great quip—something that would make Mama laugh, which would end up making her like him even more? Lord knows she does already. She wouldn't be forcing me to give him water if she didn't.

Effortlessly, he lifts her into his arms. "Where to?"

"My room," Mama says tiredly. "You people, sending me on these wild outings."

I laugh, shaking my head. "Admit it, Mama, you enjoy your visits to the hospital so you can see Dr. Demi-God Demarco."

"Hush it, now who's talking loudly?" Mama asks, only making me laugh harder.

***

"You coming over here…" I begin to say as I walk out onto the porch. He left me in order to continue installing the new lock so I could get Mama into more comfortable clothes and then get her all situated in bed. She fell asleep as soon as her head hit the pillow.

"Yeah?" Silas stands up straighter and takes the sweet

tea I'd brought out for him. He takes a drink, and once again, I'm enamored by the way his throat works.

"Is this another part of Step Ten?" I continue.

His hand tightens around the glass. "No."

I stare up at him expectantly, hoping he'll give me more of an explanation. I'm tired of him pulling back every time it seems like he's about to push forward. I need answers—more than yes and no.

"Thank you for the lock," I say. "And for this afternoon."

There's no *anytime* or *you're welcome*. All I get is a nod as he sets his glass on the railing and goes back to his work. I'm getting tired of those nods, too. Maybe Silas Manning makes my body react in funny ways, but his personality—or lack thereof—does not.

I turn around and start to head back in, but Silas' voice halts me. "Why didn't you tell me you're with Brandon?"

I keep my back to him as I try to come up with a good answer. By the time I turn around, all I have is, "I just didn't."

He runs a hand over his jaw, the other busy holding a screwdriver. His movements are always so agitated—made out of pain and meant to cause pain. "I don't get it, Rooney. I don't fucking get it."

My eyebrows pull together. "Get what?"

"Where is he? Why isn't he here?" he asks and he sounds irritated. "No man should leave a girl like you when you need him. He should be here with you. For fuck's sake, I'm here."

I've had the same selfish thoughts about a million times. I want Brandon here. I need someone. It's been on the tip of my tongue to beg him to come home, and I'm pretty sure if I did, he would. But at the same time, I don't want him to. When he's been home, he's tried to distract me—to take my mind off of what's been happening. In the short term, that might feel better, But I need to face this so I can find acceptance.

"I can't ask him to choose me over his future. We've only been together a year, and we're too young for that."

"Rooney." He shakes his head, the motion tight. He brings the screwdriver behind his head to grip with both hands, muscles flexing. He rolls his head back to the sun, but it's not to bathe in it. One of that few things Brandon's ever said about Silas is he always has the intention of hurting himself. "I've known you for less than a fucking week and I would never choose my future over you." He lets out a humorless laugh that makes me feel sick. "Not that I have a future, so I guess the choice is pretty damn easy."

I swallow down the bile in my throat. I take a step forward, into his space. I tilt my head up to see him. He slowly lowers his face until he's meeting my gaze.

"You're alive, you know that? You're alive and my mama's going to die. Maybe you think you're ruined and you ruin everything, but I don't care. I don't care, because you get to live while she's gonna die. You need to stop acting like you're nothing, and like you have nothing. You *have* a future, you just don't want to face it. So start facing it, and make your life important—make it turn out right, even if it's been wrong so far—because some people don't get that chance, okay?"

By the end of my speech, I'm crying. All the stress from yesterday and today is boiling over onto Silas. Even if it's all true, he doesn't deserve for me to berate him in the middle of him trying to do something nice for me. Still, I can't bring myself to apologize. The tears clogging my eyes and the ache constricting my chest make it impossible.

The screwdriver clatters to the ground and it takes me a minute to comprehend what's happening before his arms are wrapping around my waist, pulling me against him. He's touching me—holding me. Comforting me. And I was just yelling at him. God, who's the monster? The man who's done terrible things and is doing his best to avoid causing more trouble, or the girl who's letting the situation get the best of her and lashing out?

I wrap my arms around his neck and bury my head against his chest. He's all sweaty from working outside, but I don't care. All I need is this—someone to hold me while I fall apart. All this time, I've been letting myself cry, but I haven't given myself enough time to shatter.

Sometimes I feel so close to it and I force it away, then by the time the feeling comes around again, it's worse. I know if I could just let it all out, then I wouldn't feel so out of control. This is the first time I've felt comfortable enough to do that, because I know Silas can handle it. If he can handle himself, he can handle me.

The longer I cry, the more his arms lose their statue-like hold and mold to my body. They tighten around my waist and his fingers press into the small of my back. I fall deeper into him, wanting so much for this to last. But I guess I'm just getting my hopes up, because it won't.

I finally pull myself together and ask, "Do you believe in Heaven?"

One of his hands curls into a fist. His embrace goes rigid again, but he doesn't drop his arms. "I believe in Hell, so I guess then I have to believe in a better alternative."

"Can I…will you run away if I go too deep?"

"Only if it's about me," he answers. "I can't go there."

I nod, because I can agree to that.. All I need is to tell someone what's been rattling around in my head. I have no one else to tell it to—no one who won't judge me. You don't understand something like this, until death has touched you.

"If we sit down, will you still—will you keep holding me?" My voice sounds a lot like that of a scared child.

He remains still and I'm pretty sure he's about to say no, when "yeah" comes out of his mouth. We take a seat on the porch steps and he hesitates before he wraps an arm around my waist. I melt a little too willingly into his side, closing my eyes.

"I've never gone to church other than when I went

with a friend once. I'm not sure if I...if I believe in God or in heaven. I don't know how I can if I can't see it. That terrifies me. What if Mama dies and she's just gone—she's not thinking or feeling or living anymore? I don't want that for her."

Silas' fingers trail up my ribcage and then back down, his touch making my skin tingle, even with my tank top as a barrier. Why do I feel this way with him?

"We don't get to know what exists until we finally do," he says in a slow drawl, like he's trying to find the right words. "But you've got to believe there's something watching all of our decisions. Our mistakes. There's something out there to reward us for living."

"You think we need to be rewarded for living?" The words tumble out of my mouth before I can stop them. There I go, digging just like I said I wouldn't. "I'm sorry."

He exhales through his nose. "I do, Rooney. Only because I need there to be a punishment, as well. Life can't be this meaningless—we can't do terrible things or do good things, we can't go through terrible pains or no pains, and have it not mean anything."

"Mama says she's walked both sides of the line," I say softly. "I hope she doesn't get punished for that."

"Your mama is a good person. Sometimes good people do bad things, but it's not a reflection of their character."

I bring a hand up to his stomach and fist his shirt in my hand, holding him here. "You're a good person."

"No I'm not, Rooney."

I'll argue with him someday. I'll tell him he is a good person—how he's like Mama in that he's only made bad decisions. If he had an ounce of bad in him, he wouldn't be here holding me. Even though he wants to run, he's trying his best to stay.

"Do you think about this a lot?" he asks.

"Every night when it's quiet and dark. I wake up thinking it, too."

"Same here," he says in a whisper, like it's some kind of

secret. "Step Three: made a decision to turn our will and our lives over to the care of God."

"Have you—done that, I mean?"

His fingers catch the hem of my shirt and his jagged nails kiss my skin. My breath catches and I feel his entire body go completely still.

"No."

CHAPTER NINE

Silas

"Someone called for you while you were gone," Dad says when I walk by him.

Like always, he's reading a non-fiction book—looks like something about Hitler. Teaching world history at the high school is no doubt the best place for him. Brandon and I never had him, thankfully.

"Thanks," I mumble and head for the answering machine.

Talking with Rooney wore me out. I need to start pulling back before she finds a way into my head, but I keep letting her get closer to me and that's a fucking selfish thing to do. I shouldn't let myself crave her—want her.

She's just so damn pretty and her sweetness…being around her is like a breath of fresh air when I've been suffocating in toxic fumes for too long. But she's my brother's girl and I won't take her from him. I won't ruin her by knocking her down until she's a shell of herself. Yet I know tomorrow I'll be over there again, doing whatever I can to see her. To interact with her. To bask in her sunlight.

Man, this is bad.

I play the message.

"Hello," says a grainy, older voice.

Shit, not him. Stupid fucking Bob.

"This is Bob calling for Silas. I wanted to make sure you had my number so you could get in touch with me. Don't hesitate to if you need to. We're two sides of the same coin, kid. We'll talk on Tuesday."

I erase the message and lean on the kitchen countertop, my hands pressing as hard as possible into my skull. This time, the throb is welcome. Since the accident, a lot of people have told me to go to hell. What a lot of people don't get is I'm already there—living a life where I know what I've done and I can't come back from it. Who knows, maybe this life is my hell. Maybe I'll just live it over and over again, repeating the same mistakes, which is the punishment I deserve.

"Took down the number for you, already. It's on the side of the refrigerator," Dad tells me as he walks by me. He reaches into the fridge and pulls out a soda. "Might need it, someday."

I glare at him. Sure, he acts like he's all high and mighty because he got away from drugs—because he cleaned up his act. He thinks he's got it all figured out, but I know damn well he doesn't. No one does. If we did, we wouldn't be addicted in the first place.

He ignores my glare and pours the soda into a glass. "How's Rooney?"

My pulse spikes for some unknown reason. Did he see me holding her? Does he know while I was fighting so hard to not to look at Brandon's girl, I've been fucking lusting like mad over her? How even though she was crying and telling me secrets, my dick was hardening and I was dreaming of burying myself deep inside her? "Fine."

"Just fine?" he asks.

I walk over to the kitchen table and fall into the seat. "This is killing her, Dad. What the hell do you expect me to say?"

His jaw drops and he stares at me. Shit. That outburst was out of character. Not something I meant to do and definitely don't plan on doing again. If these people see the smallest bit of a crack, they'll shove their fists through and clang around at it until it finally breaks open. They'll hate what they find when they do, and I'll just be fragmented and unrepairable. I'll spring a leak and it won't plug up until everyone's drowned.

Slowly, Dad's mouth closes and then he chuckles. "That's what I thought."

"What did you think?" Mom asks as she walks into the kitchen, carrying a bag full of books for Dad and her to devour later. They always do this whenever she's about to make another book order.

"Just that I need to get my ass on the treadmill," Dad supplies, giving her a wink. He kisses her on the cheek and then heads down the hallway and into the basement.

"Your father acts like if he misses a day he'll blow up like a toad. He should try walking in a woman's shoes and see how he feels about toad-ery." Mom sets her bag on the table and then shakes her head. "How's Rooney?"

Why the fuck do these people think I should know this shit? Can't they find out themselves?

"Better," is all I answer, which has to be a step up from my previous answer, right? I stand up, because this is enough communicating for one day. You can't go around breaking patterns and shit, or else people jump on you fast. But I still find myself pausing on the way out the door. I've got an idea I can't seem to shake loose. Something I want to do, but can't do alone. I hate asking for help, but if I'm gonna keep working at making all of this easier on Rooney by going above and beyond Step Ten, then I need help. "Do you think…"

Mom's ears literally perk like a chihuahua's. "What, sweetie?"

Suddenly this all feels uncomfortable. Wrong decision.

Abort plan now. Except it's too late. Mom's a damn chihuahua all right—a chihuahua with a bone. "I'd like to do somethin' for Rooney."

Her grin widens and she's nodding before I even state the plan.

There's no question one of us is under Rooney's spell. But I'm beginning to wonder if it's both of us.

***

I stop outside Rooney's bedroom door and I'm not sure why. I keep doing this and I keep getting caught. Mom and Billie—which she demanded I start calling her— have declared I shouldn't go into a secret ops career, which they're right about.. Rooney could open this door at any second and I'll just be standing here like an idiot.

Mom walks down the hallway toward me, grinning from ear to ear. This shouldn't make her happy. I mean, she loves Rooney because she's Brandon's girl. She shouldn't be smiling at me the way she is. I'm not standing outside of Rooney's bedroom door because I'm a gentleman who wants to open it for her. I'm not a mind reader.

No, I'm standing here because I'm a sick bastard. Every time I walk past this door, I imagine what she might look like in there. I think about what she's wearing. The last time I saw her, I got a glimpse of the tiniest shorts known to man, with cute-ass koalas on them. Does she wear those to bed, or did she just put them on to come outside? Maybe she sleeps in just a T-shirt, with a pair of panties on—damn, and now my imagination is running wild with what her panties look like. Are they red, black, white, pink? Then I keep thinking about the way she sleeps. On her stomach, with her ass pointing up? On her back, with those perfect tits of hers reaching sky-high and her nipples tight? On her side, where every magnificent curve is on display?

Shit, as if that's not bad enough, my mind goes somewhere else. Somewhere darker. I imagine turning the knob and walking into her room. Sliding her shirt up and tasting her nipples. Pushing those panties to the side and slipping my tongue and fingers inside her tight, wet heat. I imagine the soft moans her sweet mouth could make. The way those blue eyes of hers would light up and melt me, then squeeze tight as she's overcome by an orgasm—

Step Four: Made a searching and fearless moral inventory of ourselves.

I am a complete, selfish jackass who, if I didn't deserve it before, should be dragged to hell right now.

I think of my Steps. Of cars. Of Brandon. Of peppers. Of anything besides her, because Mom is looking at me and here soon my jeans are gonna be tented too much to hide.

It's not working.

"I think this is the first time I've seen a spark of...something in your eyes, Silas. It's good to see." Mom hugs her arms around her waist, I'm sure to keep from hugging me. "This was brilliant idea."

All of a sudden, Rooney's door opens and she's standing in front of me, looking all tired as she rubs her eyes with both fists, her hair half in a braid, half out. She's in those damn shorts again, only this time they've got pandas on them. She's also wearing a black tank top. Without a bra. Those stiff nipples are not going to make my hard-on disappear.

"What are you..." she begins slowly, her voice husky from sleep, but then panic flickers in her eyes. That's not something I anticipated. "Is Mama okay?"

She's already pushing past us and running for her mama's room. She gets there and when she doesn't see Billie, her panic rises.

She freezes the second she steps into the kitchen. We pulled one of the sitting chairs from the living room into the kitchen so Billie can sit there comfortably while she eats her breakfast—a breakfast I made while Mom got Billie ready this morning. We also did a bunch of the housework, like cleaning dishes, dusting the furniture, and organizing Billie's medicines for the rest of the week. Yesterday I could tell this was all getting to be too much for Rooney and she needed this.

"Mama?"

Billie smiles brightly. She woke up groggily and I can't imagine Rooney having to deal with this every day. I haven't been around long, but I can already see a decline in Billie. I'm sure every morning is a reminder of the short time they have left together.

Rooney covers her mouth and faces Mom and me. There are tears in her eyes and for once, I'm glad I put them there. Something good I can say I did.

Without a word, she comes running at me and flings herself into my arms. I stumble backward, but quickly gain my footing before the both of us wind up at the hospital for a round two.

Her head pops up from the crook of my neck to kiss my cheek, literally lighting my cheeks on fire, then pops back down to hiding again. Her legs are wrapped around my waist and her arms are around my neck. There's no doubt my erection is pressing against her, but I can only hope she's too distracted to notice.

"Thank you, thank you, thank you," she murmurs.

Her lips brush against my neck as she talks, and every part of my body is all too alive. She needs to get down before something she doesn't want happening, happens— my prior promises to not hurt her be damned.

"You did this for me."

"And me," Billie calls. "Now stop mauling the poor man, and eat."

Mom laughs and there's something in her eyes...something a mom with a son already invested with this girl should not have in her eyes. I'll need to make it clear I don't want Rooney that way. Okay, I do, but I can't have her. *Won't* have her.

Rooney slowly detaches herself, but stays close. She stands on her tiptoes and whispers her question into my ear so only I can hear. "Step Ten, or more?"

"More." Fuck. This girl. I hate admitting that, but I won't lie.

Her smile grows bigger as she pulls away and heads back into the kitchen.

Mom gives me a grin of her own and says, "You did good."

I nod tightly and follow Rooney. I did good, but I hope this good doesn't come with a cost.

"You're going to stay and eat with us, right?" Rooney asks.

Billie clucks her tongue. "They've been refusing. But I have a feeling you can change their minds."

Rooney doesn't hesitate. "Please?"

My heart goes still. That one word—it does things to me. I'm pretty sure I'd give up everything if she uttered it again. Anything she asks for, I'll make sure she has it.

Before I can make a fool of myself, Mom goes to the table. "We'll stay. But do you mind if I invite Travis over?"

"The more the merrier," Billie says. I can already tell she's getting tired and doing her damnedest to fight it off, mainly when Rooney's paying attention. Billie notices me watching her, and her eyes beg me to let her be.

Dad comes over and we eat breakfast. The four of them talk and laugh, but I don't say anything. I'm too busy taking it all in—taking Rooney in. Her smile is so big and so genuine, that I'm pretty sure I'll be finding ways to make her do both those things for the rest of my life. I keep catching her eye and every time I do, her smile turns up a notch. By the time we're finished eating, I'm drunk. Drunk on her. On her smile. On this moment.

I never realized I can still be an alcoholic without any alcohol involved.

When we're finished, I roll Billie in front of the

window she likes to look out of. She glances up at me, then back out at the yard, a mischievous smile making her eyes sparkle. "You wanna go out there and start mowing again?"

"Mama!" Rooney chides.

"Oh, you liked it too!" Billie says back.

Rooney's face turns red as she focuses on my parents. "Thank you for taking care of her."

"That's not—I'm not—"

"That's exactly what you're doing."

I don't have an argument for her, because it's true.

***

I'm sitting out on our back porch having a smoke, because I need one after today. I spent most of the day over at Rooney's, taking care of the shit that needed to be taken care of. Like their garage door, her car, the clogged sink. I didn't see much of her because she was spending time with her mama, but every once in a while, she'd pop out of nowhere with water or food, or just to say another quiet thank you. Each time, I felt like a fucking king.

When I was ready to head home, I went to tell them goodbye, but I found them asleep in Billie's room. My question from before was answered: she's a side sleeper. I gave myself enough time to see that and then I bolted. I knew if I took too long, I'd be starin' at her all night long.

I stretch my legs out in front of me. Part of me hopes she'll wander over here again, but I doubt she will. I can't see her leaving Billie. Billie's not even my mama and I found it hard to leave her. I could think of a million different scenarios where they both might need me, which put a pit in my stomach I've never had before. I knew I needed to leave fast, before I lost my head.

The door swings open and Dad walks out with the phone in his hand. "Another phone call. It's Brandon."

I take a drag of my cigarette. "Not in the mood to talk

to him."

"He's in the mood to talk to you," Dad argues. "Talk to him."

I take the phone from him and stare down at it begrudgingly.

"You smoke?" he asks.

I take another drag. *No, I keep the cigarettes around for the ambiance.* I'm surprised he's just now noticing. I've got to smell like a damn chimney. "Yeah."

"Bad habit."

I level a glare on him. "So is alcohol. Best of the two evils."

Dad swallows and I can tell I've pushed him away for the time being. He walks back into the house without another word.

I exhale and bring the phone up to my ear. "Brandon."

"Hey!" Amazing how I haven't talked to my brother longer than five minutes in the past few years, but he still holds the same enthusiasm, as if we're best friends. If he knew the thoughts I've been having about his girl, there's no way he'd be this nice. "Mom told me about today and I wanted to thank you for being so nice to Rooney. I feel guilty about not bein' there, but I will be soon. Until then, I'm glad you're there. She's special, isn't she?"

I tap the ash from my cigarette and watch it burn out, needing to collect myself. I purposefully keep my voice even as I say, "She is."

"I knew you'd love her. Rooney's got a way about her. Think I fell in love with her the second I saw her."

Fell in love with her? I grit my teeth. Then why isn't he here? I get she doesn't want him to give up school for her, but isn't there another option for him? Like, I don't know, *don't* go in the summer? I mean, who does that shit? Summer should be his free time.

If he did love her, there's no way he'd leave her—even if Billie wasn't sick. I know I wouldn't. Hell, I'm not sure anything would pry me away from her if she was mine.

But she won't be. Ever. Need to get that thought out now, and destroy it.

"Surprised Rooney never mentioned meeting you," Brandon continues.

She didn't mention me? Of course not. Why should she? I'm no one.

"Then again, I've had to cancel our calls the last few nights. I'm gonna call her after this, so I'm sure she'll mention it then."

"She's asleep," I say, my voice hard-edged, which trips him up. Not for long, though. He sees too much good in people to question anything—like why I was over there so late, and how I know she's sleeping.

"I'll call tomorrow, then. Do me a favor, though? Take care of her until I can get there to do it myself. It's always just been her and her mom and they're close—I can't imagine how she must feel."

"Yeah, I will." I already am. Not because of him, but for her. Only for her. Him thinking there would be any reason for me *not* to help her, makes me wonder if *he's* the one who doesn't see how special she is.

CHAPTER TEN

Rooney

Silas is walking over to the house just as I'm about to get into the car and head for the pharmacy. Rita's with Mama. They're upping her pain medication, and I need to go fill the prescription.

Silas isn't armed with his toolbox, so I'm not sure why he's coming over here. Is it just to see us? God, I hope so. Having him around is a welcome distraction, even if I don't see him the entire time he's here. Mama gets a light in her eyes when he's around, and she talks more. I don't even care if she flirts with him most of time, or tries to push him my way.

"Hey," I say when he's close.

His hair is pulled up in bun, stubble lining his jaw. His eyes tired and half-lidded, making him look as if he hadn't slept last night. "Hey."

"Mama's nurse is here. You wanna take a ride up to the pharmacy with me?"

He props a hip against the car. His gaze sweeps up my body in a slow perusal, which makes my cheeks heat. I'm wearing an older tank top—one with "XOXO" written across the chest, but since I got it, my boobs have grown, so the lettering is pulled. I also rolled up the hem of my shorts because the stress has made me thinner. Meaning more leg is showing. A sliver of my stomach, too. When I put all of this on, I felt like I rolled out of a garbage bag filled with clothes needing to be donated, but now...now I feel attractive. He's drinking me in, enjoying every piece of me I thought was ordinary and not worth looking at.

He swallows, his Adam's apple bobbing. He looks away and down at his feet, stuffing his hands in his cargo shorts pockets. "Sure."

As he walks around to the other side of the car, I take the chance to let out a shaky breath. My stomach feels like it's coiled tight. Too tight. If I could trust Mama to remain level-headed, I'd talk to her about what I feel for Silas—the way he makes me feel. But Mama wouldn't be able to listen to me without putting in her own two cents about why I should be pro-Silas, like her.

We both get in and buckle up. I pull out of the driveway and head in the direction of the pharmacy. My hands are shaking on the wheel and I know it doesn't matter—I'll still talk to Mama, anyway.

"Talked to Brandon last night," Silas tells me.

I stiffen. I have a feeling his intention is to distance us. His goal's accomplished. "How is he?"

"Fine. Kept sayin' he misses you."

"I miss him, too," I say honestly. "But I'm so busy here, that even if he was here, it'd be the same."

He doesn't look the slightest bit pleased. Though this is just his general, car-riding persona. His hand is gripping the door handle, the other one braced against the center console. His teeth are clenched, his eyes set dead ahead. He must not like cars.

"What's he studyin' up there?" he asks, but he sounds like he's only doing it to distract himself.

I purposely drive the exact speed limit to make this easier for him. As I approach the stop sign at the end of our road, I leave enough room so I can come to a stop slowly. "He's going to be a lawyer. Defense."

Evidently, he doesn't like this. His gaze narrows. "Why?"

"He wants to help people. Make a difference."

"Most of the people who need to be defended can't—shouldn't—be helped."

"Do you really believe that?"

"I know it."

"You're wrong, then. Everyone can be helped. Some people just don't want to be helped." I take a chance because we're in a car, and I can't see him jumping out of a moving vehicle. "You can be helped."

"No, Rooney, I can't."

"Give me a reason."

His gaze unlatches from the road and onto me. "What?"

"Just give me a reason. Why can't you be helped?"

His jaw pops. He remains silent, but doesn't look away. He doesn't have an answer he knows I'll listen to.

"Exactly. You're someone who doesn't *want* to be helped."

He looks back at the road. "Why are we talkin' about this, Rooney?"

Now it's my turn to not have an answer. I'm usually not this pushy. It must be Mama coming out in me. It didn't help how last night she kept going on and on about how reserved he is—how he reminds her a lot of how she was when she was younger. Self-hating and not seeing herself as worthwhile.

Growing up, Mama led by example. It seemed like every lesson she wanted me to learn, she already knew the consequence of, because she'd been through it. Don't have sex unless it's special or with someone you care about, or else you'll wind up a single mom—that conversation also led in to the how-to-use-birth-control talk. Don't do drugs or else you'll munch on everything, gain five pounds, and lose brain cells. Don't get bad grades or you'll have to repeat the fourth grade and have a godawful, vulture-looking teacher again. Don't jaywalk drunk because the police officers on duty when you're in trouble won't be hot.

For her, there were a whole lot of bad decisions and she said it was because she never thought she was worth the good ones. Until me, which was when she turned her life around.

We eventually make it to the pharmacy and head inside. "They have to fill the prescription first. So it'll be a little while."

"I've got time," he says a tight voice, obviously not happy with me.

I catch up to him and step in front of him. "I'm sorry for going there in the car. It's not my business. Talking about you is easier than—"

He halts. "Talking about you? It's okay. I get that."

"So you're not mad?"

His eyes soften. "Not at you. Never at you. I'm just mad at everything else."

"Like yourself?"

He nods. "Always."

A sadness washes over me, but I don't know what to say. I don't know how to change his mind yet. I can prove to him that I won't judge him and that I can't be mad at him, but how do I make him feel better about himself? His self-hatred is so deep-rooted.

After I drop off the script, we take a seat in the waiting area. A middle-aged couple is standing near the pick-up sign, watching us skeptically and whispering to each other.

"Do you know them?" I ask Silas quietly.

He doesn't look up, just rests an arm on the back of my chair, and does the same to the empty chair on the other side of him. His warmth is overwhelming, making my whole body tingle, and I find myself leaning in to him, so it's almost like he's holding me. "Not really."

"But they know you?"

"Everyone does."

I make sure he sees my smile before I say, "Gee, I've never been in the presence of someone so popular before."

"What can I say? I'm the town prince. The crowning's next week." He chuckles under his breath, his eyes turning wicked. His look alone sends a shiver down my spine. Not because it's scary—because it's the opposite. It's beautiful. Sexy, even prince-of hell."

"So long as you get to wear horns and play with fire, I'm pretty sure it'll be a blast."

"I'm sure it will," he says, the wicked look turning smoldering.

My whole body seems to melt into the chair. No one should have a smile with the power to stop hearts. Maybe he is from hell—a temptation sent to show how weak we all are.

"You've got a beautiful smile on you, Rooney Oliver."

My blush deepens and I drop my gaze to my knees, letting my hair shield my face. "So do you, Silas Manning."

"Neither of us really got many reasons to show them off, huh?"

He'll deny up and down about having a heart, but you tell him he's good-looking and he doesn't even try. He obviously knows he looks like a god.

"Not really," I admit. "We should try to—"

"—killed Tommy's friends with his recklessness!" the lady over by the counter nearly screams, her voice going unbelievably high as she talks to the pharmacist, who's now also glaring at us. "My Tommy could've been in that car with them!"

He draws back so fast and goes rigid, it's like I'm molten lava he can't be near. "I'm so sorry. So fucking sorry," he mutters over and over again so quietly, it's a struggle to make out what he's saying. His eyes squeeze shut and as his words pick up speed, his body starts to rock.

I cup a hand over his knee. "Silas."

His eyes fly open, blazing with more pain than I've ever seen. I didn't know a person could actually vibrate with such intensity. He stands up suddenly. "I'll meet you outside."

"Silas," I say again.

"I said, I'll fucking meet you outside, Rooney," he growls, looking at me but seeming to see straight through me.

He bolts from the pharmacy. Running, always running. This time, I don't blame him. I've never hated anyone as much as I hate this woman right now. Maybe he made a terrible, unforgivable mistake, but it's not like he's throwing a parade to shove it everyone's faces. No, instead, he hates himself so much that there's no worse punishment.

"Oliver," another pharmacist calls out. She's been in the back this entire time, unaware of the spectacle. I numbly stand and head to take the script from her.

As I'm walking past the couple, the woman says in her banshee-like voice, "You are who you associate with, and he's bad news, girl."

I freeze and glance at her. Mama always said I was sweet until I took a bite. "I could say the same to your husband."

I turn on my heels and the guilt doesn't hit me until I'm outside. I can't believe how I spoke to her. Everyone has reasons for their actions, and it's not right to judge one side because I already think I know enough from the other.

Silas isn't at the car.

Oh no, I've lost him. Literally lost him.

"I'm an alcoholic."

I spin around, my heart stilling and going numb. He's standing in front of the liquor store next door. It's been closed because of construction. His eyebrows are pulled together and he's glaring at a display of grapes surrounding a barrel. Anger is radiating from him—his fists are clenched, his jaw is so tight it might shatter, his muscles are spasming. I would be lying if I said the way he's standing right now doesn't terrify me. It does.

I really hope I wasn't wrong about him, and getting close to him won't ruin me, like he keeps trying to tell me it will.

"I need a drink so bad, I'd hand over my life for one. Probably hand over yours, too." He brings his hands to the back of his head and hits there, then roughly drags them forward over his face. "What the fuck is wrong with me? Why am I like this? What did I do to deserve this damn life?"

I set my checkbook and the prescription on the hood of the car and step toward him cautiously. "You didn't do anything."

"How do you know that? You don't know me, Rooney—who I am. So you can't know this. You fucking can't.

I flinch, tears welling in my eyes. "I don't like you like this, Silas."

"You think I do?" he roars, turning to me. The veins in his neck are popping out, seeming to pulsate with each heavy breath he takes.

"You're scaring me," I whisper.

"*Fuck.*" Everything in him washes away in an instant. He takes several long strides and stops just in front of me. He wraps an arm around me and uses the other to press my head against his chest. I immediately cave in to his touch, even though I know I shouldn't. I need to remember how it's soft and kind, how he's not the man I just saw.

His breathing still comes out in heavy pants but it softens with each exhale, slowly becoming even and controlled. As he breathes, so do I. There's a tidal wave of emotions flowing through me. Fear. Concern. Anguish.

"I'm so sorry, Rooney. That wasn't...I shouldn't have yelled at you—scared you. Shit."

I wrap my arms around his waist. "Please don't go in there."

"I won't," he says, sounding desperate and honest. "I promise."

"Thank you."

"That was my punishment back there, Rooney. It's what I get for actually doing something I want to do. For having you. Everything has a price, and I can't pay it. I can't."

"You don't have to," I tell him pleadingly. "Me caring about you is for free, because you've already done so much for me. Back there wasn't a punishment, it was a test, okay? And you didn't go in the liquor store, which means you passed. You passed, Silas."

He pulls me tighter and I feel his lips brush against the top of my head. "I wish it were that easy."

CHAPTER ELEVEN

Silas

I'm terrified I'm going to break Rooney.

Correction: I'm terrified for *when* I break her.

There'll be no coming back from that, but I'm already beyond the point of walking away. Today was proof.

Even if I was able to choose her over alcohol, there's still a chance I'll go back to my old ways. The alcoholism isn't even my biggest enemy—it's all this anger raging in me.

I *yelled* at her. I fucking yelled at the only sweet, pure person I know, which I'll never forgive myself for. I keep messing up, saying the wrong damn thing and making the wrong damn choices, and I don't know how to change it.

When I do break this girl, I'll be damned forever. I hope I am.

About an hour ago, I helped her get Billie into bed. I stuck around after we got back from the pharmacy, and continued doing shit around the house, most of which wasn't needed. I couldn't trust myself to leave, because if I did, I'd probably end up with my fist clasped around a bottle, and alcohol gloriously burning its way down my throat.

When I had Rooney in my arms, the need seemed to virtually disappear. Without her, it came rushing back. Drinking until everything is black and I've emptied my soul into my bottle has been my only way to cope. After today, I'm wondering if there's another thing, if maybe it's Rooney—if she's just something else for me to be addicted to.

She meets me in the kitchen after getting Billie all settled for the night. She holds up a baby monitor, offering me a shy smile. "I've got 150 feet."

I kick off the counter. Of all her smiles, this one's my favorite, because it makes any battle worth it. It's so kind and innocent and *unsure*. "I know a place."

She follows me outside and to a tree between our houses. "What's this?" she asks, her smile turning wry.

"I used to pull pranks on the lady who used to live here. Always hid here when I couldn't get away fast enough."

"You were a little ruffian." She laughs.

I shrug. "Someone had to be."

"If I'd have known you, you'd have done me some good. Mama's always telling me I need to let my hair down. Me making trouble would make her happy."

"Not the kind of trouble I have to offer."

"Let me be the judge of that." She looks at the branches above us. "Lift me?"

I swallow thickly as I step behind her. Shit, I'm going to touch her. Not anything huge, but something a lot more intimate than a hug, which has definitely got my pants becoming unreasonably tight.

Without thinking, I trace my fingers down her sides before I grip her hips. She shivers and my hold on her tightens. Holy hell, she feels good. I can easily imagine leaning forward and pressing my lips against the soft spot behind her ear as my hands pull slowly down to her shorts. I can see myself working her until she's screaming out my

name, her Southern lilt begging me to take more—
everything. It's something I'd get addicted to, right quick..
The taste of her…the feel of her…

She leans back into me with a soft noise that sounds a
lot like a moan. Shit, shit, shit. Without thinking, I was
pressing my erection into her back, letting her feel just
how much I want her. Fuck me, a moan like that…God,
now I know I'll have something to add to my visual
tonight when I take a shower. Fucking damn needs.

I lift her up before I can take this any further. "Grab
hold of the branch." She does as I tell her, not saying
anything, but her hands are shaking. "Hey, Rooney?"

"Yes?" she asks, her voice wavering just as much as
those hands.

"I've got to grab your ass."

"Okay."

I do as I say, trying my damnedest to ignore the
softness of her butt. I fail miserably. For god's sake, is
anything on this girl not perfection? She manages to grab a
hold of the branch and pull herself up.

"You're aiming for the next one up."

I follow up behind her, nervous as hell because all I can
see is her falling and cracking her head open. When she
finally sits down, I let out a relieved sigh. I take the spot
beside her, laughing because she's breathing so hard.

"What?" she asks.

"You gonna make it?"

She elbows me. "Not all of us grew up climbing trees
and terrorizing neighbors."

"Where'd you grow up?"

"Kentucky."

"How'd you wind up here, then?"

"Mama always wanted to live near the ocean, so we
packed up and moved when I finished high school."

"That's random," I point out.

"Mama lives off of spontaneity. Life's full of surprises,
so she's bound and determined to surprise it right back."

"Sounds about right."

She tilts her head back to see the stars. "She was diagnosed two months ago," she whispers.

"How long did they give her then?"

"Six months." Her voice cracks and her hand immediately comes up to brush away her tears. "Our time together keeps getting cut short."

I wrap an arm around her waist and her head falls onto my shoulder. My damn brother should be here holding her. She's his, not mine. So why am I glad he's not here—that I'm the one who gets to hold her?

"I don't have anyone else, other than her. I don't have a father or grandparents or any siblings. I don't even have a cousin. It's always just been us. I'll be alone when she's gone."

I lay my cheek against her head. "That's not how it's gonna be. You're gonna have my parents and Brandon. They'll be there for you."

"And you?"

No matter how I answer, it'll be a lie. If I say I'm leaving, I'll remember all of the reasons why I shouldn't, and end up staying. But I'll end up going if I say I'll stay because I'll remind myself of all the consequences I offer her. "I'll do whatever's best."

She wrings her hands together in her lap. "I hope you stay," she murmurs.

"Me too," I say, telling the honest truth.

We're quiet for a long time, her letting me hold her and me doing my best not to do more than hold her. Holding her is a gateway drug.

"Can I ask you something?" she asks in a whisper.

"Yeah." She could rip out my soul, take all the answers she wants, and I wouldn't even mind until tomorrow, when I wake up with a gaping hole in my chest.

"Those steps—those are because you're an alcoholic?"

"Step One: We admitted we were powerless over alcohol—that our lives had become unmanageable," I recite. "It is. They're the Twelve Steps."

She merely nods, unfazed even though she's associating with someone so unhinged. She doesn't need the likes of me in her already-chaotic life—she's got enough to worry about. But, she won't admit it—I'm not even sure she can see how much of a danger I am to her.

"Is that what's on your back?"

Her wondering about my tattoo catches me off guard. A lot of girls I've fucked for a release and a good time were curious, too. Not in the way Rooney is—they saw it as something sexy, something dark to explore. Rooney's curious because she cares—she cares about me.

I got the tat as a way immortalize the importance of staying sober. I spent my savings on it, because why the fuck shouldn't I? Not having the money to find a place to sleep at night or to get a bite to eat felt like the perfect sacrifice. I've always been closer to death than anything or anyone else, so there was no use changing.

"All twelve of them," I answer.

Her eyes go wide and she leans back, breaking free of my hold. All my red flags go up as images of her falling backward, and hitting her head or breaking her leg, flood my imagination. If I'm not going to allow myself to break her, I ain't going to let gravity do it, either. I grab her wrist, while my other hand clamps down over her thigh.

"I'm okay, Silas," she gasps, her gaze falling to my hand.

The length of my hand is about the width of her thigh. Her bare leg beneath it is soft, but firm. Toned. Holy fucking hell, more for my imagination. There's no doubting these babies could link behind my back and hold on to me with an out-of-this-world strength. It would mean I could easily kiss her and take her up against—

Step Twelve: Having had a spiritual awakening as the result of these Steps, we tried to carry this message to alcoholics, and to practice these principles in all our affairs. It's the only Step that matches up to this. Rooney ain't alcohol, but she's pretty damn close. She's a whole hell of a lot more addictive.

She has a bad enough way without you adding to it. Don't ruin her.

I slowly remove my hands and clench them on my own thighs. She exhales and continues in the direction she was going. Her hands dance down my spine to the hem of my shirt and she lifts it, her touch like a ghost's.

"You won't be able to see it in the dark," I tell her, voice gravelly.

"You're right," she agrees and drops my shirt. "I can't."

She sounds so disappointed, it's cute. "Later."

"Later," she confirms. "Did it hurt? It looks like it would."

It hurt like a motherfucker, which I refuse to admit. "Not really."

Her eyes start to glimmer and I know she knows I'm lying. She lays her head back on my shoulder. "Mama wants you over tomorrow." She hesitates before she adds, "I want you over tomorrow, too."

I can't break free of her, yet. The only thing I'll let tear her away from me is if she tells me to get lost. So long as she wants me, I'm here. Even when she doesn't, I'm not so sure I'll be able to leave.

"I'll come over, then."

CHAPTER TWELVE

Rooney

"Do you have a bucket list, Silas?"

Silas stops guzzling his water, and gives Mama a confused look. He came over here directly after his run, not even bothering stop off at his parents' house. He's still in his athletic shorts and a sweaty T-shirt that reveals he was on his high school's track team. Even his choice in sports is running.

"Not really, ma'am."

"Hmm." She's in the kitchen again. Today has been a good day, so I was able to get her up and dressed, then walk her in here, all without needing Silas. I was glad how, when Silas saw she was all settled, he didn't use it as an excuse to leave. Instead, he asked if he could have a glass of water and followed in behind me. He's been drinking it, idly chatting with Mama—well, Mama's been chatting him up and he's been doing his best to reply with more than one word—while I've been washing up dishes. Our dishwasher's broken, which I know I need to tell Silas about. I keep waiting for him to say he's done fixing things for us.

"I don't, either," Mama says.

I glance over my shoulder at Silas. The more and more I'm around him, the more comfortable I am with him, which also means my attraction to him is getting out of control. If he would've laid another casual hand on me last night, I probably would've attacked him with my mouth. I know he was feeling it, too, he's just got better self-restraint than me.

Brandon. Brandon. Brandon.

"Mama doesn't need a bucket list because she just does whatever she wants to do," I explain to him, excitedly. Silas grins at me, his eyes sparkling with humor. But then they flicker to my lips and as my heart thumps in my ears, the humor washes away from his face and his eyes spark instead of sparkle.

Mama coughs and when I start for her, she holds up a hand. "I'm fine. A cough is a cough. Not much hand-holding needed." We both know there is, but she's putting up a front with Silas here. "I've never seen the point of a bucket list. If you want to do something, why not just do it now? But I get it now. Mine's not really a bucket list, though. It's more of a list of all the events I'm going to miss when I'm gone."

"Mama..." I murmur.

"Don't be sad," Mama says back, although she's just as sad, too. She steeples her hands on the table and continues with all of the confidence in the world, "I've been thinking that you two should get married."

Married?

What?

I shouldn't be surprised. Mama's plans have always been a little bit...out there. But still, *married?*

Silas has frozen, mid-drink.

I'm just as still, but I'm still *and* gaping at him. Married to Silas. A piece of me might actually want that. Why wouldn't I? He's been taking care of me, holding me up, and trusting me. Then there's also the things he does to my body just by looking at me, and I'm pretty sure if he did more, I might spontaneously combust.

Brandon. Brandon. Brandon. God, he needs to come home soon.

"Mama…Silas and I can't get married. We don't even lo—"

Mama's eyes light up and she's looks between us both, probably seeing something we don't. "I'm not talking about the real thing. I'm just thinking a fake ceremony. You in a dress, Silas in a suit. The vows, the cake, the dance, the garter. Something new, something old, something whatever." Her excitement tumbles over into another cough and she struggles to compose herself. "I'm not going to get to witness a lot of things in your life, Rooney, so I'd like to experience this—even if it's fake. This way you'll have a memory of me for the real day, too."

When you're losing someone you love, you're constantly aware that it's happening. It's impossible not to, when part of your heart is dying along with them. Accepting it and talking about it is what's hard—impossible. You have to face how you'll keep on living even when they can't. She'll miss all of the important parts of my life. When I graduate college, when I get married, when I buy a house, when I decorate it, when I have babies, holidays, confrontations, special events.

"We can do it in the back yard. It'll just be us and Silas' parents, maybe someone to 'officiate' it. It won't need much planning, so we can do it soon. What do you say?" she all but pleads.

How do I say no to her? I look to Silas to find he's watching me closely, following my every expression. He looks like he's about to run, and I wouldn't be surprised if he does. I might just run right with him. He closes his eyes tightly and clenches his fists. *He's going to say no.*

"We'll do it," he answers.

***

"Are you sure you're okay for us to leave, Mama?"

Mama narrows her eyes at me as she rests her arms on her chest. Silas and I moved her to the bed a little while ago. "Positive. I feel good today and I think with medicine in me, I'll be driftin' off any minute now. Besides, I know for a fact you left last night and everything was fine."

Panic strikes. Did she need me and I wasn't here to help her? "How did you—"

"Don't worry. Nothing was wrong. I could just hear the two of you a little bit outside. I'm glad to see you're getting close. You need someone, and I think he can be it."

"Mama, I have—"

"Brandon, I know it." She shakes her head, too tired to argue. "I'm okay for you to go. I want you to tell the Mannings, and I look forward to hearing what they have to say. Not your kid gets married without actually getting married."

"You're crazy."

Mama motions for me to lean down and give her a kiss. She plants one on my cheek and says, "I'm damn crazy, but it's the good kind of crazy."

I can't do anything but agree with her. I make her give me a second kiss. I always fear I won't get another. She never complains, and sometimes even asks for a third.

Silas is fiddling with the dishwasher, cursing. Something about the sight makes me laugh. His attention shifts to me and is look his not a happy one.

"Why didn't you tell me this damn thing wasn't working?" I can't stop laughing and Silas only frowns at me. "Not funny, Rooney."

"Yeah," I say, unable to catch my breath. "It is."

He stands up and shuts the dishwasher, then stalks toward me. He stops in front of me. One of his fingers tilts my chin up while the other tucks the loose strands of hair behind my ear. His eyes are almost churning, like they were the first time I met him. This time they're not scary. They're just intense enough to make my lungs stop working.

"You've got enough to deal with around here—you don't need washing every damn plate on top of that," he explains in an abnormally low voice. "From now on, if there's anything you need done, you tell me. Got it?"

Awe washes through me. "You want to be there for me."

"Someone's got to be."

When it's just you and another person all your life, you forget there are more people out there to rely on. It's probably why when Mama got sick, I found it so hard to accept help. I could barely even tell people. The only reason why Brandon found out was Mama blurted it out one day.

Ever so slowly, he leans his forehead forward to rest against mine. A jolt of electricity shocks its way through every square inch of my body, leaving behind chill bumps. Both hands slide to my cheeks and cup them. His thumbs make small caresses beneath my eyes.

"You wanna know something?" he asks, his breath tickling my nose.

His lips are so close to my own, the taste of cigarettes and mint teasing me. I wonder what it'd feel like to kiss him. I'm beginning to be afraid this attraction thing is building and building and before too long, I'll do something we'll both regret.

"Yes," I answer distractedly, my voice barely audible.

His lips part and I can't help but watch them as they do. What would they feel like? They're so full, so they'd have to be soft, right? Or maybe they'd have a rough edge, just like he does.

"I care about you, Rooney. More than I should. But damn, do I care."

At that, he drops his hands and puts space between us

by going to the door and waiting for me. I stand there, staring at where he just was, and pressing a finger to my lips. Even if he didn't kiss me, I can feel the ghost of a kiss. It will haunt me for as long as he's in my life.

Thank God my body finally begins to work, because my mind sure isn't there. Silas is like being in the middle of the nowhere without reception. Disorientating and frustrating, but an adventure.

I slip my flip flops on and we go outside. He looks at me expectantly, then a smile tugs at his lips as he shakes his head. "Lock the door."

"Oh." I quickly do as he says. I've gotten out of the habit of locking it. At least we'll be safer—not that Collette is an unsafe town. I'm pretty sure its crime rate is virtually zero. Well minus...

No, I won't think about Silas' past until he brings it up. I know him well enough now to not judge him based on his past.

"So are you sure you're okay with this?" I ask for the thousandth time since Mama dropped the wedding bomb on us.

He shrugs. "This is what your mama wants, so I'm not sure how I couldn't be."

My heart flutters. How did we go from him basically telling me he didn't care about Mama's sickness to him saying these sorts of things?

"Do you think your parents will be okay with it?" By his parents, I mean Brandon.

Another shrug. "Sure, yeah. More importantly, are you okay with this?"

More than I should be. "There's no else I'd rather be fake-married to, Mr. Manning."

"Good, Mrs. Manning, because I don't see your mama takin' no for an answer."

"That word's not even in her vocabulary."

We make it to his house and he takes us in through the back door and into the kitchen. His mom and dad are sitting at the table, both drinking coffees. They've got a few piles of books in front of them and a book in his hands. Mrs. Manning sees Silas first and gives him a sad look—it's a look I've grown used to seeing her give him. Those years he was away put more than just time between them. I'm sure she wonders why her son is choosing to befriend me, rather than bridge the separation between them. I know I do.

Her gaze shifts to me. "Rooney!"

"Hi," I say with a wave.

Mr. Manning looks up from his book. "To what do we owe this pleasant surprise?"

How do we go about explaining this? Coming from Mama, it didn't sound crazy because it's just a Mama thing to say. Coming from Silas and me, it'll sound like we've lost it.

"Mama asked if we'd do somethin' for her so she can have the experience before she…" I let my voice trail off and everyone nods, knowing the words I can't bring myself to say.

"Sure, sweetie," Mrs. Manning says. "We'll do anything we can."

I give her an uneasy smile. "She wants us to, um, get married. Not for real, but just—"

I cut off, noticing both their jaws are dropped. Mr. Manning's hand is clenching his coffee cup and Mrs. Manning is hugging her book to her chest. All of a sudden, that book is thrown to the table and she's coming toward me with a big grin, her arms wide open.

"That sounds like a wonderful idea!"

"You think so?" I ask, glancing up at Silas. He looks just as confused.

"Yes!" She pulls me into a hug as she rubs her hand down Silas' arm. "I'm so proud of you for agreeing to this, Silas."

If anything is going to make him run, it'll be his mom's comment. I don't think Silas wants anyone proud of him.

"We were hoping you would come," I say and she nods excitedly. "That you'd maybe help us take care of a few things. Like finding a nice spot for the ceremony, and baking a cake and stuff."

"Of course!" she says, clapping her hands. "You two will be so cute!"

Silas clutches the back of his neck with his hand. "You do know this isn't real, right?"

She waves him off. "I know. But that doesn't make it any less important. Oh, Travis, isn't this wonderful?"

Silas' dad is still staring at us, looking lost. Eventually, his wife's words sink in and he brings a hand up to scratch his head, reminding me so much of Silas, it makes my stomach do a little flip.

He looks at Silas and says, "Yeah, it is."

When I follow Mr. Manning's gaze to Silas, I find him staring down at me with a blank expression, carefully guarding himself from the situation. But those soulful eyes of his give him away—they're searching for something. I'm not sure what the something is, and I'm not sure if he likes it or if he doesn't.

I'm not sure if he'll run or if he'll stay.

CHAPTER THIRTEEN

Silas

I'm not sure how I got myself roped into this. I expected it to be like two kids playing pretend—we get dressed up, say a few words, and then we're done.

Evidently, Mom thinks this wedding thing needs to be a big deal. The woman's got something coming if she thinks she can condense what takes most people a year or more to plan, into the span of a few days. If you ask me, that's just askin' for a train wreck.

Here she is, even trying to order a bouquet of flowers, as if we actually need one. It's a *fake* wedding, so I'm pretty sure *fake* flowers would be doable.

Reminding myself how this situation is artificial is paramount, because if I don't, I'll let myself want things I can't have. Yet I can't stop this charade of pretending I'm excited. I hate how when I don't, or when I downplay the wedding, Rooney's smile slips away. She looks about as disappointed as I feel about this not being real.

I shouldn't have told her I care about her. I think it's made her think she needs to care about me back. I don't want her doing that, because then when I leave, she'll actually notice my absence. Yet I still want her to care. So damn much.

Brandon had better come home soon, or else he'll find himself walking back into a clusterfuck when he finally does. If he was here, then maybe I'd back off. Then again, probably not. But he needs to be here to knock some sense into me and fight for what's his. If he's not careful, she won't be his and she'll be mine and if we ever reach that point, then he deserves to have lost her.

Figuring she wants some time with Billie, I haven't gone over today. A good thing, since I think we need some space between us. She's going shopping with my mom for a "wedding" dress, and I can't imagine absence being easy on her or Rooney. Billie shouldn't have to miss this.

When Mom brought up taking Rooney, Rooney said she couldn't leave Billie alone, so I offered to stay with her. I'm not sure I deserve Rooney's trust, but I could tell she thought leaving Billie with me is safe. The thing is, the entire time I'm over there, I'll be dreamin' up the dresses Rooney's trying on, and the one she'll choose. I won't be a good keeper for Billie if I'm too busy fantasizing about her daughter.

I'm glad they didn't invite me along, too. Not because it'd be boring, but because I wouldn't be able to sit by and *watch* as she tries on dress after dress, one showing off her body better than another. Hopefully they'll settle on a trash bag, so I'll be capable of stringing a few words together during the ceremony, instead of swallowing my tongue.

After I got home, I found Mom waiting for me. She basically coerced me into spending some time with her, which is really just a polite way of her making me sit around while she gabs the day away. Her favorite topic is the wedding, not that I really expected anything else.

"Oh, I think I'll call up Pastor Wallis and see if he'd be interested in doing the ceremony."

I do a double take, coming out of my thoughts. "That's not a good idea."

"Why not? This isn't about you—it's about Billie. If he turns it down for any reason other than prior obligations, I'll be outraged."

"Mom, they were all part of the con—"

"He preaches forgiveness and second chances all the time. If he's not willing to integrate either of those into his own life, then he's a hypocrite."

"Mom..." I let the words trail off because she's already searching through the phone book for his number. There's no use. She won't listen to me, and the devil knows I won't listen to her, either.

Mom finds the number and dials. She's buzzing with excitement, but I know it's gonna disappear in a matter of seconds.

"Hi Pastor Wallis, this is Karen Manning—oh, I'm fine, thank you. I was wondering if maybe you'd agree to doing us a favor. You see, our neighbor is ill and doesn't have much longer, so she wants to have a fake wedding ceremony so she can see her daughter get married." She pauses and her face brightens. "Oh, she'll be marrying Silas—you're busy? You just said that you...that's fine. I understand. Thank you," she hangs up and then quickly finishes, "you damn jackass."

I'm more surprised by her reaction than his response. "He said no?"

"He said no. She's *dying*, for God's sake. Who refuses to do something for a person who's dying?" Mom slams the phone down into its charging station. She slumps down into one of the chairs at the table. "The store will *definitely* not be donating to the church book drive this year."

I roll my eyes and walk over to the window facing Rooney's. Mom's not the vindictive type. She's a good person—she'd have to be, to stand by my side. Me, I'm nothing like her. Instead, I'm clenching my fists because I'm close to driving over to the church and reminding the good pastor about why he should be offering everything he can to Rooney and Billie. There wouldn't be a whole lot of God in my actions, either, unless the word was spelled on my knuckles. The most Mom will do is ignore him the next time she sees him in town.

I know I'm overreacting. I fucking knew this would be his answer, but it still sets my teeth on edge. All because of me. Because I screwed up in the worst way possible, and now my mistakes are casting a stupid fucking shadow on a girl who's the light in this world.

If Rooney and Billie don't deserve a broken dishwasher, then they sure as fucking hell do not deserve a last wish gone wrong because of some man who can't even follow the words he preaches.

"Silas," Mom says loudly and I jolt. She must've said my name a few times already. I'm too lost in my rage to care. "I'm sorry. I shouldn't have done that. It's my fault," she apologizes.

"No," I grate out, the words tasting like sand, "it's not."

"Silas…"

"This is because of me. It's *my* fault." My nostrils flare and I trudge past her toward the door. I'm not sure what I'm heading for but I have an inkling. It ain't alcohol I turn to for solace anymore.

"Don't do anything you'll regret," she reminds me in a stern voice.

"I'll always regret being around Rooney," I tell her honestly. "Except I can't stop myself."

"I meant—"

"I know what you meant," I say and I know it comes out harsher than I mean for it to. "But I don't need a drink."

Mom gasps and all my anger dissipates. Now I've gone and hurt her, too. I'm just a ball of eternal sunshine. I turn around, purposefully make my expression blank, and try to relax. "Don't blame yourself. Blame me."

She takes a step forward, her hand reaching out to me,

but thinks better of it, and retreats. She draws her hand to her chest. "I never have and I never will."

She should. I wish she would, because if she would scream and yell at me. Then, at least, I might be able to accept her feelings. I just don't get how unconditional love could be that strong. She should hate me, even if I'm her son.

"I'll figure this out, Mom. Don't worry about it. I'll find someone else."

And then I walk out. When I'm outside the door, I stop and punch the wall, letting out all of my frustrations. Now I've got finding someone who doesn't hate me on my list of shit I have to figure out.

CHAPTER FOURTEEN

Rooney

I was never one of those girls who grew up dreaming about their wedding—Mama always seemed to be doing it for me. I always made a point of reminding her how step one to wedded bliss was actually finding a boyfriend. But even though I never put much thought it, I still know one thing for sure: she should be here with me to pick out a wedding dress. That's the thing mothers and daughters get to share—something to look forward to—and it's just a reminder of something else we'll lose.

At least Mrs. Manning had the smart idea to video chat with Mama while I try on the dresses, so she can take part in the experience. I'm not sure this would be as fun without hearing her "oohs" and "ahhs" or "NOOs!"

Of all the dresses I've tried, there hasn't been a yes. She keeps saying how when the one comes along, I'll know it.

Every time tells me, guilt curdles in my stomach. I'm beginning to think "the one" has come along—and I don't mean a dress.

I'm not going to let my mind go there right now. I need to focus on this moment and store it away for later. I slip out of a dress that was a hard no. Mrs. Manning and I picked it up on purpose, to make Mama laugh. It's honestly probably the ugliest thing, and Mama's speechless reaction was priceless. It was one of those moments I wish I could go back in time and record, because it brought out so much life in her.

We're been at a little dress store Mrs. Manning suggested, which is just outside of town. She said she always wished she had a daughter to come here with. The store is packed with dresses, leaving barely any room to walk. Mama would absolutely love this place—she's kind obsessed with clothes. Before we had to sell off a lot of our things, she had a closet full, plus about half of mine. The same with shoes.

I slip into the next dress and do my best to zip up the back. When I turn to face the mirror, I let out a gasp.

This is the one.

Even if it's not technically a wedding dress, it's white, which'll make Mama happy. It falls mid-thigh, with three-quarter-length sleeves and a Queen Anne neckline and a lacy-bohemian style to it.

All of a sudden, I feel beautiful. Looking in the mirror, I don't see myself. I see my mama. I see her beauty in me—I see how she's with me, even if she's not here.

Happy tears well up in my eyes and I hope that Mama likes this dress just as much as I do.

When I walk out, Mrs. Manning is talking in a hushed voice. She sees me and cuts off, looking guilty. Okay, weird. The guilt washes away when she gets a look at me and the cheesy smile that's taken over my face.

"Oh, Billie!" she says excitedly and then turns the phone around so that I'm in the video. The closer I get, the better Mama can see. Her jaw drops unexpectedly and so does my heart. She doesn't like it.

Then she squeals like a madwoman. No one would think that she's sick, reaching that octave. "That one's—"

"Billie!" I hear a door open, followed by stomping.

"Shit, Billie are you—"

"I'm fine! Get out! You can't see the dress!" Mama yells.

"You just damn near sent me into cardiac arrest. If somethin' would've…" Mama's glaring up at what I'm assuming is an unhappy Silas as he speaks in a very serious, very worried tone. "I can't even see her."

Mama lets out a huff. "Fine. Have a seat. Just not within viewing distance." She looks back at the phone. "Our conversation will make him even more excited to see you on the big day."

I want him to be excited. I want him to be speechless. I bite my lip and flatten out the dress. "So you like it?"

"Love it!" Mama says.

"You're beautiful," Mrs. Manning agrees.

"I already have a few ideas for your hair that I will not speak about with a certain someone in close proximity," Mama tells me.

"You can talk about whatever the hell you want. I probably won't understand it," Silas interjects.

"You better understand it on the wedding day," Mama says sternly. "You better see how beautiful she is."

"I already do," Silas says quietly, making me wonder if I've heard him right. I glance up at his mom. She's staring down at the phone, which is still facing away from her, with an odd expression—as if it's a foreign object she can't seem to understand.

"You better," Mama mumbles. "Are you gonna get shoes while you're there?"

"I was thinking I could borrow those sandals—"

"The wedge ones? With the jewels? Oh, those are my favorites!"

That's the reason why I made sure we kept them. Giving them away would feel like letting go of a piece of Mama.

She claps her hands. "Well, you go buy that one and get here *fast* so Silas can scram and then you can try it on for me."

I laugh. "Okay, Mama. Hey, give me to Silas for a second."

"Only let him see your face!" Mama warns and then hands over the phone to Silas.

I grab the phone from Mrs. Manning. I'm worried Silas will have seen me already, but when I look down, he's busy looking like he's met his enemy as he tries to figure out how to angle the camera. He finally gets it right and gives me a sheepish look. "Not used to using these things."

"Don't worry about it," I laugh. "Thank you, again."

"Anythin' for you, Rooney," he says. "Just like I told you."

Step Ten. I give him a smile and say, "I'll talk to you later, Mr. Manning."

He nods. "See you then, Mrs. Manning."

A flutter runs through my chest as I turn off the video call so Silas doesn't have to do it, and hand the phone back to his mom. She takes it with a look of awe on her face. "That's the most...he doesn't really talk anymore."

I nearly spill my guts to her and tell her how Silas means so much to me—how it's not just him changing, it's me, because we're changing each other. But then she'd realize what I feel for Silas is much stronger than it is for Brandon, and she'd hate me for it. What mother wouldn't hate a girl for pitting her sons against each other?

Before I can do anything I might regret, she slips her phone into her purse and grins at me. "I'm paying for your dress."

"No, you can't—" I argue, but there's already defeat in my voice. I know it's pathetic, but I can't afford to say no to her offer.

"Rooney, sweetie," she says, cutting me off. "I want to do this for you. I feel so helpless watching you go through this, so let me do what little I can. Besides, I think Silas is really going to love you."

Does that mean she knows how I feel—is she okay

with it? And isn't there something missing to her sentence? Like an, I don't know, *going to love you in that dress?* Saying just the *going to love you* part is a little like dangling me over a cliff.

I don't have the courage to question her, so I give her a shaky smile. "Thank you."

There's a knowing look in her eyes and it dawns on me how maybe in saying nothing, I was saying everything.

CHAPTER FIFTEEN

Silas

On Tuesday, I take my usual seat at AA and slump down, prepared for another hour in hell. Maybe I like the program and the steps it provides, but all I see it as is an hour away from Rooney, where she might need me. I can get why she carries around a baby monitor. Maybe I need to invest in a cell phone.

I was honest with her about where I'm at tonight. I might've mumbled it like I had a mouthful of mush, but the point got across. She even offered to go with me, saying maybe Mom could sit with Billie for the hour. I told her there's no way I'm bringing her here.

Her life's tainted enough—she doesn't need to hear the sorrows of other people. She's too good for the likes of us, because she can handle her problems. We can't. That's why we drink, or why most of us do it, at least.

Today, I've got a reason to be here other than it's court-mandated. If Bob wants to help me so bad, then I've got a request for him.

He arrives ten minutes before the meeting and I shoot him an agitated glance. How the hell am I supposed to ask him to officiate the wedding? In my entire life, I never planned on speaking to him, much less asking the man for anything. This'll probably make him think we're best friends from now on, too.

If there was someone else, I'd be asking them, but there isn't. In high school I had friends, sure, but most of them hated my guts back when I stared drinking, way before the accident. I don't have a lot of family, either, because both my parents are only children and their parents are gone. My parents don't even have a whole lot of friends, something I'm to blame for. I'm up a creek, my lifeboat's sprung a leak, and Bob's the only tape around.

"You got somethin' on your mind?" Bob asks after I've glanced his way one too many times. "'Cause if you do, I've got ears."

I run my hand down my jaw. I can do this, as long as it's for Rooney. I can do this. "You free on Thursday?"

Bob raises an untamed, gray eyebrow. "Might be, if you tell me why I need to be free."

"I, uh, I'm getting married."

His eyebrow pulls to meet his other one. "Married? You find someone who likes that attitude of yours?"

I grimace. "It's not for real. The girl's mama's got stage-four cancer and she's on borrowed time. We're tryin' to make sure she gets to see Rooney walk down the aisle."

"I'm sorry to hear that. No girl should lose their mama," Bob says. "But what's my role in all this?"

"We need someone to officiate the wedding. You don't need a license or anything, just read from a book. I don't have too many people in my corner and Rooney and her mama don't have any close ties outside of my family—"

"Just tell me when and where, kid."

Relief washes over me. I figured this was gonna go one of two ways, either with me pissing him off by being a jackass, or with me on the floor, begging him to do this. Without saying much else, I give him the address to my parents' place and a time, then slide back down into my seat and pull my hood up over my head, trying to hide. When I'm called on, I shake my head in refusal, which earns me an exasperated look, but I could give a shit. They don't know I'm sitting here craving something much stronger than alcohol; I'm craving Rooney's smile.

***

The next day, Rooney doesn't come to the door when I knock on it, even though I know for a fact she's in there. For a split second, I regret installing a damn lock. With it there, I've got two options ahead of me, and both piss me the hell off. I can sit and wait patiently while my mind plays over all the possible reasons why she's not opening it, or I can bust the door down and have to re-install the damn lock. I know which one I'll be doing, because I sure as hell am not waiting around and acting like I'm all polite while my girl's on the other side of the door, dealing with something she might need me for.

Wait.

My girl?

When had she gone from my brother's girl to mine? She's not. She can never be. But the thought of my brother coming home to her and getting all of her damn smiles and her words, even her tears, makes me want to wrap my bare hands around his neck and throttle him. I want her only in my arms, those lips gracing only mine, only my words whispered in her ears

The door finally opens and Rooney's standing there, eyes frantic. I could seriously fuck up whatever higher power is putting this in her life. Whoever said God only gives us what we can handle was some sort of masochistic son of a bitch. Just because we can handle something doesn't mean we need to face it as a test of strength.

"What is it?"

She looks up at me and blinks tears away. "It's just a bad day." Her shoulders begin to tremble and she brings a hand up to cover her mouth as a sob fights its way up. "A really bad day."

"Hey," I say, swallowing down all the raw emotions building up in my throat. If there's anyone who can give her a shoulder to cry on, it's me. The stoic statue. But she's even managing to bring my emotions out. "Come here."

I press my hand against the back of her head and guide her to my chest. She comes without hesitation and even in a moment like this, it makes me feel good. Too damn good, which is enough of a reminder as to why I'm not meant for her. I shouldn't enjoy getting to hold her in a circumstance like this.

I take a step around her and close the door.

"What are you doing?" she asks, pulling back.

"You'll see." I lightly push her head back. I leave one hand braced there, my thumb rubbing small circles, while my other arm wraps around her waist. I pull her even closer. "Now scream."

As I speak, my lips brush against her ear in a soft, barely there kiss. If I wasn't holding her, I wouldn't have noticed her shiver. Wouldn't have felt her immediately snuggle into my chest. Wouldn't have heard her soft, little gasp. I shouldn't want her at a time like this, but I do. Every time I lay my eyes on her, I want her. Not just so I can be inside of her—and *fuck* do I want that—but so I can have every single last piece of her that makes her, her.

Mostly, I want her to want me back, which is worse than any sin I've ever committed.

"What?" Her voice is muffled and I can imagine the adorable, confused look she's be sporting.

"Scream. No one'll hear you. Try it—you'll feel better."

She shakes her head, like she's not going to, but then all at once her whole body goes rigid and I feel her lips part against my chest and she's screaming. So loud and with so much force, it seeps past my skin and echoes throughout my insides. I can't help but smile. That's my girl.

Not my girl.

I run my hand down the length of her hair. "Did it work?"

She pulls away, shocked. "I don't feel as close to losing it."

"You wanna tell me what's going on?"

She tights her arms around me and sighs. "She's just not doing well today and it's on the bad days where I have to face that she's...dying. She won't eat, she won't talk. She looks so exhausted. I can't...I don't know what to do, Silas. I don't know how to make this easier for her."

"You already are making it easier. All of this is up to her." I hope she sees what I mean, because I don't want to have to say it. As long as Billie chooses to fight, she'll continue on, but when she gives up, she's gone. All Rooney can do is keep her comfortable, and enjoy the time they have together.

She doesn't answer me, which I'm glad for. Vocalizing Billie's mortality is hard, and I know it must be unimaginably worse for Rooney.

She pulls away and stands on her tiptoes to press a kiss against my cheek. Her soft lips against my skin send a shock wave of heat through my body. It's the closest thing I'll ever get to a real kiss from her. It's enough and not nearly enough, all at the same time. My stomach muscles tighten. I need more. I need her.

The thing is, she's looking at me a little like she needs me, too. Like she *wants* me. Those blue eyes are exceptionally bright and her lips are pursed as she falls back onto the balls of her feet. If I just leaned down, then I'd easily be able to capture those lips with my own, and based on her look, she wouldn't stop me. She'd let me take from her what belongs to my brother and I'd enjoy it, because even if it's wrong, for once in my life, I would have a taste of perfection. Of the goodness she exudes.

"Rooney." I swallow thickly. "What was that for?"

She tilts her head, hair falling loose around her face. I catch it and twist it around my finger. She blushes. This close to her, I can feel her cheeks heat, which reminds me I'm a damn idiot for thinking you can fly close to the sun.

"A thank you," she answers.

"You don't need to be thanking me. This is all—"

She looks away suddenly and manages to shrink down into herself by wrapping her arms around her middle. "Step Ten?"

I wasn't going to say that, but I'm glad she thought I was. If not, I might've told her about how this is all for her. For Billie, too, but mainly for Rooney, because at the end of the day, Rooney's the one who's going to have to deal with this and find a way to keep moving forward. I've never wanted to do anything for anyone in my entire life, and then Rooney stepped in. Being around her is the first time I haven't just *wished* I could be better, but I've tried to *be* better. She's the only mistake I can't bring myself to regret. I'm afraid that even when I've ruined her, I won't regret it.

CHAPTER SIXTEEN

Rooney

My heart starts hurting when he doesn't answer me, which tells me all I need to know—he's here for me because of Step Ten. He's still righting his wrong toward me. I didn't mind it at first, because I wanted Silas in my life, even if he didn't come across as the most warm and cuddly type of guy. Now I mind it.

We've come so far from when we met, and I want him to be helping me because he actually wants to. I don't want to be an obligation, or something he feels bad about. The more I get to know him, the more I'm putting my heart out on the line—letting the attraction turn into something *more*.

It's not something I can keep doing if I'm nothing but Step Ten. If Silas leaves me, I'll have lost one of the most important people in my life. I won't be able to take losing him *and* Mama.

For once I need him to choose staying over running. But Silas is always running, and I just wish he'd start running *toward* something, instead of away.

I squeeze my eyes shut. Nothing really matters, I guess.

If he stays or goes, the damage is already done. I already care too much.

I woke up at four this morning to Mama crying out in pain, the sound so broken and wretched, it'll be in my nightmares for the rest of my life. When I got to her, begging her to tell me what was wrong, she just kept sobbing about how everything hurt. It was too soon for her pain medication, so she had to endure it. The entire time, she was begging me to just let her die.

I know the Mama from yesterday wouldn't feel that way—not when she still has her good days. She wouldn't give up and would keep fighting as long she can. But this Mama is the one who's worn down by her illness and who's just ready to move on—the one who doesn't see life without pain anymore.

I lasted about an hour before I gave her the medicine, an hour earlier than I was supposed to, and she slept for a while. She hasn't eaten or talked since—she's just been staring again, thinking those thoughts I know have to be about death.

"I never say anything right with you," Silas says, sounding defeated. "I keep trying…I keep thinking if I keep you at a distance, I won't hurt you. Problem is, I can't. Always seems like it hurts you more."

I open my eyes and stare at the porch floor. "It does."

I hear his footsteps behind me and then he's resting his forehead against my shoulder, his arms wrapping around me. I can't help the way my body immediately sinks into his. I'm all talk.

"You are my Step Ten, Rooney."

My heart goes from hurting to aching. I'll never give up on Silas, even if I am Step Ten. "I know."

"But you're so much more…you're…I care about you. Too fucking much. I break everything, Rooney. There are things I can't take back. People I've ruined. I can't let you be one of those people."

"Then don't."

All of his muscles seem to coil with tension. "You say that like it's easy."

I lean my head against his shoulder and lay my arms over his. I use enough pressure so he can't let go without forcibly removing himself. "It's easy because I know you. I know your heart and I know you won't hurt me."

"Not on purpose," he adds, solemnly.

I grip him tighter. "Not even then," I say, hoping my sternness comes across as confidence.

"Rooney, you're too good. You see too much good."

"Is that a bad thing?"

He sighs. "Sometimes."

I shake my head. "You do know there can only be one if the other exists, right?"

"You're the good, I'm the bad."

"We've all got good in us. We've all got bad."

"Not you."

I close my eyes. The truth is on the tip of my tongue. To tell him how it's the bad in me wanting to be with him instead Brandon—that I'm willing to break the bond of two brothers so I can have what I want. Instead, I go with something different.

"I have a stack of books on my bookshelf from the library I belonged to in Kentucky. I stole them," I blurt out.

Silas doesn't say anything at first, but then he bursts out laughing, burying his face deeper into my neck. His lips brush against my skin and his laughter makes everything in my body tingle. I can't help but laugh along with him, even more tension washing away.

I love his laugh. All rumbles and cracks, still like he hasn't done it in forever. It'll be my mission to make sure he laughs more. Laughing is good for the soul.

He starts to pull away and my arms automatically tighten. Silas' laughter cuts off. "What's wrong?" he demands.

"Don't go," I say, sounding desperate. Probably

because I am.

"I'm not. For as long as I can be, I'm done running," he promises, and I actually believe him. He'll stay until he can't, or until he *thinks* he can't, when life is too messy and unorganized for him to handle. "I was just gonna go in and make you lunch."

"Oh." A tsunami of relief washes over me. "You do know you can visit without doing something for us, right?"

"If I don't have my hands on shit that needs to be fixed, I'm gonna have my hands on…never mind."

Hands on what? He can't surely mean his hands on me, can he? An image sears through my mind, a lot like a scene you might see on a daytime soap, where Silas is kissing me. Hands, everywhere. Lips, everywhere. Naked, exploring…

I can feel his erection pressing against me, hot and needy, wanting everything I do. Probably more. Part of me hopes more. The other part…the other part is terrified. Terrified because the only way to get anything with Silas is to take a leap of faith. Not just because I'll need to break up with his brother, but because if I tell Silas I want him, he'll react in the worst way. He'll remind me of all the reasons why we can't be together and then, without a doubt, run. Fast and far. Then I'll be alone, and I don't want to be alone. I don't want to give myself to him if he's going to run. And I don't just mean my virginity—I mean my heart and my thoughts and everything else you can give over to somebody.

Only, I think he already has all of that—heart, thought, everything. I have no choice in the matter.

Silas clears his throat and in an instant, he's stepping back from me. I can't look back at him, but I hear him shift, the distinct sound of jeans crinkling. "So how's about that lunch?" he says, his voice deeper than I've ever heard it.

Breathe normally, I remind myself. I think I may need to steal some of Mama's emergency oxygen.

All I can muster is a stiff nod. Luckily it doesn't matter,

because Silas is already pushing past me and heading into the house. I remain in place for a while, trying to get myself under control. When I hear the soft clatter of pans followed by a string of even quieter curse words, I finally go in.

His back is to me and he's gripping the counter, a pot just to the side of him. The way the muscles in his arms are flexed, he looks like he might have enough strength to rip the counter out and fling it clear across the state. He murmurs another curse and then sighs exasperatedly as he slams a hand against the counter.

Maybe he doesn't want to want me. He must not, if the thought of us being together makes him this way.

Mid-curse, his attention snaps back to me, as if he's just realizing I'm in his vicinity. Not like this is my house or anything. He straightens, jaw tensing.

I head over to the baby monitor and listen. I'm met with her even—well, even for her—breathing pattern. I set the monitor down and reach below to the drawer with the utensils. "What are we having?"

Silas finally begins to move. "How about soup and a grilled cheese sandwich?" he asks. "This way you can warm the soup up for your mama if she gets hungry."

How does he go from scary to kind in less than a minute? He has so many sides, and while some make me question my feelings for him, most only make those feelings grow. Deepen. "That sounds good. The soups are in the pantry."

He walks over and grabs a can. He starts working around the kitchen and I realize he probably already knew where the soup was. He has to know where everything in this kitchen is by now. I hold up a spoon, feeling awkward and unsure of what to do while he preps everything.

"Silas, I—" I begin, no clue where I'm going.

He shakes his head sharply. "Not right now."

"Okay," I whisper, dropping my arms to my sides. "Sorry."

The butter knife clatters to the countertop and then the next thing I know, he's turning around and stalking toward me. He cages me in, his arms on either side of my body and his hands gripping the counter edges.

"Never be sorry, Rooney. *I'm* the one who's sorry. I'm putting myself first and that's just…I can't do that."

"How are you…Silas, I don't think you—"

"Let's leave it alone, okay? I hate seein' you upset and crying, and all I want to do is give you a break. I want to see you smile because your smile…damn, it makes life worth it." His eyes are pleading. He raises his hands to cup my shoulders. "I want to do everything I can to make this easier on you and me messin' with your head only makes it harder. So, I'm gonna make us some soup and you're gonna take a seat and let me take care of you, okay?"

I do exactly as he says. I watch him alternate between stirring the soup and flipping the grilled cheese. When he's finished, he sets the food on the table and takes the seat beside me with a grin. His grin looks a lot like a mixture of a thousand different emotions, but there's something in his eyes that seems like he's confused about it all—like he's never experienced any of this before.

"Thank you, Silas," I say, as I dip my spoon into the soup. "My life's better with you in it."

He doesn't look like he agrees, but he doesn't disagree, for once. "Mine is, too. A whole fucking lot better."

***

About an hour after Silas leaves, I change into my pajamas and head into Mama's room.

"Rooney?" she says softly. "I'm glad you're coming in here."

"You miss me that much?" I ask her, trying to joke. When Mama's the one joking around, I can always follow along and usually I actually end up feeling happy. When

I'm the one, it always feels so unnatural and wrong.

"Only a smidger.." She gives me a tired smile as I lie down beside her.

She looks better than before—there's some color in her cheeks whereas before she looked like a washed-out painting of herself. Her eyes are a little brighter now, too, which is nice to see, compared to the dull, lifeless ones looking back at me earlier. Those scare me because they're checked out, like I've already lost her.

"Oh, what can I say. I always miss my baby girl."

"Me, too." I curl under the covers, facing her. She rolls onto her side, her bones popping and cracking, but she's not affected. By now, she has a higher pain tolerance. "How are you feeling? Did you eat the soup Silas made?"

She nods. "It was tasty and went down easy." She reaches over and runs her fingers beneath my eyes, rubbing the bags I'm sure are permanent by now. "I'm feeling better, but I wish you wouldn't worry so much. There's not a whole lot either of us can do about this."

"I can't help it. You're my mama."

Her eyes go wide. "Since when? Nobody's told me."

I laugh. "If you don't remember giving birth to me, then we have other problems on our hands."

"I'd say we do, because it's impossible to forget a thing like that. It's like a horror film. Put it on the screen and it'll be instant birth control." She drops her hand back to the bed. "You are the best thing to ever happen to me, even if labor was the worst thing. If you wouldn't have come along, my life would be empty and sad. I can't—I can't imagine not having you through this."

"I can't imagine not being here," I say, my voice shaking. I can't seem to do anything but cry anymore. It's a mystery how my tear ducts are still functioning "I love you, Mama."

"I love you, too," she says back, her voice soft and scratchy. "When I'm gone…"

"Mama—"

She gives me a look and I cut off. "We have to face it."

"I have, Mama. I just don't want to *talk* about it. It"—I look down at her blankets so I don't have to see her face—"scares me."

"It scares me, too. It's all I can think about." I glance back up and her eyes are closed tightly. "But we need to talk about it, or else it'll be even scarier when it happens."

I nod. I know what she means, but it doesn't make things any easier. Nothing will ever be easy about this.

"How about we talk about it after tomorrow, huh?"

"Okay." My stomach does flips out of nervousness and excitement. Our non-wedding is tomorrow and I'm feeling just about everything a girl can feel. You'd think I'm getting married for real.

Mama's eyes light up. "You should try on your dress for me."

"Again?" I say, trying to draw out the word like I'm exasperated, but I'm not. I totally want to, even though I've already tried it on several times for her. "If I must."

It's hanging on the inside of her closet. I quickly put it on and swirl around. I don't bother to zip it up, only hold the back together as best as I can. "I love this dress."

"So do I," Mama agrees. "I'm not sure Silas' gonna know what to do with himself."

I hope not. I only give a shy smile.

"Be honest with me? Do you like him?"

"Yeah, Mama. He's my friend."

"Honey, you two are as far from friends as we are from Texas." She pats the bed. "You need to talk about this, so let's talk. I promise to stay unbiased."

I smooth out my dress and sit down. I'll have to iron it anyway, but there's no use making it any worse.

"So," she says, obviously trying to keep her voice from sounding too excited and too gossip-hungry, "do you like him?"

I blush. "I do."

Mama lets out a small squeal. "How much?"

"Too much."

"You can't like somebody too much. Why do you say that?"

"Because I'm with Brandon. And even if I wasn't…Silas doesn't want me."

"He wants you, sweetie. He looks at you with the sparkling eyes."

Mama's always said when someone really, really cares about another person, their eyes sparkle. I've seen that in Silas' eyes, but I know him well enough to know whatever he feels, he'll keep it hidden. "Maybe he wants me *that* way, but not in the way that counts. He's so afraid of hurting people—me especially. He'll run, Mama, and I don't need that kind of hurt."

"So you'll stay with Brandon because he'll stay?"

I nod. It sounds like the right reason to me.

"Do you really love Brandon?"

"I do," I say softly. I link my hands and stare down at them. "He's wonderful and kind. Cute."

"But you have stronger feelings for Silas?"

"I love Brandon like a friend. But Silas…" I hope she'll get the picture. A friend doesn't make a girl feel the way Silas makes me feel. Friends don't cause butterflies and chills and things I've never felt before. "I just don't want to be alone."

When I glance up at Mama, her eyes have softened. "You won't be. No one will ever let that happen; you're too sweet for anyone to ever leave you on your own. Even if you end things with Brandon, I guarantee you he'll still be here. I may not be a fan of him *with* you, but I do like him. He's a good guy and he'll stand by you. I have a feeling that given the chance, Silas will step up, too. No matter what happens, if you need him, he'll show up. He's proved it many times now."

"So what are you saying?"

She takes hold of my hand. "That you need to do whatever you feel is right, and have faith that everything will turn out the way it needs to."

"Mama…"

"I've lived my life running scared of love and pretending I don't need anyone. Don't make my mistake. If you learn anything from me, learn to love and to need people, but not rely on them."

I slide down into the bed. If this dress is going to get ironed anyway, who cares? I wrap an arm around her waist, careful not to put too much weight on her. "I've learned everything I know from you."

"And I've learned a whole heck of a lot from you, too," Mama tells me. "But I think we still have a lot to learn from each other."

"Me, too." Sadness creeps in. Mama and I still have time together, but when she's gone…*all* of our time will be gone. I have to take in as much as I can, and keep her with me as long as I can. Every day we have together is special and it's time to start focusing on what we have, instead of what we don't.

CHAPTER SEVENTEEN

Silas

I knock on the open door of Mom's office, though it's more like a library. There isn't even a spot for a computer on the desk because she's got so many books. Her collection seemed huge before I went off to jail, but now it's even worse.

She looks up from her chair. I guess she expected Dad, because her whole body jolts in surprise. "Silas?"

I take a cautious step in and glance around the room. Among the books are a lot of pictures. The younger ones show I was just a kid being raised by normal, loving parents, and how I should've grown up to be a normal, loving kid Obviously I didn't. Even before I started drinking, my eyes are dark and emotionless and there's a carelessness to me—like I don't give a fuck about what gets destroyed. I know exactly when I started drinking, because the pictures stop. The only way anyone could've taken any of me would've been to hog-tie me down.

I didn't see the point of it all—of family and friends and life. As long as I had a drink in my system, I didn't much care about anything else.

"Everything okay?"

I tear my gaze away from the room and look at Mom. "Yeah."

She sets her opened book face down to save her page. She always used to get so pissed at Brandon and me when we'd dog-ear pages. "Is there something you want to talk about or…"

I swallow and run my over my jaw. "My hair."

Her eyebrows draw together. "Your hair?"

I grit my teeth and nod. "I'd like to cut it."

"Okay," she says, still confused. "When?"

"Tomorrow before…" I trail off because she knows and I don't want to talk anymore. Talking to anyone outside of Rooney and Billie makes me feel too open. Too vulnerable. Aside from my complicated feelings toward Rooney, being around them is easy. With my parents and everyone else, I know they'll expect more. They'll want answers and growth and socialization…all shit I can't give.

"Before the wedding? We can do that." Her gaze dances over my hair as if she's already cutting it in her imagination. "You'll look so handsome. I'm sure Rooney will like it."

I don't want to look handsome. I've purposefully kept my hair long because I thought it'd make me more unapproachable. Little did I know the guy-bun, or whatever the fuck it's called, is popular. But I've kept it anyway because I'm not out to impress.

What I do want—and why I'm doing this—is because I care what Rooney thinks. I want her to see I'm doing everything I can to make tomorrow special for her and Billie.

"How short do you want it?" Mom asks, attempting more conversation.

"Gone."

"That's doable, too," she says.

She goes to touch my hair and I instantly flinch away and she nods, disappointment in her eyes. I want to be more for her, but I can't, and it's best she realizes that now. "Maybe a buzz."

Whatever she does will be fine. At least this'll give her something to do and will make tomorrow special for her, too. She's been the best kind of mom and it's not her fault I turned out the way I am.

I'd snapped at her earlier today when she asked me if Rooney and I will have a first dance. My jackass remark, "How the fuck should I know?" hurt her, so I'm trying to make up for it because it was another mistake in the growing lists of wrong-doings.

"Thanks," I say tightly and then head back out into the hall. I keep telling myself distance is key, and then the next thing I know, I'm doing the opposite. I'm breaking my own rules—my own steps. I've slipped back into my old ways, except this time I'm not so sure I can be stopped.

***

Whenever I try to sleep, I see them. I see their smiles, their bruised and bloody faces, I see the blank spots in people's lives that were left when I *stole* those faces. Living with myself was easier when I was in prison, because prison was punishment. The same when I was living on the streets. Then I came home…and even then it wasn't so bad.

Since I met Rooney, though, everything's flooded back.

I don't know if it's guilt or fear or just self-destruction, but it's all coming back. When I'm with her, it's fine, but when it get away from her…shit, it's like some sort of switch has been flipped. Kind of makes me want to stay with her forever, and stay away from her all at the same time.

I groan and sit up from my spot on the back deck. Not getting any sleep is going to be horrible, especially since it's gonna take a lot of willpower to keep from wanting tomorrow to be real.

I fumble in my pocket for my smokes and then start for the tree I climbed with Rooney. *Our* tree. Damn, I need to stop thinking in those terms. We don't have anything together and we never will. Except for tomorrow.

Well, I guess it's today, by now.

I glance up at the window in Rooney's room as I approach the tree. I haven't been in there and it's quickly becoming one of the top things I think about when I'm over there. That, and fucking her. Telling her how much she means to me. Holding her. Holy hell, there's a lot I think about when it comes to her.

Her room's completely dark. She must be asleep. Good, for two reasons. First, it keeps me away from her. Second, if Rooney's in bed, then Billie's safe and comfortable.

I lean against the tree and light my cigarette. I should really quit. Maybe I've been smoking these damn things because I know they can kill you, but after seeing what Billie's been going through, it feels wrong to smoke. I'm in perfectly good health—I shouldn't be welcoming cancer while other people are suffering from it.

As I'm blowing out a puff of smoke, I see Rooney walking toward me in the dark. She's dressed in a hoodie I'm pretty sure might be Brandon's—a good reminder of what's mine and what's *not*—and a pair of the shortest shorts known to man. They've got sheep and stars on them, which should be juvenile, not downright adorable. Sexy, even.

"You know I ain't supposed to see you before tomorrow, right?" I call as she gets closer. "Bad luck, I hear."

She laughs softly. The sound sends chills down my back and makes my cock harden. "I don't think you and I can have more bad luck."

"I don't think we can, either," I say.

She comes to stop in front me and it takes all my willpower to stop my gaze from worshiping her body.

Every time I look at her, I want to let it roam over those legs, let it kiss the soft mounds of her breasts, hug her hips, and then finally land on those juicy lips of hers. I'm surprised I haven't died yet, trying to deny myself of her. "Shouldn't you be asleep?"

"Couldn't, again." She pulls her bottom lip between her teeth, and damn, what I wouldn't do to lean down and pull her lip between *my* teeth. "I saw you out here and I thought I'd come over. You couldn't sleep, either?"

I raise a hand and drag it roughly through my hair. The way she watches the muscles in my arm...it's too much. As long as I don't take a misstep with her, I know I'll be able to contain myself. The second I do something—kiss her—I know there'll be no going back. I'll want more, I'll take more, and the only way I won't is if I leave her. I'll take all the damn torture the world's got to offer over leaving her.

"No," I answer.

"Help me up?" Rooney asks, releasing her bottom lip and glancing up at me.

She turns and my hands instantly find her hips. We go through the same routine as the last time, and I get caught by all the same traps. Running my hands down her back, smelling her, grabbing her ass. With every touch, she has a response—a shiver, a moan, a sigh—and it all affects me. It all makes me want to bare my fucking soul to her and then rip out my heart, stick it on a platter, and serve it to her. She's gotten to me so much that by the time I start to follow her up the tree, I'm adjusting the evidence of my arousal. It's not like I can go home and take a quick shower—which my parents will no doubt find strange at two in the morning. Then again, I am an adult who's survived *prison time* and can therefore do whatever the fuck I want.

I let out an aggravated breath, because nothing's going to calm me down, and then I climb up after her.

She stares down at her legs, watching them dangle,

swinging slightly. I watch them, too, captivated by them. She's so tiny, but those legs…they could go on for miles. No doubt they'd fit perfectly around my waist. Bad thoughts, wrong thoughts. I'm so screwed.

"I hate sleeping," she says. "Sleeping means there's going to be a new day…and I'm always so terrified it'll be Mama's last."

The sadness in her voice has me nearly falling off the tree limb and crumpling to the ground. I wish she didn't have to go through this. I want to take all the sadness away from her. I don't know how to, though, so I settle for slipping an arm around her waist. She immediately sighs into my side and lays her head against my shoulder.

"I hate it, too," I tell her quietly. I can't help but brush my lips against the top of her head. "It's the only time in my life I can forget…and I don't want to forget."

"Because then you have to wake up and relive reality all over again."

This girl gets it. Even though we've taken completely different paths and are completely different people, she gets it. With her, I feel like I could just about tell her anything, which terrifies me. I don't want to know what happens when she finds out what I did. I don't want to see the look of disgust and hatred in her eyes.

"There's no one else like you, Rooney," I admit quietly, because I'm afraid to say it too loud.

She doesn't say anything, just sinks even farther into me. I'm pretty sure we could get closer on a molecular level, and it still wouldn't be close enough.

"I like it when you hold me," she whispers. "Is that wrong?"

"Yeah." I won't lie to her. I won't pretend being with me is okay. I shouldn't be looking at her or wanting her, not when I don't even deserve to be her friend. "But it's right, too."

"I think it's more right than wrong," she tells me.

I'm not sure who reaches out first, but we both watch

as our hands link together, mine rough and hers soft.

"I'm glad you came into my life, Silas. I don't think I could do this without you. I couldn't breathe until you came along."

I couldn't, either. I've been drowning all my life and she's my life raft. "Someone needed to be here with you."

"And you won't go anywhere?" she asks. "I can't lose you, too."

I can tell she's pushing for me to say I'll stay with her. I've seen it in her eyes and I've heard the question without her even asking it. I can't make any promises because I know I'll have to break them. "I'll be here as long as you need me, Rooney."

There's still a long journey ahead of her, and she knows it. I'd definitely rot in hell if I left her during any of this. When I'm sure she's good and ready—and when my brother's pulled his damn head out of his ass—that's when I'll let her go. Even if it means chaining myself to this very tree to keep from going after my brother, and claiming what I want.

"I'll always need you," she tells me. She tilts her head back and looks up at me. Her eyes are so bright, glistening like the stars above us, and it makes my heart beat hard, and irregular. "Silas. I think you're my best friend."

My voice catches. "You're mine, too, Rooney."

She sets her head back down. "Question?"

"Yeah?" Fuck knows, I'm an open book with her. She could probably ask me anything and I'd tell her all of my deepest, darkest secrets and then some. I won't go telling them to her without her asking me to, but the second she does ask, I know it'll all tumble out.

"Tomorrow," she starts and, from the shy tone of her voice, I can guess she's probably blushing, "are we going to write our own vows?"

My eyebrows go sky-high. This is why I'm a guy. Guys don't think about this sort of girlie, sentimental shit. "If you want. Or we can say whatever the traditional speech is."

"I think I'd like to write our own, if that's okay?" she asks, her uncertainty clear. "I think Mama would like it better. But you don't have to put a whole lot of work into it or anything. Just say whatever."

"Whatever, huh?" I ask. I raise my eyebrows and let and a smile tease at my lips. I've never smiled as much as I do with Rooney. Even as a kid, I was never the carefree type, while Brandon always was. I was the one who overthought everything and spent a lot of alone-time, brooding. Mom used to say Brandon and I were the difference between sugar and salt.

"Not whatever. Just what's true."

"Ah, so I shouldn't talk about aliens," I say.

"No," she says in a stern voice. "That was a secret. A secret you're supposed to take to the grave. No one needs to know about my people or my origins."

She sounds so serious, I can't help but laugh. I wish I would've known her before Billie got sick. I wonder if she would be like this, or maybe losing her mama has caused her to step out of her shell.

"Sorry, I thought it was okay to tell. I guess I shouldn't have sent out the directions to Area 51 to everyone and their uncle."

She playfully slaps my chest. "I'm rethinking the best-friend status. My people are in danger because of you."

"You can't rethink our status," I tell her. "It's etched in stone."

"You're right, it is. You're irreplaceable."

"Damn right I am," I say. With my thumb, I gently caress the length of her index finger. I try my damnedest to ignore the chills spreading down her legs. And I fail. Miserably. I release her hand and trail my fingers down her thigh to her knee. More chill bumps rise in wake of my fingers.

"Cold?" I know damn well she isn't, so I don't know why I'm asking. All I know is if she lies and says yes, then I need to back off If she says no, then…well, then I don't know.

She hesitates, her whole body rigid. When she looks up at me again, her eyes are as round as saucers, extra shimmery, and her lips are red from her pulling them between her teeth so much. Holy fuck, I want to taste those lips. I want to trace the length of her body with my hands. I want her to know all of the things I feel for her, but can never say out loud.

"No," she whispers.

I swallow and look away. Why did I even ask? I wasn't going to like the answer, regardless. "You should probably get home. Tomorrow's a big day."

She slips out of my arms. I risk a glance at her and see a blush has crept up over her cheeks and she's looking down at her thigh, where my hand was. Shit, I'm gonna hurt her no matter what I do. Be with her, run from her, stay, leave. It's all just gonna be one mighty mistake, with consequences.

"Hey," I say, catching her chin. "This is on me. I'm not—"

She meets my gaze with determination. "You're *everything*. And you're afraid of everything. I'll see you tomorrow."

We stay silent as we climb down. All I can think about is how this girl might be shy and quiet, but she's also fierce. She's exactly what I need and maybe she's right—maybe I'm just setting myself up for disaster on purpose, so there's no alternative option for me to ruin.

CHAPTER EIGHTEEN

Rooney

Even after the way last night ended, I wake up nervous and excited. Both emotions are tangled inside my belly, tumbling around like shoes in a dryer. Something felt like it changed last night—like Silas and I are stepping into new territory.

"It's very normal to be nervous," Mama says from her wheelchair, "or so I've heard."

"It is *very* normal," Mrs. Manning provides. She's standing behind me and finishing up my hair.

She put a flower head band in my hair, according to Mama's advising, and I think it's going to really set off the dress. She's already done my makeup, too, so all I have to do after this is slip on my dress. I can't wait to see the finished product—for Silas to see it.

"I couldn't even think straight on mine. My maid of honor was so worried I was going to forget my vows, she memorized them for me."

"So you wrote your own?" I ask.

She squints, not quite happy with the setting of the headband. "We did. Is that what you and Silas are doing?"

I nod.

Her eyes widen. "Really? I wouldn't have thought Silas would've gone for that."

"You'd be surprised at the lengths Silas takes for her," Mama points out.

"I bet," Mrs. Manning says and a look I don't recognize passes between them. " Go put your dress on."

I go into my bathroom and carefully slip on my dress. I've spent more time than I should have imagining what Silas' expression will look like when I walk down the aisle. I want him to look at me the way you see a groom looks a bride, like his life hadn't really started until that day.

"Rooney?" Mrs. Manning calls through the door. "I hate to bother you, but Brandon is on the phone, and he's hoping to catch you."

All my excitement washes away. I drop my gaze from the mirror. I suddenly feel wretched and disgusting. I'm a terrible person for wanting Silas the way I do.

I open the door and Mrs. Manning holds out the phone, with a strange expression. Almost disappointment.

"Let me zip you up, first." I take the phone from her and turn around. She zips me up, and then says, "Travis is here to help me with your mama. He'll meet you on the porch."

Mr. Manning is being kind enough to walk me down the aisle, since I don't have anyone else to do it. "Thank you. For everything."

She only grins. "Don't keep us waiting. We're all too excited."

I laugh and bring the phone up to my ear. "Hey."

"Hey. I hear you're getting married to Silas. Talk about betrayal," Brandon jokes. He wouldn't be joking if he knew the turmoil in my heart. "Why's this the first time I'm hearing about this?"

"We haven't talked." It comes out more bitter than I intend. Probably because I want sweet, stable, normal Brandon to be the one I want—except if Brandon is so sweet, stable, and normal, you'd think he'd be here for me. Not just *here* here, but making more of a point to call me or get in touch with me, rather than only talking to me for a few minutes every few days. Before, it didn't matter because I didn't know what it meant to be cared for or to be put above everything else, but now I do.

"I know and I'm sorry," he says, sounding genuine. "I've been a terrible boyfriend and I'm going to make it up to you. I've got a massive surprise for you."

I'm an awful person. I shouldn't be this way toward him. He doesn't deserve it—he's a good guy and I'm sure if he could be, he'd be here. Me, on the other hand, I think I used to be good. "Okay."

"You don't want to know what it is?" he asks.

"It wouldn't be much of a surprise if I knew," I point out.

"Are you ever not perfect?" Brandon asks with a chuckle. If he only knew. "So, you and Silas must be close, if you're already at the marriage stage."

I can't help but smile at myself in the mirror. "I really like your brother. He's...he's a great guy."

Another laugh. I do not like that laugh. "Never thought I'd hear those words."

"Why not?"

Brandon's quiet for a second and then stutters as if I've thrown him off balance. "No. Shit, no, Rooney. I don't mean—I agree with you. He's just never let other people see that. Half the time, he never even lets me. I'm surprised he's this way with you."

I am, too. But I'm not about to admit it. "When you come home and get to talk to him, you'll see. He's just been through a lot and it's hard to understand unless you've been through a lot, too."

"Yeah, but, Rooney, you didn't—he..."

"I know," I admit. "Are you...have you not forgiven him for..."

Brandon lets out a breath, and I can imagine it clearly.

Only it's not Brandon I picture doing it, it's Silas. They're so much alike, but it's only Silas I see. "Sometimes I don't think I have. But other times I do. He's my brother and I love him, Rooney. Isn't that enough?"

"Not always."

"I guess not," Brandon says quietly. He clears his throat and quickly changes the subject. "Send me pictures? Mom said you look beautiful."

"I will," I promise. "I'm sure your mom will send you a million, too."

He chuckles. "Wouldn't doubt it. I'll let you go, then. I love you."

"Love you," I repeat and I'm not sure if I'm saying because I have to, or because I want to. If I've always felt the way I do now, or if I've just changed.

I'll let today be a happy day, and then I'll figure it out.

***

"Hey, kiddo, you ready?" Mr. Manning asks me as I step out onto the porch.

I glance down at my bouquet, filled with pretty purple and yellow flowers, and blush. "I think so."

"Well, you look beautiful as always," he tells me and my blush deepens. He loops his arm through mine and helps me down the steps, since I'm in Mama's tall shoes. He leaves our arms linked and starts walking me back to where the wedding's set up. "The natives are getting restless—particularly your mama. She's got a lot of life in her, that's for sure."

I can't help but laugh. "No doubt if we don't get out there, she'll charge in here, find me, and drag me out."

"Hold up. Got to text the wife."

We pause and he texts Mrs. Manning to start the music. From where we are, I can hear it begin playing. Nothing traditional, just a romantic song to make the day more special.

"We better go," Mr. Manning says as we start walking again.

We round the corner and my gaze immediately finds Silas beneath a wooden arch. He's the most handsome man I've ever seen, dressed in a tan suit that fits his body like it was crafted with the sole intention of him wearing it. What shocks me is his hair is short now—cut close to his scalp, his stubble only slightly shorter. It makes him even more striking, his caramel eyes unhidden and sparkling, and his lips full and apple red. He looks like something out of a magazine, not someone who used to be in prison and lived on the streets. I barely even register the scar going from his ear and down his neck, because it's just another piece that makes him beautiful—mesmerizing.

His gaze meets mine and I gasp. It's not friendly or welcoming, which would calm my growing nerves. Nope, Silas isn't capable of easy. He has to look at me with the most intense, soul-consuming stare I've ever witnessed. His gaze roams down my legs and then back up, paying special attention to the hemline of my dress, my hips, and the swell of my breasts. By the time it lands back on my eyes, I've forgotten how to breathe.

He swallows and the closer we get, the more his stare intensifies, until I'm standing right before him, my skin on fire and my heart beating so rapidly it's rabbit-like.

Silas leans forward. His lips brush against the sensitive area behind my ear as he whispers, "You're a gorgeous sight."

My blush deepens. "You're handsome, yourself."

He straightens, a grin tugging at his lips. He takes my hand and pulls me toward Mama. "No use in you holding these," he tells me, and then takes the bouquet from me. He places it in Mama's lap and kisses her cheek. "For another gorgeous woman," he whispers, so only she and I can hear.

Mama blushes. Actually *blushes*. I've never seen her do that before; I didn't even think she was capable of it.

147

Maybe she's the one who should be marrying Silas. Then again, after this little show of perfection, she might have to fight me for him. I have no doubt I'm looking at him with a swoon-face. As if all the swoon happening inside of my body needs to be shown on the outside, too.

Mama reaches for my hand and squeezes. "My pretty girl," she says in a hoarse voice.

I lean down and kiss her other cheek and then let Silas lead me back up to the arch. There's a man standing just behind it. He has a book in one hand, while the other is fisted around a cane to help him stand. He's obviously been weathered by age and there's a haunted look to his eyes I recognize because I see it in Silas'. But there's also kindness there.

"I'm Bob," the man says, "and I'll be officiating your wedding. Or whatever this is."

I smile at him because he doesn't seem like he's putting this down in any way, he's just generally not sure what to call it. I don't think any of us do. Except for Mama—for her, this is real.

Silas faces me and takes my other hand. The look in his eyes is exactly how I dreamed for him to look at me, and more.

Bob holds up his book and begins to read. I don't hear a lick of what he's saying and I wonder how many people actually do. I'll bet everyone is just as distracted as I am, just as nervous, and just as lost. It's all good, though. There's nothing bad about this moment. Not the butterflies in my stomach or the flush in my cheeks, not the way his look makes me feel special and loved, not even the fact that this is fake, even though I want it to be real.

My stare drifts from his eyes to his lips. When the kiss-the-bride part comes, is he going to kiss me? Or will he go straight for the cheek, or the forehead? No doubt Mama will expect the real thing, and throw a fit if she doesn't get it. But what about me? Do I want the real thing?

His lips part and chills rush throughout my body. Yes, I

do. I definitely do. I can't even think about all the reasons why I shouldn't, or the consequences that will follow.

He makes such a big deal about me being good, as if it's something ingrained in me. Really, it's a conscious effort I make every day. Up until now, I never really had a reason to stray away from making the right choices. No one else except for Silas has made me want to take chances, and pray there's something there to catch me.

His lips part again, but this time it's so he can talk. Oh God, I've been completely blanked out this entire time.

"This is the part where you say your vows," he reminds me with a wry smile.

"Oh." Even though I love all of his rare smiles, this is my favorite. The blush on my cheeks is probably flaming, and could be an alternative energy source. "Right. My vows."

He shakes his head, smile still there. "This was what you wanted."

I glance down at our hands, and draw in a breath for courage. Last night after I left Silas, I kept writing and rewriting what I was going to say in my mind. It was on a constant carousel and no matter how hard I tried to stop and fall asleep, I couldn't. When I did, finally, I'm pretty sure I dreamed about it. Now I can't remember a single word or how I was supposed to begin. No wonder why people write these things down.

"I had planned what I was going to say, but I, uh, forgot them," I manage to admit, with only a slight stutter.

"You're fine," Silas tells me.

His thumb strokes the inside of my wrist, calming me enough to get some of my thoughts together.

I can do this. It's just Silas. And Mom. His mom and dad. Some random guy I don't know, but seems like a nice person. It'll be fine. I'll be fine.

"You came into my life when I needed someone. Not just anyone, either; I think I—I think I needed you, in particular. You've been—*are*—everything I need. You've been strong when I've needed to be weak, you've been quiet when I've needed someone to be with, you've just been my best friend." I pause and notice he's looking at me with an awed expression, like he can't believe I'd feel this way. I can't believe he can't believe it. He should. It's all so true.

"I'm not sure how many people would just instinctively know what I need like you do. Letting me scream, giving me a tree, letting me in—it's all stuff I'm not sure anyone else would be okay with. But you are, and...and that makes you one of the best people I know." His brows pull together and I know he's fighting an internal battle to not argue with me. Good thing he's in a position where he can't. He has to listen to me, and accept what I'm saying. I squeeze his hands.

"Silas, I plan on keeping you in my life as long as you're willing to have a place in it. No, you'll *always* have a place in it, whether you want it or not. You just have to choose to claim it. You've become a part of me and my life, and I can't imagine being without you. You're it for me."

Silas' lips part as he tilts his head, his gaze searching for more. Hearing what I've just said and believing it are two very different things.

I draw in a shaky breath. "Your turn."

He blinks and offers me a half-smile that barely even curls up the left side of his lips. It's enough to make my heart beat madly. I hope he can't feel my pulse through my hands.

"My turn." He does something I don't expect: he slides his hands from my own and then brings them up to my neck, his thumbs resting along the curve of my jaw. Yeah, if he wasn't feeling my pulse before, he is now.

"My life's always been going in the wrong direction...I've always been heading in the way I shouldn't be. And while you know my reservations about our friendship, the day I brought you and Billie food was the best day of my life—until today, at least. It was the day I finally felt like I was doing something right. Not just because of my dumb steps, but because you're involved, and nothing with you…nothing with you can ever feel wrong. I haven't believed in a lot—not in goodness or strength or loyalty—but then I met you, and you're everything I didn't believe in and now *do* believe in. You're some sort of angel, giving me light and guiding me through the darkness. I'm not sure if I'm *everything,* but you are. *You* are everything, Rooney."

I don't know what possessed me to tell him that, yesterday. I just want him to see he's so much more than what he thinks, and how he can be even more if he just lets it happen.

He takes a step closer and we have no choice but to tilt our faces into each other's. He's so close, our chests are brushing, and there's barely any space separating us. "You're some sort of haven and risk, all wrapped up into one, but you're worth it all. So worth it, that I'm agreeing to marry you and so long as it's in your best interest, I won't leave you. Ever."

His words do something to me—make me feel both safe and scared, because the only thing to really fear is the safety disappearing. But I won't let fear rule me, because if I've learned anything, it's life is short and there's no room for dwelling. You get one or two chances, or sometimes you get none. You take what you get and you make the best of it.

Silas is the best of it.

He doesn't put distance between us during the "I dos." I try my best to listen, but being so close to Silas makes it nearly impossible. He smells too good, looks too strong, and holds me too perfect. Plus, it's not like he's easy on the eyes or anything.

"Do you have the rings?" Bob asks.

Rings? I didn't even think about the rings. I glance nervously over at Mama, but she's grinning at Silas like he holds all the answers in the world. That's just fine, as long as he can make wedding bands materialize out of thin air.

I should know Silas takes care of me. He releases my face and drops a hand into his pocket. He holds up a solid gold band for me to take and then winks at me as he reveals another, thinner gold band with a line of diamonds on it. I gasp. Why do I doubt him?

He shrugs, giving me a sheepish look. "You can thank your mama."

I glance over at her. "They were your grandparents'," she explains, tears filling her eyes.

"Mama, I—"

She waves me off. "Silas already argued me up and down the steep side of a mountain. I want them to be a part of this." She lets out a small yawn. She's usually had a nap by now to keep her going. This has to be tiring her out. She's paler than normal, too. "Now continue with the ceremony."

I look back to Silas, and take the ring. Our fingers brush, which does nothing for my nerves. Or my knees.

Bob tells us how the rings are a symbol of eternity and then he has us both repeat after him, before we slip the rings on each other's fingers. As Silas does mine, I notice his hands are shaking—he's just as nervous as I am. I don't acknowledge it because I don't want him to know I saw his weakness, not that I think it's a weakness. If I had the time, I'd explain to him all the reasons why I think his shaking hands are a sign of strength. It shows he's human—how he's worried about making this right, and bad people don't worry about what's right.

When the rings are secure on our fingers, I know what's next. Except I don't—I really don't. I'm going to leave it up to Silas. Cheek, lips, or forehead, it's whatever he prefers. I won't start it, but I won't end it.

"You may kiss the bride."

I see all of the possibilities flicker behind Silas' eyes. I can see his skepticism and terror, but his need is the most visible—his want. Maybe he's not as emotionally tied to me as I am to him, but our bodies are almost being pulled together. Everything he does, I feel, and I think it might be the same for him. Like half of him belongs to me and half of me belongs to him.

He seems to make a decision, bringing his hands—shaking even more—up to my face. He slowly tilts my head back with his thumbs, inclining his head toward mine. His gaze searches my own, looking for some sort of permission to take the next step.

You have my permission. You have all of me. I can keep telling myself today is for Mama—and it is wholeheartedly for her— but this kiss isn't. This kiss is for me.

My lips part in preparation and I plead him with my eyes to close the gap. He seems to sense it, because the next thing I know, his soft, incredibly full lips are brushing against mine with the softest yet strongest kiss I've had in my entire life. It's the perfect kiss. The kind where the black and white movie ends, with the camera circling around the man and the woman as they embrace, wrapped up in each other's arms, passionately kissing. I want to fall as deep into Silas as I can, without a life jacket and no way to float back to the surface. I'd happily drown in it. I never want this kiss to end.

Silas pulls away and distantly, I hear clapping, but I can't function beyond seeing Silas' confused, curious eyes as they lust over what we just shared. I can still see the conflict there, but now it's like he sees the choice. I'm not sure if it's the choice he thinks he should make, but it's the one we both want.

He brushes his thumb along my lip. After our kiss, everything seems possible. Like I can do anything. Even us.

***

"Sweetie, it looks like your mama is starting to go down for the count," Mrs. Manning says to me.

I don't have to glance over at Mama to know it's the truth. I've been watching her like a hawk. I've gotten good at knowing the exact point when she's had too much, because I have to know it, or else she won't say anything. She doesn't want to admit when she's fading, not even to me. She's had to stay awake and interactive for a longer time than she has in a while. She's putting a lot of effort into doing it and I'm proud of her for it, only we both know she's going to pay for this later. She's going to be exhausted and cranky. I just hope tonight doesn't end with anything worse.

I nod at Mrs. Manning and then head over to Mama. I crouch down in front of her wheelchair. She rolls her head forward tiredly, her eyes half closed. She's not tired enough to refrain from giving me a look of disapproval. "You're going to get your dress dirty."

I roll my eyes. "If I don't fall in your shoes first."

"You've worn heels before."

I twist my ankle so she can see the backs of my feet. "I'm a size bigger than you are."

She snorts and I know where she's about to go before she even starts. "You had to give somewhere. Those bigger feet are your price for having bigger boobs. If I had yours, I wouldn't be complaining."

I blush, but I don't chastise her.

She takes my hand and brings it into her lap. "You look so beautiful and mature."

"Thank you, Mama," I say. "I get it from you."

She doesn't even try to deny it. She just squeezes my hand. "Are you enjoying yourself?"

"I am." I'm enjoying this more than I expected I would. I thought maybe I'd only see it as a memory of Mama, but it's so much more. It's a memory of Silas, too. I know I'll tell my kids and grandkids about today with tears and smiles for a long time to come. "Are you?"

She looks over at Silas. Bob's talking, but Silas is just sort of standing there, playing the part, nodding and answering when needed. His gaze is fixed on me. He doesn't even blink or look away when we catch him—instead, his gaze seems to burn darker. The kiss stirred something, and he hasn't been hiding any of his hungry looks. I'd be lying if I said I don't like it.

"This is all I wanted for you, and more. I didn't expect…I never thought I'd get to see what I'm seeing between the two of you." She lets out a small cough and his expression goes from lust-filled to worried. His attachment to Mama makes my heart swell with pride. "I'm more than enjoying myself. This is the best day I've had in a long time."

"Me, too."

She grins at me, but falters as exhaustion settles back in. I stand up, because my knees are getting tired, and point over to where Mr. Manning is plugging in the stereo to the extension cord, while Mrs. Manning takes pictures of the wedding cake. I was right in telling Brandon she'd take a lot, all of which have been uploaded to Facebook already. Silas hates it, but I'm thankful this is being documented.

"Why don't we do the dance and cut the cake, so you can head in?" I ask her. "You have to be getting tired."

"I don't want to ruin today…" she says, her voice wavering.

"You're not," I tell her quickly. "Mama, today wouldn't even be happening if it weren't for you. The only way you could've ruined it was by not coming up with the idea. Don't be worried if you need to head to bed."

"I think I do," she admits and I know it's hard for her.

I motion for Silas to come over to us. He says something to Bob and then heads over. He lost his suit coat in between the ceremony and now, so he's only in a crisp, white button-down that shows off his lean body. All shaved and cut, he looks like he's straight out of a business magazine, but one for extremely attractive people. I recognized he was good-looking before, but now he's so handsome that words seem to have become a problem around him at times.

"We're going to dance and then cut the cake," I tell him.

He comes to a stop beside me and grins down at me. His smile is so open and rare that it steals every single square inch of air I've got. "Sounds good to me."

He leads me over to the stereo. They haven't gotten the song I picked out playing yet, but Silas wraps his arms around my waist anyway, drawing me close. We haven't interacted since we walked down the aisle to the recessional song. He kissed me chastely on the cheek and squeezed my hand, but then we went our separate ways: me to Mama and him to tell Bob thank you.

"She doing okay?" he whispers in my ear.

I try to hide my shiver by wrapping my arms around his neck. "She's tiring out fast."

"I wish she could enjoy this more."

"I do too," I admit. I can't stop my fingers from dancing over the base of his scalp. "You cut your hair."

He nods. "Do you like it?" The way he asks it makes my heart squeeze. He sounds worried and hopeful. Like a little boy looking for verification.

"I love it. Why'd you do it?"

His thick lashes lower, shielding his eyes. "For you."

For me? He cut his hair for me? So I would like it? His words strike me speechless. Only Silas.

Before I can form a logical thought, the music clicks on again. I faintly hear Mr. Manning congratulate himself, while Mrs. Manning makes a whooping sound, but I'm focused on Silas as he squeezes my hips and begins to sway to the music. I'm pretty sure if he doesn't remove his hands, my dress might catch on fire from the heat of his touch. But it'd be the good kind of fire. I'd gladly throw myself in the flames if it meant Silas would continue touching me in this way.

I move farther into him and lay my cheek against his

chest. He immediately tucks his chin against my head, as if this is something we do all the time—like we fit together and he knows exactly how. My eyes drift closed and suddenly it's only me and Silas, dancing to our first song, married and in love.

Here, I can pretend this is real and that Mama's going to be around for when we have babies and she'll be there to grandmother them and teach them all of the things a grandma has to teach her grandkids. Only she'd probably refuse to go by "Grandma" and would teach them things normal grandparents don't teach. We probably wouldn't have a conventional family, but it'd be the one we'd all like—the only one that matters—because marrying Silas, and Mama living, is my perfect and untarnished world, even if it can't exist.

Silas' hands slip from my waist and circle around to my back, with his pinkies resting just above the curve of my butt. He's touched my butt when he's helped me up into the tree, but this time, his touch feels more intimate. Scorching.

I curve in to him and that's when I feel him, hard and needy, pressing against my stomach. An ache unfurls between my legs and I realize just how much I want him—more than I've wanted anyone else. Who am I kidding? There hasn't been anyone else and there never will be. The only one who exists in my heart is Silas.

These touches are torture, but it's a good torture. It's a torture I want to get worse and never end. I bite my lip, trying to hold back a moan. I never moaned before I met Silas. Not even over food.

The song ends and we stop moving, but neither of us lets go. I want to stay wrapped up in his arms until neither of us can stand.

Reality sinks in and I realize that isn't possible. Not with everyone staring at us, like I know they are.

I'm not ashamed of the way I feel about Silas, but I am ashamed because Silas'—*Brandon's*—parents are just a few feet away. I have no doubt Mama's smiling like a madwoman, but the Mannings? They've got to be disappointed, probably about to call up Brandon and explain to him all the reasons why I'm a horrible person who doesn't deserve his, or Silas', time. And lord knows what poor Bob's thinking.

Silas clears his throat. When he speaks, it's deep and rough, like he's barely able to do so. "Guess it's cake time."

I step away from him, keeping my head down, my hair shielding my face. His hand drops from my waist, but he twines his fingers through mine. Some first dance. It was probably the dance to end all dances, if it doesn't end me first.

Our cake would be worthy of a real wedding, rather than a fake one, with only a few people in attendance. I'm not sure how Mrs. Manning got someone to make it on such short notice, or how much it cost her, but I'm glad. It's white and pink, made to look like a bird cage. Along the side of the door and going to the top is a line of flowers, each so intricate they look real.

I glance up just in time to see Mama's grin, which is all I expected and *more,* as Mr. Manning wheels her over to us.

"Don't smear it on each other's faces," Mama says, her smile so huge I'm surprised it fits on her thin face. "Just feed it to each other."

Feed it to each other? Don't people usually do this part with their hands? Does that mean…does that mean Silas' lips are going to touch my fingers? Vice versa?

"My sister did smeared it at her wedding. Got cake all over her three-thousand dollar dress," Mrs. Manning explains. "Blue does not come out, no matter what you do."

Mr. Manning snickers. "I thought it was funny."

"It was," Mrs. Manning says with a laugh. "She deserved it. You don't, Rooney."

"Plus, it's not very picture-perfect," Mama adds.

I glance up at Silas and find him staring down at me. His eyes are searching for something, like he's trying to solve an equation. There's a shine in them, though. A shine that makes me think about how all the variables are worth it, even if he can't see it.

"I guess we shouldn't do that, then," I say in a quiet voice I barely recognize.

"No," he answers. He cuts out two pieces and puts them on separate plates. He holds up one plate and uses his fingers to tear off a chunk of the cake. I do the same and my gaze meets his. He's smiling at me—really, really smiling. Just behind him, his mom is watching him, grinning just as big as Mama is. I'm glad Silas is the reason she's happy

I can't help but giggle as he raises the cake to my lips. "Are we really doing this?"

"Your Mama might force feed us if we don't," he jokes.

"I will," Mama pipes up.

"I guess we better, then," I say and raise my hand up, too.

He feeds me at the same time I feed him and I'm sad when his fingers don't touch my lips and mine don't touch his. I faintly hear Mrs. Manning's phone snapping pictures. The cake tastes absolutely wonderful—it's strawberry. My favorite. I'm not sure if they knew that, or if it was a lucky guess.

Silas licks the rest off his fingers. "Tastes good."

Mrs. Manning looks proud of herself. "I knew you'd like it. You've always had a sweet spot for strawberry cake."

My mama coughs, but it's not a bad one. It sounds a little like she's trying to hold back a laugh. "So does Rooney."

***

"Thank you again," I tell Bob as he gets into his car.

He smiles up at me. "Miss Rooney, I can tell you're a wonderful girl. I'd do this about a thousand times over for you and your mama. For you too, Silas."

He only gets a stiff nod from Silas.

"All right, then," Bob says with a laugh. "Hope to see you again, sweetheart. See you next week, Silas."

Another nod.

Bob only shakes his head and shuts the door. Silas and I both turn around and head back over to my house. Silas' mom was nice enough to offer to help Mama into bed.

"Bob seems like a nice man," I say. "How do you know him?"

Silas' shoulders roll forward. He seems angry with me, all of a sudden. "He's from AA."

I don't say anything else. I've already prodded enough and I don't want to risk ruining today. As soon as we step into my house, his mom appears in the hallway, closing Mama's door behind her. "She's already asleep. I think today wore her out."

My body relaxes. When Mama's asleep, I always breathe better. I know I could just as easily lose her in her sleep, but at then it would be peaceful for her. "Today was a good day, right?"

"Today was a good day," Mrs. Manning says reassuringly.

Beside me, Silas nods. "Today was a good day."

I don't know why, but all of a sudden I tear up. My eyes flood with tears and then they're rolling down my cheeks and splattering against the hardwood floors while my shoulders jolt up and down. Silas immediately draws me into his arms. This has to be second-nature for him. Me crying, him holding me together, pulling me back from going into full-blown panic mode.

I just can't seem to stop this. Crying is set on repeat. But everything feels so sad—so ominous. No matter what I do, she's going to die. What does it matter if she's lived these moments, or if she's made it through another day? In the end, I'll find her lying still and cold and *alone*. All of this happiness is attached to a time bomb that'll eventually go off, only to leave me left with its empty, lonely destruction. This is only a pretend world, because it's going to disappear.

Today and tomorrow and yesterday…it's all going to bleed together until one day it's all just gone. It feels so close, but I can't reach it. I don't *want* to reach it. I know I have to and that makes me want it all to just end now so I can just get all of the pain and suffering over with. The terrifying part is how wanting this all to end goes hand in hand with Mama dying, and I'm not ready for that.

I'm just not ready for anything.

I'll never be ready.

Silas' hand runs up and down the length of my spine as he whispers something into my ear. I don't listen to him; he's not going to say any of the things I need to hear. Even with Silas here, I'm lost and alone. He can't save me. He can't save Mama. *My* mama—the woman I'll need every day for the rest of my life, even if it's just to tell me a way to wear my hair.

I'm going to have to face a world without her. I can't…how am I supposed to move on? To live out my life without her? I know she'd have to leave me eventually, but now? When I'm not even twenty and she's barely even forty? Maybe I should think of myself as lucky to have had our time together, but I don't feel it. Not when I should have at least twenty more years, and have her in all of the important moments of my life, rather than the fake ones.

"Rooney, listen!" Silas yells. He's shaking me. There's a look of pure terror in his eyes—more emotion than I've ever seen in him. "Listen and breathe with me, Rooney."

It's then I realize I'm gasping for air—that I can't breathe and I'm on the verge of hyperventilating. I'm in a full-blown panic attack, over nothing. Right in front of Silas and his Mama. On my fake wedding day. While Silas holds me in his arms on the floor.

"Listen," Silas says again.

I finally manage to listen and when I hear Mama's breathing—even breaths. She's okay. She's still with me. She's alive. Mrs. Manning has the baby monitor pressed up against my cheek. I'm not sure how either one of them realized it was what I needed, but I'm glad for it.

Silas cradles me even more firmly against his chest and I focus on synchronizing my breathing with his. He's shaking.

"I'm sorry," I whisper. I didn't mean to worry him. I don't want him to be afraid that I'm going to go into a panic attack when he's around me, or be afraid to be my friend.

"You're okay, Rooney. You're okay," he says against my hair, pressing a soft kiss there. "Shit, that was the scariest thing I've ever been through."

"I'm sorry," I say again.

"No, no, no." He pulls away and angles his head so his gaze is locked with mine. "Don't ever be sorry. I'm just glad we were here. You shouldn't have to go through that—or any of this—alone." He presses me back against his chest, looser this time. "What happened, Rooney? Did we do something? I can't fucking live if I'm the reason for what just happened. You—"

"It wasn't...you didn't do anything wrong. I just got scared. Overwhelmed with everything."

"Today was a long day," Mrs. Manning interjects. "Even if it was a happy one, it was still emotional." She bends down to our level and brushes the hair away from my cheek. My other cheek is mashed against Silas' chest. "You've got to be tired. You've been going non-stop for months, now."

"I have to," I tell her numbly.

"I know." She lets out a long breath and then gives me a sympathetic smile. "Why don't the two of you go take a walk? Get some fresh air? I'll be stay with Billie. She'll be fine with me."

"I'm worried—"

"And I'm worried about you," she tells me sternly. "Silas, too. You need a break. A huge one—but this is what I can give you, because I know it's something you'll be willing to take. So take it, okay?"

"Let's go," Silas says urgently. "Some fresh air will do you good."

"Okay," I agree, because he's right. "I'm sorry."

"Rooney, stop apologizing," he commands.

"Okay."

He stands and he helps me up. My body doesn't feel like it belongs to me anymore. It's lifeless and uncoordinated. Tired. "We'll be back soon," I say.

Mrs. Manning smiles at me. "I know. But take your time."

I quickly change into a pair of tennis shoes and then we leave out the back door. We go beyond our tree this time, farther than the radius I established, and into the thick line of trees behind our homes. We keep walking until I can't see our houses anymore. Silas seems pretty sure-footed and I wonder how many times he's come back here—if he has a favorite path from when he was a kid.

I always thought it would be fun to walk back here, but Mama got sick, and I never got around to taking the chance. It wouldn't have been fun, anyway. Not when I didn't have someone to enjoy getting lost and finding myself with.

Silas slows down and glances over at me. He runs a hand roughly down his jaw. "You fucking scared me, Rooney."

"I'm—"

He cuts me off with a look, which clearly says he really meant for me to stop apologizing. "Do you know what you do to me?" he demands.

I shake my head, taken off guard by his question.

He turns and I halt in my tracks. He grits his teeth and his hands clench at his sides. "You do *everything* to me,

Rooney. I can't stop it, either. It's like you've turned something on inside of me and I can't seem to do anything but drown. You're all I think about and all I care about and all I *want*." He brings his hands up to the sides of his head. I can tell his fingers are itching to run through the hair that's now gone. "I'm supposed to be nothing. Do you know what I did?"

My voice gets caught in my throat. My eyes have to be as wild as his are.

"I killed two people. The third...the third is in the hospital. *Forever.* All because I needed to get plastered one night and decided I was sober enough to drive. Well, I wasn't. And now...now I have you in my life and you're not a punishment. You're some sort of angel and prize and redemption and how the hell am I supposed to handle you without breaking you? How am I supposed to love you, when I was never made to love? When no one should ever fucking love me?"

Is he saying he loves me? I'm not sure, but it doesn't matter. Whether he loves me or not, I already have a stake in this. I've already gone and fallen in love with *him*. Loving him was never a choice, or something he could stop. Even the things that should've scared me off have kept me around because he's Silas—the Silas who cares deeply and shows more than tells. The Silas who I count on and miss and need. My Silas.

I take an unsteady step toward him and bring my hand up to his face. He flinches, but doesn't pull away when I run the back of my hand down his cheek. "I'm already yours, Silas. You have me. There's no going back."

"You know," he says, his voice sounding rough and raw. "You know what I did. How can that be if you know? How?"

His desperation brings another wave of tears to my eyes. I blink them away. I can't cry. He needs strength. Sureness. He needs to believe me. "Because it doesn't matter. Not to me. I don't know the you who hurt people..

I only know you now as the person who's everything I could ever want or need. You're good to me. You have me because I belong to you."

Silence hangs between us. I'm not sure if he's going to run away or embrace me. Probably both. Silas is never one to pick only a single direction.

He surprises me by doing neither. Instead, he kisses me.

He doesn't kiss me softly or tenderly, like during the ceremony. He kisses me with the same intensity of the words we were sharing. Like we're not just being drawn together, we're being thrown together in an unstoppable, impossible-to-ignore type of way. I welcome it. Desire it. Need it. I kiss him back in the same exact way he kisses me, a way I've never been kissed before.

Our lips mash together in a war, both of us fighting for something, unsure if we're on the same side or not. His tongue flicks out across my lips and inside, seeking and tangling with my own. He doesn't ask for an entrance, he just takes. I happily give. There's nowhere else he should be.

I've always been shy and unsure and nervous about letting anything go too far, but not with Silas. I'm not even sure there's a line to cross, when it comes to him. If there is, I think I've already dragged my toes across it, to make it disappear.

Silas' strong arms lift me up and I immediately wrap my legs around his waist and hook my feet. His hands roam down to grip my butt, forcing me to grind against his impatient erection. I'm just as needy and there's no stopping my moan. He captures it with his mouth, a guttural groan erupting from his throat.

My back meets the a tree and it only registers for a split second that we're in the middle of the woods, before I'm lost again in Silas and his perfect, unyielding kisses. My hands grip the of his neck. My nails have to be digging into his skin, but if it mattered, he'd stop. He hasn't. If anything, I think it's spurring him on.

This time, I'm the one moving my hips up against his, searching for any sort of relief I can get. Through his pants, his erection meets the fabric of my panties. I wonder what it'll be like when there's nothing separating us.

I've never let myself get so far ahead of myself before. I'm a virgin and it's always terrified me to think about taking the next step. But with Silas? I think I could. Easily.

His lips leave mine and I whimper, their absence way too noticeable. They trail down the underside of my jaw, down my neck, over my chest to the swell of my breasts. He's panting just as heavily, his whole body shaking like he's on the verge of losing control. I know I am.

Without so much as any warning, Silas' hands leave my backside and release one of my breasts out of the top of my dress. I'm too shocked and lost in him to really care or be self-conscious. Especially when his eyes suddenly glaze over with a look of awe.

"Fucking beautiful," he murmurs.

I can only moan in response. Silas' thumb brushes over my nipple and it strains, sending an electric shock straight through my body. "Please.."

Silas' brows knit together. "This…Rooney, I…perfect…"

"Silas," I breathe, arching in ways I didn't think possible.

Those eyes darken and then he leans down, capturing my breast in his mouth. I cry out and claw blindly at the back of his head. He sucks and flicks at my nipple, grinding his hips against mine until I'm writhing and mumbling unintelligible things, heading toward something bright—something I'm pretty sure I might die if I don't have.

All of a sudden, it feels like I'm suspended and then flung in a reverse direction…or maybe up toward the heavens. All I know is it's wonderful and perfect and something I'm not sure I can keep living without. It's like lightning and fireworks and the beach all wrapped up into the best kind of feeling. My whole body sags in a sigh, with only Silas holding me in place.

"You liked that, huh?" He chuckles against my collarbone. He's still straining against his zipper, but I don't have the confidence, even after what we just shared, to help him out. Maybe later.

I nod happily.

"Me, too. You're like every dream I've ever had. All I've ever wanted."

I'm able to pull away slightly. I brace my hands on either side of his face. "You are, too."

His eyes widen and he stares at me. A slow, almost prideful grin pulls at his lips—they're swollen and red from kissing mine. He looks a little lost, maybe even bewildered. He kisses me again, soft and tender this time, and then helps me fix the top of my dress.

I'm sure my hair looks like a mess. The dress, too. Oh god, how are we going to face his mom? She's in my house and we'll have to pass her to get there. I will, at least.

Worry shoots through me and I immediately pale.

"You okay?" Silas asks worriedly.

"Perfect," I tell him with a blush. Everything we just did replays in my mind. The fact that he saw my boobs—that his mouth was there. That he kissed me and touched me and loved me. "More than perfect. I'm just thinking about the walk of shame back into my house."

Silas throws his head back and chuckles. When he regains his composure, he runs a hand down the side of my face. "We'll figure it out. Rooney, that was...I've never..."

I have no doubt Silas is experienced—if he wasn't, I wouldn't feel so great. But there's something in his eyes telling me all of the experience in the world hasn't prepared him for this. This was completely new for him.

"What are we...what was that?" I feel a grin pull at my

lips as I wrap my arms around my waist. "Because I want it, Silas. I want you. Only you."

He stares at me and I see something in him click. He goes from the man who was just kissing me and saying sweet things, back to the man who was on my front porch, telling me he didn't really care about my sick mama. He's shut down, no longer caring. He's hiding himself away to protect me and himself and everything else he thinks needs protecting.

"Shit," he mutters.

I suddenly feel sick to my stomach. He can't just shut down on me, walk away. Not after what we just did. Not when I'm in love with him.

"Silas, no. Don't. It was right. You know it was. We can be together—"

"No we can't, Rooney." He puts space between us. "You deserve more than me. You deserve to be happy and with someone who can give you everything. I'll destroy you like I did those people. I'll tear you down until there's nothing left to build, and you'll hate me. I can't have you hating me. Not you."

"I could never hate you, Silas. And I know you won't destroy me," I tell him and try to close the distance. "Me, you—this...Silas, you can't walk away from it. Please don't. *Please.*"

"Rooney, you have to see this is wrong!" he yells.

"It's not. It can't be."

He starts shaking his head. "That's my fault. This is all my fault. I should've showed more restraint—tried harder to stay away. Now everything's all fucked up. Us, your heart, your relationship with Brandon..."

"I'll break up with him," I say, desperate for anything to make him want to stay with me. To make him go back to where he was, just a moment before. "I don't feel an ounce of what I feel for you, for him. It's you, Silas. You're the one I want."

"No. Don't fucking break up with him." He lets out a

breath so strong it slices straight through me. "Just, no. You don't get it. All I am is poison and this right now— what's happening—is just a fucking preview of what's to come, if anything more happens between us. This entire time, I've let my feelings for you and my liking of your mama override the truth. The heart of all of this is you're nothing but a Step. You're a way to make it easier for me to sleep better at night, nothing more. If I have to live my entire life with my guilt, then I at least needed something good to keep me going. Something good to suck up and make my own. But I won't do that...I'm done using you. You need to go and just get the fuck away from me, forever. You don't need me right now and I sure as hell don't need you messing with my head."

A breath wrangles free and I choke out a sob. I'm about to double over right here—have another panic attack, lose it completely. My heart feels like it's been broken all this time and Silas repaired it, only to shatter it completely. All this time, I've been a Step to Silas, and in some ways I think he's been a Step to me, but I thought we were more.

The worst part is, I can't bring myself to hate him.

Instead, I run. I run until I'm my legs are bloody from the sticker bushes and my dress is torn. I run past Silas' mom and her gaping mouth. I run straight into my room and I bury myself under my covers and pray when I wake up—if I ever fall asleep—that this was all a nightmare. I pray everything's okay and I wake up tomorrow morning with a chance of doing today over again. Mostly, I pray Silas comes into my room, apologizes to me, and tells me he loves me.

And once again, I'm wishing away another day I'll never get back.

CHAPTER NINETEEN

Silas

You're nothing but a Step.
I sure as hell don't need you messing with my head.

I wake up with the worst hangover I've ever had. Not because I went out and got drunk—although I did want to, and had to hold myself fucking back from getting one. I know where every bar in the county is and I'd planned out exactly what I'd order at each. Just thinking about it, I can practically smell each drink. All I wanted to do was wash away everything I said to Rooney, and drown myself. I especially wanted to get rid of the memory of our kiss. Shit, it's still haunting my lips. My breath. Maybe I *could practically* smell the drinks, but I can, without a doubt, smell Rooney. Still taste her. The feel of her skin beneath my hands is even still there. Prominent.

This hangover ain't from drinking. It's from Rooney—from giving in and giving up, on more than one account.

I don't know what time I finally fell asleep against the tree we made out at. I couldn't face walking back, because I knew if I did, I'd go straight to her and apologize and try to redeem myself. There's some sort of pull on me and it leads me straight to her. She's the new taste I can't shake.

After spending the night out here, I have no doubt my parents are assuming the worst. I would, if I was in their position. An alcoholic doesn't stay out all night picking flowers. We find a drink and we forget ourselves. Doing that would make it easier to bury all of this—especially since I'm pretty sure I might've fallen in love with Rooney.

As soon as my probation's up, I'm skipping town and leaving her behind. At least then, maybe one of us can find peace. I know it won't be me.

I manage to stand up, my body sore and stiff from lying propped against the tree. Mom's going to kill me for getting my suit dirty—at least there's no mud. I pat out what I can, until I'm presentable. Smelling like the earth is a step up from smelling like whiskey and beer.

I keep my eyes cast down as I pass Rooney's house. It's already become a routine to go there every day, and I hate breaking it. What's gonna suck is how by losing Rooney, I'm also losing Billie. Billie's carved out a spot in my blackened heart. I'm not sure how, but I do know her mischievous smile, honest heart, and love for Rooney has made the crater impossible to ever fill, even with more darkness.

The first thing I hear when the door swings open is Mom's laughter. For a split second, I hope it's Rooney. Maybe what I said last night wasn't bad enough to keep her away, no matter how much I want her away from me, I want her with me more.

I stop dead in my tracks when I realize it's not Rooney. It's my brother.

He's sitting across from our parents at the kitchen table, looking like your typical boy-next-door, college-success, parents'-favorite son. Hell, he's everyone's favorite of the two of us, mine included. In the few years since I'd last seen him, he'd gone from a kid to a man. Hair all shaggy, eyes bright, smile easy. He looks just as carefree, like he's ready to spring into action and save kids from a well in a moment's notice. I used to idolize my little brother, but now I kind of want to punch him in the perfect mouth. He's everything I want to be and he has everything I want. He has *her*. Fuck, I want her.

"Look who came home early!" Mom cheers.

Dad stares down at his coffee on the table in front of him, like it's the holy grail of avoiding awkward conversations. Wish I had a mug of my own so I could do the same thing. Instead, I've got to acknowledge my brother or get the hell out of Dodge. One's better than the other, because I'm feeling violent.

Brandon gives me a nod, but then stops and grins.

"Nah, give me a hug." He stands, shorter than me, and comes at me with his arms wide open. He wraps them around me and I just stand there stiffly. Doesn't he know what a shithead I am? Can't he see how much I hate him because he's got the girl I'm in love with?

He steps away, not at all affected by my non-hug. He stuffs his hands into the pockets of his khaki shorts. He's wearing a polo shirt for God sakes, like he's going golfing. Why does he have to be the opposite of me? He makes me feel like shit on the bottom of a shoe.

"My professor let us turn in our term paper in early, so I got to skip town sooner. Here for a week. Figured my girl could use a good kind of surprise."

His girl. I can't listen to this. I feel like I'm going to hurl. "She'll like that."

If he's caught off guard by me talking to him, he doesn't show it.

"Hopefully, I'll be able to get her mind off of…things," he says.

If that's what he's going to try to do, then he's in the wrong. Rooney doesn't need him trying to distract her from what's going on with Billie. She needs to face it— digging her head in the sand will only make the loss her hurt more. My brother may love her, but he doesn't know what she needs. Not like I do. Even he doesn't deserve her.

He can do whatever the hell he wants. Maybe I'm not thrilled about it, but I cut myself out of her life. Severed it, really, then soldered it. Loving her doesn't mean a thing in the end, if I'll only burn her for loving me back.

"I'm going on a run," I mumble.

"You won't stay and visit?" Mom asks.

I know I should. He's my brother. But I've never done anything right, or done what I should do, so why start now? I can't face him, knowing where my mouth was last night, knowing Rooney was willing to choose me—*me*! Who the hell chooses me? And why? I shouldn't even be a choice. I killed those people and the girl is still in the hospital, so how the hell does that make me worthy of someone like Rooney? Is it because the world's fucked up and gotta show me all of the things if I was a better person?

"Nah, I think I'm going to head on over and see her," my brother says, covering my ass as usual.

He's always taken care of me, as if we're reversed in age. We used to play baseball together in high school and I once chose to get drunk in the field with a few of the cheerleaders instead of going to practice, so he acted like he was sick—said I was too, and couldn't be there. Another time, I hosted a party at our house while our parents were out of town. The couch got ruined with God knows what, and he told them we had a few of the guys from the team over, things got rowdy, and they spilled everywhere. It was believable 'cause everyone knows Brandon didn't drink—doesn't drink—and no one faults him for it.

Funny how when you're young, it's made out to be cool when you drink and you're a pussy when you don't, but for him it wasn't like that. He was cool for not drinking. Brandon never needed alcohol, or anything else, to fit in and be liked. Maybe it was because he had me to be compared to.

All my life, Brandon has stepped up and taken the blame. Then a time came when he couldn't—when I'd gone too far, gotten in too deep, and the consequences were too huge. Somehow, he still managed to forgive me. Get past it. Maybe the town hasn't, but my parents have, Brandon has, even Rooney has. But me? I haven't, and I never will.

***

I take an extra-long run until I feel like all I've been doing is running circles around the town, avoiding one specific place. Well, two, if you count Rooney. But when my body finally tells me it's time to stop, I find myself running past my house—toward the place on the curvy road with two crosses. By the time I get there, my shirt is soaked through and my legs feel like they're about to give out.

This time, there's no doubting I'm a sick bastard. I really am torturing myself—reminding myself of the unsurmountable guilt that is weighing me to the ground like an anchor. These crosses are a reminder of what I do to people. How while I'm weighed down by guilt, there are people who'll never walk this earth again. It makes me sick—*I* make me sick.

One of these crosses belongs to Victor Daniels. He went by Vic. I didn't know him—he was a year ahead of me and he was involved with the academic team and band, so we didn't roll in the same circle. From the way people talk about him, he was a cool guy. Big heart, friendly personality, huge sense of humor—those are all the things his loved ones said on the stand at my hearing. As they were implying all of the things Vic was, they were also implying all of the things I'm not. Someone deserved to die, and it wasn't him. His mother even burst out in tears, asking why the drunk driver always lived, and the ones doing the right thing had to die. No one had an answer.

There was only silence. Then it was pointed out—like they had to further nail my soul to the devil's palm—that he was going to be a ER doctor. He was going save people, some of whom might've been just like him. A person was going to save lives died, while I lived. Fate is fucked like that.

The other is Melanie Parker's. I knew her because she was my age. I even went out on a few dates with her, fucked her in Tommy Brady's parents' bedroom once at a party. She was a wild one, but she must've settled down when she started dating Vic. She was going to college to be a journalist and was in a sorority and the honors program. Her parents liked to point out she was on the right track in life and she was constantly talking about her future plans: working for a news station, starting a family, owning a little white house with a picket fence. She had a future ahead of her, and I stole it away.

Then there was Maggie Jonas. Maggie…shit, I still can't think about her. Can't face her, because she's alive but she's not living. She was Melanie's best friend since they were three. They grew up next door to each other, went off to the same college, moved in to an apartment together. She wanted to be a computer scientist. God, all of her professors came to my hearing to tell about all the potential that disappeared with her.

I ended every single one of their futures because I decided to go out and get drunk, then thought I was sober enough to drive. I couldn't even walk straight, let alone operate a vehicle. I was even going in the wrong direction—away from home and toward another bar, probably. Wasn't their fault they were coming home from college for a visit. One curve cut too short, and it was all over.

Victor and Melanie died instantly. They were in the front seats. Maggie…she survived. But she didn't survive in the way that counts. No, she's in a hospital room where she'll haunt me for the rest of my life. I saw pictures of her at the hearing and I got sick right there in the courtroom. By then, she was healed up, but she was on a ventilator—a machine the only thing keeping her alive. She's not brain dead, but she'll never wake up again. Even if she does, she won't be a person anymore. She won't be Maggie, the shy, sweet girl I remember who always kept Melanie out of trouble—who always blushed whenever anyone talked to her, and spent most of her time reading. But she was a beast on the volleyball court, I remember that. Not anymore. Now she's in a place between life and death, the decision to keep her or let her go resting on the shoulders of the people who loved her.

I would give myself over willingly if it meant they were all safe and had their futures intact. I can't. All I can do is keep running, keep punishing myself, and remind myself of all the things I can't have.

***

I walk the rest of the way home, listening to my music and trying to turn my brain off. I'd give my left nut for a huge glass of ice water and a shower to relax my aching muscles.

I pull my headphones out of my ears and stop in the middle of my driveway. I drop down onto the concrete and do a few quick push-ups, then stand and stretch out my arms, legs, and neck.

"Silas!"

Shit. All the tension I just stretched out is gone. I clench my fists and glance to my side. My brother is sitting over on Rooney's front steps. She's sitting beside him, her baby-monitor-best-friend clutched to her chest. Of course Brandon's got his arms wrapped around her. I get it, she's his. Still doesn't mean I don't want to rip his limbs off and steal Rooney away and climb a tall building, then beat my chest.

"C'mere."

I should just pretend I can't hear them, walk away. But Brandon knows me too well and before I can, he's coming toward me, Rooney in tow.

This is clearly torture for her. She honestly looks like she's about to burst into tears. There's anger there, too, similar to what sparked the first day I met her. Her hair is a wild mess of curls, still done up from yesterday. I'm surprised she didn't go home and try to wash me, and the memories of me, away.

She stumbles to a stop and her baby blue gaze settles on mine. Just as quickly, it flicks down to the ground. Mine drifts to Brandon's arm as he wraps it around her waist. He kisses the top of her head.

That's my move—holding her, kissing her head…mine. *No, his.*

"What?" I all but growl.

Rooney tenses and sucks in her bottom lip. My brother gives me an easy smile. He doesn't know me to be anything but hostile, so this is normal to him. "Well, I was asking her about yesterday, and couldn't get much out of her. Thought you could enlighten me on it."

"There were pictures," I tell him, voice hard. I refuse to relieve any of it.

His eyebrows knit together. "Rooney won't show them to me."

She won't? Yeah, she probably doesn't want him seeing the depth of yesterday—the kiss, the dance, the cake. It was like we were two cords wrapped together and pulled taut, ready to snap. The snap being our time at the tree.

"They aren't much," I grumble. Wrong answer. Rooney's gaze rises back up and there's hurt there. A lot of hurt. My stomach turns over. What does she want from me? What does she think I can give her that Brandon can't? Why *me?* "They'd mean more if it was you."

He grins and kisses her again. Damn kisses. "Probably. But that might be jinxing us, huh?"

Then my brother does something to make me want to

pound his fucking teeth into his brain: he winks. What the hell is that supposed to mean?

My glare must be something, because this time he catches a whiff of my anger and straightens. He brings his free hand up to the back of his neck and scratches. "So we're about to call in a pizza. You wanna eat with us?"

"No." Call in a pizza? Eat with them? Even if the situation wasn't sure to be awkward, I wouldn't agree to it. I'll do definitely do something regrettable.

"Really?" he asks, going into his lawyer-mode. He's always got an argument. He likes reason.

"No."

Rooney slips out of his arm and takes a step back. "He said no, Brandon. Let's just go…"

"I thought you two got along?" he asks.

We both shake our heads, but it's Rooney who talks. Her voice is soft, like some sort of breeze rolling over me. "He was only doing the wedding. Nothing more."

Disappointment washes over me. *Nothing more*. Right. She's put me in my place, just like I've put her in hers. Weird thing is, Brandon looks disappointed, too. I don't know what he was hoping to get out of this exchange.

Rooney's grip tightens around the baby monitor. "Can we go back over?"

Brandon smiles, cool and easy again. "Sure." They start walking away, but then he turns and calls over his shoulder, "Hey, stop over later if you can. Seriously. I miss you, man."

I only shrug. "Yeah."

CHAPTER TWENTY

Rooney

In the two days since the wedding, Mama's health has changed drastically, and it's scaring me. She's barely done anything except for sleep. I've had to beg her just to get her to eat a pack of crackers. She doesn't talk, either. Only mumbles syllables here and there, which is especially terrifying because Mama *always* talks.

I think it's time to face that if she keeps getting worse, I have to call Rita and ask her to set up hospice. I'm not sure how much longer I can keep doing this.

I haven't been sleeping because I've had too much on my mind—Mama, hospice, the part that comes after. I'm constantly worrying. I'm also waiting for the next shoe to drop, constantly expecting something bad to happen. Every minute feels like it's going to be the final minute. I'm beginning to realize my memories of sick Mama are taking up more room than those of healthy, happy Mama. Taking care of her, seeing her sick, watching her waste away—I don't want those to be the only memories I'm left with. I want to remember the strong, vivacious, mischievous Mama who raised me, and this isn't her.

"I didn't realize how sick she is," Brandon says.

We're sitting on the couch in my living room, watching some random movie. I think Brandon wanted to kiss me, but I couldn't bring myself to let him. It doesn't feel right anymore. Whatever safety Brandon used to bring me was just an illusion. Now that I know what it feels like to be truly safe with someone, I don't think I'll ever find it again. This only tells me what I already know I have to do.

"Why didn't you tell me?"

I pull my fleece blanket tighter around me. We're on opposite ends, which couldn't be more true about our relationship. Well, about me, I guess. He keeps trying to close the distance, but I open it right back up. I'm running and he's trying to catch me.

Hilarious, considering it's the same reason why I'm so heartbroken about Silas.

"She's dying," I remind him. "She's never going to be good again." Brandon eyes go wide and I realize I'm being not being considerate. He means well. Maybe I don't like him the same way I used to anymore, but I do like him as a friend. "Sorry. I'm just—I'm tired."

Brandon's eyes soften. "Of course you are, Rooney. I can't imagine how you couldn't be. If you need to bite my head off, I get it. It's what I'm here for."

My shoulders relax and I let out a weak laugh. "That's not what you're here for. I doubt you came home early for me to snap at you."

"How do you know that?" he teases. "Can you read my mind?"

"Like a picture book."

He gasps. "Are you saying I have the brain of a child?"

This time my laugh is real. "Who picks his nose."

He chuckles and tosses a piece of popcorn at me from the bowl in his lap. "But you know what, since you're my girl, then you've obviously got to be a nose-picker, too."

The *my girl* does something to my stomach. Not a good something. I muster a grin. "Your logic makes no sense."

"Makes all the sense. Listen, I was thinking you and I could do dinner tomorrow? I think we both need a night out together. Mom said she'd stay with your mom. I think Silas is gonna, too."

I doubt Silas will. When he walked away, he walked away for good. I don't foresee him looking back. The things he said to me...it was like he was sharpening a blade and driving it deep, slicing my heart in half. I still find myself missing and wanting him, needing him. For every sad or bad thought I have about him, I have twenty that aren't. Twenty that make me want to beg him to give us a chance, or at least be my friend. It doesn't seem fair how he can just walk away when I can't stop loving him.

"Would you be okay with that?" Brandon prompts. The look on his face is so hopeful. Why can't I want him? He'd be so easy to love.

"Yeah," I say and my voice is uneven. "But I don't want to be gone too long."

He nods. "Just dinner."

"Okay."

"Okay," he says with a big, cheesy grin.

This dinner will be good for us. Hopefully, it'll set us in the right direction.

CHAPTER TWENTY-ONE

Silas

My brother has been talking since we started eating dinner. He's always been talkative, even once got sent to the principal's office for it, which was his one and only act of rebellion.

I never really noticed it because we've always canceled each other out. He's outgoing and I'm *not*. Now it sort of pisses me off. Not sort of. It *definitely* pisses me off.

I want him to stop talking so he'll finish his meal and I can dig in to the fucking fantastic cake Dad baked, then disappear and have a smoke.

The more time I spend around Brandon, the more I come to resent him, especially since his favorite topic is Rooney. What I'd give to hear about his classes or some dumb professor he's got. Hell, he could talk about paint drying and I'd hand over something of high value.

He's been going on about the day their day together. I know I could probably talk forever when it comes to her, but I don't want to hear someone else talk about her. Yeah, so what? I'm jealous of my little brother. Fucking green-eyed monster is what I am.

He stabs his pasta with a fork and pauses for the first time in what feels like a millennium. "Her mama...she been doin' this bad the whole time?"

A lump immediately forms in my throat. Hopefully his definition of "bad" looks a lot like mine and Rooney's definition of "good" for Billie.

"What do you mean by bad?" Mom asks. She sounds concerned, herself.

"She's not eating. Sleeping all the time. Won't talk."

That's definitely bad. Worse. Shit, I hope the wedding didn't wear her out. She had such a great time, and I would hate to see the memory ruined for her. I work my jaw and gather up the courage to ask, "How's Rooney?"

Mom eyes me and Dad is obviously trying his damnedest not to.

"Okay," Brandon answers. "Sad."

Sad? There's got to be more than that. *Sad* is when you wake up and the day's rainy, or you see a dead deer on the side of the road. What about devastated, depressed, lonely, withdrawn? All of those things I know she has to be feeling and I can't seem to wrap my head around why Brandon's here, rather than there with her. There's no question she's worth skipping a family dinner, or fifty.

"But I think tomorrow will be good for her."

I glance up and Dad looks just as confused as I am. As far as I know, he was just gonna get Rooney out of the house. It's great and all, but he looks like a kid who just walked into a candy store. Mom seems to know what's going on but she looks...hell, I don't know what she looks like. Definitely not happy, that's for sure. She's smiling, but it's a fake smile.

"What's tomorrow?" Dad asks.

My brother grins and sits up straighter. "I'm going to propose."

Three things happen simultaneously. Mom's grin slips and she struggles to regain it. Dad's jaw drops, along with the fork in his hand. And I nearly jump across the table and murder my little brother with my bare hands. Propose? The hell he will. They've only been dating, what, a year? She doesn't even love him—she can't tie herself to him forever. Does he even love her, either? The way she deserves to be loved? The way *I* love her.

Shit, there's that word again—love. And man, is it true—I do love her. Too much, and I don't even know how to handle it—how to love her. I don't know how to give her what she needs, let alone give my future to her, when I don't even want a future most days.

If she says yes to him, I'll have no choice but to skip town. There's no fucking way I can spend the rest of my life watching him and her have the life I want with her. No fucking way.

"Isn't that great?" Mom finally asks.

"I know we've been apart a lot, but I love her and I know we'll make a great team," Brandon adds.

Team? What the fuck. Marriage isn't a game. You're not looking to score in marriage. Well, you are, but not in the way he's talking about. There aren't any points or rules or plays, just each other. *Team.* Fuck me.

Dad clears his throat and picks up his fork. "You sure now's the right time?"

Brandon nods, obviously having thought this through. "It'll be good for her to have some excitement. Her mama, too. Don't get me wrong, the fake wedding was good and all…but this is more. This is real."

I'll shove real right up his ass. The wedding meant everything to her mama. To Rooney, too. An engagement is only gonna remind Billie and Rooney of all the things Billie's gonna miss out on.

I swallow and try to simmer down all my anger. I take another bite of my food and then throw my napkin on the table. "I'm gonna go have a smoke," I grumble and stand up. "Good luck with…" I let the words trail off because I can't say much else without erupting in a storm of emotions that definitely won't be your typical, brotherly congratulations.

He goes right into talking about how he plans on popping the question and I disappear as quickly as I can, the door slamming behind me. I could give a shit about the damn door when he's going to *propose* to *my* girl.

Maybe she's been with him longer, but there's no way in hell he knows her as well as I do. If he did, then he wouldn't think staying hours away while her mother is terminal is a good idea. I doubt he knows her sad tears from her about-to-freak-out-in-a-panic tears, or when they're just happy tears. I doubt he's made her moan the way I have—I wonder if he's even made her come, just by his mouth on her breast. Hell, I hope he hasn't made her come at all. The territorial red flashing across my vision tells me I don't want to know. I don't need murdering my brother on my rap sheet.

I pull up the couch cushion on the chair and take out my pack of smokes. Mom finally figured out I was smoking and the next thing I knew, two packs disappeared. So I've been trying to hide them from her.

I set the cushion in its place and then fall back into the chair. As I prepare myself a cigarette, I can't stop from glancing over at Rooney's. There's not a whole lot of answers in looking her way, but I do it anyway because she's somewhere inside of that house. I wonder if she's thinking about me, too.

Who am I kidding? I'm being selfish. Her thoughts are probably on Billie, as they should be.

The back door opens. My neck pops as I look away from Rooney's. I bring the cigarette up to my mouth, draw in a breath, and release a cloud of smoke.

Mom rolls her eyes but doesn't say anything. She takes the spot beside me and glances at the pillow and blanket I jacked from the linen closet. They're sitting in an unfolded heap next to the grill. If I was smart, I'd put them somewhere where the ants won't get in them. But I don't care—bug bites are nothing.

"Are you ever going to start sleeping inside?"

I shake my head.

"Why? It's got to be uncomfortable and cold out here.

"It's what I know," I reply. God, it is. Hell, I know worse than this. The feeling of cold concrete beneath my ass. The need to keep a hand protectively curled over my nuts while the other one clutches the wallet housing what little money I have to my name. Before that, sleeping lightly, so you don't find yourself on the wrong side of a foot or a fist or a knife. Not having enough sleep after hearing people constantly calling out or yelling or cursing or banging their cell doors, until the guards finally get fed up and snap.

She swallows and looks away. Her blond hair is pulled back in a tight ponytail, and for the first time, I notice the wrinkles just beside her eyes and at the corners of her lips. I always thought Mom was beautiful and she still is, but I've managed to age her, just like I did Dad.

"You belong with Rooney."

I jolt at her words and then immediately freeze. The cigarette butt falls from my hand and nails me in my jean-clad thigh and even though it burns, I ignore it. Did she seriously just say that? Am I losing it? Is she?

"You heard me," she says softly. "You belong with her."

I slowly regain consciousness and shake my head.

She reaches across and brushes the butt off my leg. She winces. "Are you okay?"

I shrug.

She laughs, but there's no humor in it. "That's one of the reasons why you belong with her. You've always been so silent. Your dad and I used to worry you were behind because you wouldn't talk, but then we realized you knew how, you just didn't want to. Didn't like to. But you talk to her. She makes you smile and you make her smile and you guys look at each other...you look at each other like I've always wanted you to find."

189

I clench my fist and set it on my thigh. "She's with Brandon, Mom."

"I know. And I never thought I'd condone one of my sons spending so much time with the other's girlfriend, or that I'd be okay with you falling in love with her, but I am. I hate it because I promised myself I would never play favorites—that I wouldn't let one get away with something, especially if it was unfair to other. But I could see it the first time I saw you and her interact, and there was no denying it at the wedding: you two belong together."

She pauses and seems to mull over her words. "Your brother's always made it easy to love him. But you haven't. And I don't mean I haven't loved you, because I have, every second since you were born, and I realized what it meant to love someone so much you'd sacrifice the whole world for them. Even when you didn't want me to, I've loved you. But you haven't wanted me to. You haven't wanted *anyone* to because you don't think you deserve it, so you've pushed everyone as far away as you can. You've isolated yourself. I knew if anyone ever won your heart, they would be worthy of it, and they would be someone who you couldn't let go—they'd be the closest thing to a tailor-made soulmate. That's who Rooney is for you."

"So what? I'm just supposed to steal her from Brandon?" I bite out my words, each one sharper than the next. "He's better for her. He deserves her."

"But you love her."

I don't answer her, which was an answer all in itself, I guess.

"I knew it." She reaches a hand out and draws her fingers down over the scars on the side of my face.

These stupid fucking scars should've been a whole hell of a lot worse. I stiffen.

"You can't steal her from Brandon because she's already yours. If he proposes to her and she says yes, then *he's* stealing her from *you*."

No, he's not. She's wrong. "Brandon wouldn't see it that way."

"No. Brandon loves her, but not even remotely the way you do." She drops her hand and offers me a sad smile. "You owe it to her to love her and be with her. You have Rooney's heart and it wouldn't be fair for you to walk away. If you do, then it'll be the mistake you can't come back from. Everything you've done will be nothing, compared to the way this would haunt you."

I don't agree with her, but I won't argue with her. I bring the cigarette up to my lips and take another drag. "She's going to say yes to Brandon. It won't matter."

"You really think that?"

I'm not sure what she means, so I nod. Of course I do. If I were her, I'd choose Brandon. He can give her everything. What I can give her is the opposite: nothing.

"Then you have a day to realize how wrong you are before there's no turning back."

I stare straight ahead, her words repeating in my head like they're on a record. We sit in silence for a while, me as rigid as can be with more ash landing on my legs. Eventually, she stands and heads back inside, leaving me to sit there and think and stew.

I've got Twelve Steps to avoiding my addiction to Rooney, and for some reason I can't remember a single one.

CHAPTER TWENTY-TWO

Rooney

When Brandon mentioned going out, this was not what I expected.

It started with him arriving ten minutes early—Brandon's always early—with a bouquet of roses. He used to do that a lot, mainly for Mama when we first started dating, but once we got more serious, those bouquets became few and far in between. Tonight's roses are just another reason why Brandon is perfect. But as more and more time passes since I let Silas turn my head, I've realized no matter how perfect Brandon is, he's not perfect for me. I thought Silas was, and I guess I was wrong, but it doesn't mean I'm wrong about this. I'm not.

He made reservations at one of the fancier places in town. It's an expensive seafood restaurant and bar. And I mean *expensive.*

"What are you getting?" I ask, trying to scope out what price range I'm going for.

Brandon laughs. "Get anything you want, Rooney. I've got this." He leans across the table and points on the menu. "The shrimp scampi is really good. So are the scallops."

"I'll get the scallops."

The smile Brandon gives me eases my nervousness. He's going to hate me by the end of this dinner. I've been going over how I'm going to start our conversation, and it sounded good in my head until it came time for me to actually do it. Now I've pretty much forgotten everything and what I can remember, sounds terrible. Like, ready-to-throw-my-face-in-the-scallops terrible.

Mama's eyes fluttered open when I went to tell her I was leaving, and she called me by her own mama's name, then fell right back to sleep. She was up last night, pain shooting throughout her entire body. She was in so much pain she was almost delirious, completely unaware of who I was. Getting her to take her pills was one of the worst things I've ever gone through. I've heard Mama curse before, but she's never cursed at me. Last night, she did. I couldn't do anything about any of it.

Before Brandon and his mom came over, I called Rita and asked her if she'd come over tomorrow so we can decide our next step. I hate doing this is, but it's necessary, and there's nothing else left to do.

The only reason why I'm okay leaving Mama with Mrs. Manning is because she'll probably sleep the rest of the night.

Our waitress eventually comes over to drop off our drinks and take our orders. Once she leaves, I pull my drink toward me and stare down at it, the awkward silence thick. I'm not sure when to broach this conversation. Before we eat? After? When we're in the car?

I lift my gaze to find Brandon watching me, looking a little nervous, himself. Does he sense I'm about to break up with him?

He clears his throat and fidgets by running a hand down his jaw. He looks so much like Silas that a pang hits my chest. Now or never.

"I think we need to take a break," I blurt out. My skin

flushes and I look away. Crap.

Brandon stutters out something I can't decipher. He places his arms on the table and leans forward. "What? You can't mean—"

"I do," I whisper. "I think we need some time apart."

A gap of silence follows. I shrink down into myself, wishing I had a time machine. This totally could have started better.

"Rooney," he says slowly, like he's trying to work this out in his head. "You've been under a lot of stress and I can't imagine being in your position. If I had to face losing Mom...I can't even think about it. I can only imagine how something like this can make you see things different. Question life. But you have to know how much I love you and that we're meant to be—"

He cuts off as the waitress walks over with our side salads. She sets them down and gives us a wide smile. "Your food will be out shortly."

"Thank you," I say, voice shaking.

Brandon doesn't say anything until she's gone. "We're meant to be together, Rooney."

I link my hands in my lap and stare down at them. "I don't think we are. I don't—I've changed. I *do* see things differently and I have been questioning life, but it's more than that. I'm realizing how short it all is and how I can't..." I try to figure how to put the next part so it sounds kind. *I can't spend my life with a man I don't love* sounds a little harsh. "I can't reach the end and have regrets."

"So you think I'm a regret?" he asks, an edge to his voice I've never heard him use before.

I flinch.. "No, no. You could never be a regret. I'm just saying I don't know what I want anymore." I do, but I won't tell him what I want—*who* I want. It's not like I can have Silas, anyway. "The only thing I want to do is spend time with Mama. I can't think beyond that."

His demeanor changes and compassion softens the sharp edges. "That's what's going on here? You need time apart so you can dedicate it to your mama? If that's the case, all you have to do is ask, Rooney. I'll step back and we'll go on a break. I'll give you the space you need. I get it if she's the reason why you're doing this. I'm sure everything but being with her feels like a waste of time."

I don't have the heart to tell him it's only half the reason—how the other half is that I just don't want to be with him. Maybe we'll go on this break and drift apart, or he'll find someone who steals his breath away.

Brandon shifts and reaches into his pocket. He pulls something out and discreetly sets it on the table in front of us. A ring. An *engagement* ring. Suddenly the nice dinner and Brandon's nervousness clicks. Here he was, planning to propose to me, and I just broke up with him.

"I can do a break, Rooney. I'll show you how much I love you and remind you of why you and I belong together, then I'll give this to you when you're ready. I should've known now's not the time, so that's on me. But I do know the way I feel about you isn't going to go away, so I'm going to keep trying. I'm going to be here for you, I'm going to hold you, and in the end, *we're* going to come out stronger, okay?"

"Brandon, I—"

"I know. Not now, okay? Give it time." He picks the ring back up and slides it back into his pocket. "This'll just give us a story to tell our grandkids."

He laughs, but I can't even muster up a smile. Luckily, the waitress comes out with our food, so he doesn't notice. He really does expect a future—he expects our love to win out. He doesn't know the only love I have for him now is as a friend. I'm not sure it was ever more, at least not more than a crush.

I stare down at my food. We have the rest of dinner *and* the ride home. Getting through the rest of this evening is going to be interesting.

***

I jolt awake and I'm not sure why.

Mama? Oh no, I hope she's okay.

I blindly search for the baby monitor but it must've fallen off the bed. I don't waste time looking for it and stumble out of bed, and run for her bedroom. My heart is racing so hard I'm pretty sure it's in one of the Derbys. I throw open Mama's door and it takes my eyes a minute to focus in on her.

She's still, lying on her back with her hands resting on her stomach. She looks pale and her features are twisted in her never-ending pain, but her chest is rising and falling. Not in a healthy way, but in the way that's her new normal. She's asleep; the noise wasn't her.

I step back out into the hallway and walk to the kitchen. The clock on the microwave says it's about two o'clock in the morning. Mama was asleep when I got home, so I said my goodbyes to Mrs. Manning, who surprisingly didn't ask about the dinner at all. Maybe Brandon texted her and told her. Though she didn't act awkward, like I'd expect her to if she knew.

Once she left, I crawled into bed and finally fell asleep when my racing thoughts decided to take a breather.

"You're just tired," I say to myself, knowing I won't be able to fall back to sleep with my heart rate through the roof.

There's a soft knock on my door. Was that what woke me up? And why is someone knocking on my door this late at night? It can't be anyone good. Should I call the police, or maybe the Mannings? I don't know—

"Rooney."

I go completely still.

Silas?

Without another thought I go to the door, and swing it open. Sure enough, it's Silas. His hair has grown slightly and his five o'clock shadow makes him look tired, just like the bags underneath his eyes do. Those eyes, though—

they look devastated. Like something terrible is weighing on him, sagging down his shoulders and breaking his spirit. Oh God, did something happen? Is that why he's here?

"You can't marry him, Rooney," he tells me, his voice like he's spend a thousand years in the desert. "You can't marry him because I love you."

CHAPTER TWENTY-THREE

Silas

I don't know what the hell I'm doing. I know why I'm doing it—I just said it to Rooney. But I don't remember consciously making the decision to come over here. Hell, I remember making the conscious decision *not* to come over here.

I purposefully made sure to avoid Brandon and my family tonight, especially Mom. I didn't want to know if Rooney said yes, because I knew I wouldn't be able to hold myself together I'd be one heck of a hurricane ripping through town, either by going after my brother, or heading straight for the bar.

The shitty part about avoiding them all was I wasn't even sure if Brandon came home—if he might've come here with Rooney, instead. The thought he might be here, holding her, celebrating their engagement in ways I don't want to imagine, was gnawing at every fiber of my being.

She swallows as she stares up at me, eyes wide and glassy. Shocked. She's wearing tiny shorts that barely cover her ass and have little Hello Kitty's on them, and a pink tank top that leaves little to the imagination. I can see the faint outline of nipples I remember too well—can still taste. Her hair is a long, tangled mess, showing she hasn't been sleeping soundly. *If* she's been sleeping.

That only makes me pissed, even if I'm turned on by the sight of her. Someone should be here—she should be able to count on someone else so she can get the sleep she needs. I'll bet she hasn't gotten a good night's sleep since this thing started.

Her lips part and form a little circle as my words sink in. Damn it if I don't want to grab her and kiss her until those lips are marked by me. How the fuck did I manage to get myself into this? I was going to stay as far away as a man can get from the girl who has his heart. I was gonna make sure she was safe from me and lived a life she deserved, because I can't give her either of those. She's a standard that not even the best of people can reach. The thing is, all this time, I've been thinking of myself as the villain in our story, but I'm not. Not for now, at least.

The villain's Billie's cancer. It's not just her it's poisoning, it's the people who know and love her.

"You love me?" Rooney asks in her soft voice that is always my undoing.

A shiver runs down my back as I take a step forward. She doesn't move back, but instead grips the door knob, letting the door support her weight. I get as close as I can to her and tilt my head so I'm looking down at her. She inclines her gaze to match mine. Those round eyes are sparkling like rare diamonds. If those babies don't own me, then I don't know what does.

"I love you," I repeat.

A pretty smile pulls her lips. I wonder if she's been smiling enough lately—lord knows I didn't give her many reasons to smile when we were first met. If I'm going to let her throw her life away on me, then I might as well make it worth it. I need to make sure she smiles and laughs and feels loved, even if I'm at a loss as to how to make any of it happen. She's worth figuring it out for.

I bring my hand up to cup her chin, and run my thumb along her bottom lip. "There's that smile I can't seem to get enough of."

She blushes and it's too much for me. I close the space between us and plant a feather-soft kiss on her lips. It's nothing like when we were against the tree, but it's also nothing like our first kiss, either. This one is for reminding the both of us I'm here and also for reminding us what the connection between us feels like. Just this simple brush of lips is enough to bring my body to life and make her sigh and lean in to me. Her hands leave the door knob and fist in my shirt.

If I don't get this girl vertical, fuck knows I'll take whatever she'll give me. I didn't have any trouble making her come against a tree, and I damn won't have any trouble against a door. At least it's smoother than a tree.

When I pull away, her eyes are closed and that blush has deepened. She's breathing hard, like that kiss was some sort of major physical activity. I'd be lying if I said it wasn't; it was the best kind of workout and I want more. Her eyes flutter open and as soon as her gaze meets mine, it flickers down so she's staring at my chest.

"Why are you here?"

I swallow and tilt my head back. From where I'm standing, my view is half stars, half door frame. "Because I can't stay away. Because I love you. Because thinking of you saying yes to Brandon—"

"He didn't ask," she says, cutting me off before the words are out. "I broke up with him before he could."

Shit. While a part of me is relieved, the other part of me feels bad for Brandon. Poor fucking guy. A girl like Rooney cutting him to the chase has to have left him heartbroken. Still, my relief outweighs any sympathy by a fucking landslide. I don't know what I'd do if she'd said yes.

Who the hell am I kidding? I know what I'd do, and it wouldn't end well for Brandon.

I run my hands down her arms and slide them to grip her hips. My thumb innocently brushes over the small sliver of visible skin. She shivers and I realize it might not be *that* innocent. I'm aiming for this reaction. "Why?"

She draws in a sharp breath and moves farther in to me, gripping my shirt tighter. She tilts her chin up, turning her gaze back on me. "I don't love him."

My other fingers slip beneath the fabric of her tank top, at her waist. Her skin is too soft for me not to touch. "Why?"

Her lips tremble. "I love you."

I want to kiss those lips until I've got them memorized. Too bad I can't go there—yet, anyway. Later, I will. Right now, I need to clear some things up. Especially since we've both admitted those three big words to each other. I and love and you go down a serious path, where there's no turning back.

"What I said the other day—about you needing better than me? It's still true, Rooney. Maybe I meant for my words to hurt you, but they weren't a lie. I'm fucking terrified about feeling the way I feel about you. I've never..." I pause and force myself to look at her. If I look away, I'll pussy out. I won't feel the compulsion to bare my soul to her. If I'm not going to hurt her, I need to start letting her in. "I've never loved anyone as much as I love you. I never thought I was capable of loving anything, but then I met you and now...now I can't help but worry some higher power's giving you to me to love just so it can take you away from me when I ruin you. I don't think I can—"

Her hands release my shirt and she brings her hands up to my cheeks. "You won't."

"How do you know that?"

"I just do." She stands on her toes. "If *I'm* wrong, then it's my fault, because I'm tired of you running and me letting you. From here on out, Silas Manning, I'm chasing. I'm chasing until my feet are raw and my heart is pounding and I've run a hundred miles past my limit. I'm chasing you because I love you and if I don't chase you, then I'm in the wrong. This is out of your hands now. If *you're* wrong, well, then we can be happy and in love for the rest of our lives. So let me chase you, okay?"

I close my eyes and let out a breath through my nose. I can't believe I'm letting myself do this—letting myself have her. I'm an idiot and genius all in one. "Okay."

I choose to let Rooney close the distance, because this has to be her decision. Even if she says she loves me, I need more verification. Maybe I sure as hell won't be the one to end this, but I'm not about to go starting it. If I let her take the lead, then it'll lessen the regret I'll feel at every wrong turn from here on out.

Her arms link at my neck and her fingers massage the back of my head in a way that almost has my eyes rolling into my skull. I swallow hard, because fuck me if a touch as light and as innocent as that one has my cock springing to attention like a soldier prepared for the best, most blessed battle of his existence. A battle he's only set up to walk away from in glory.

Her lips part and I know if she doesn't kiss me, I'll be regretting *that* for the rest of my life. Not just the case of blue balls I'll surely die of, but because I won't have gotten another taste of her. Something to for me to clutch on to and harbor like a damn burglar.

"You wan*t me* to kiss *you*, don't you?" Rooney asks, those lips pulling up into a wry smile.

I mirror her smile, even though I don't have any feeling outside of my swelling cock and the weakness in my knees. "How'd you know?"

"Because I want *you* to kiss *me*."

I lean my forehead against her, giving in the slightest bit. "If you kiss me, you're mine for the rest of our lives. Damn it if we've only known each other for a short time, because it's enough for me to know we're going to last. I'm in love with you as much as I love you, and that ain't going to change, even when we've got grandkids."

Her eyes sparkle. "Silas."

"Hmm?"

"Are you done with your speeches?"

"Yeah, why?"

She answers by closing the distance. By pressing her lips against mine, by parting those lips without hesitation and letting my tongue sweep inside to meet hers. Her frame lines up with mine and a moan comes from one of us, maybe both, and it gets lost somewhere between us.

Her hips grind impatiently against me and I know they're needy for what I have to give, and fuck knows I've got a lot to give her and she'll take it—she'll take it and come hard.

"I ain't doing this against a damn door," I mutter and lift her up to carry her. Her legs immediately wrap around me, like they did when I pressed her up against the tree, and I walk us back to her room, kissing her like a blind man without a care in the world. I don't even bother to pay attention to where I walk because if we go down, I'll fall with her on top of me and keep taking. As long as we're vertical, I'm fucking content.

Rooney murmurs something in disappointment as I stop kissing her to lay her back on her bed. I can't help but grin at the disgruntled look on her beautiful face. Red lips pouting, eyes longing, cheeks flushed and on a bed; it's like something out of a fantasy I never let myself have.

I take my shirt off and throw it somewhere off to the side, enjoying the flare in Rooney's gaze. I've been looked at a lot of ways, but not by someone who matters, and if it wasn't for my need for her pulsing through my veins, I'd praise something almighty.

I cover her body with my own and weld our mouths back together, because they should never be apart after this. My hands run up and down her body, reveling in the smoothness of her skin and her luscious curves. Goddamn, this girl is perfect.

While I'm exploring, she is, too. Her fingers dig deep into the muscles of my back, into the base of my neck, sometimes even finding their way down to my ass. The more my hips grind against her, the more they go there and the more she moans.

I lean back, breaking free of her, while my gaze roams all over her body. Since I'm all about lists, I've got one for all the things I want to do to her body. Deciding which one to start with is the hardest thing I've ever done in my entire fucking life.

Rooney pulls her lip between her teeth and gives me a shy look. Damn, that good-girl look of hers. My cock twitches and I know she feels it because she sighs, her lips falling apart.

"I want you, Silas," she whispers, her voice filled with need. "I want you to have me."

I bring a hand up to her face and run my thumb along her cheek. "I thought I already do have you."

"N-no," she stutters. She closes her eyes tight. "I want you to...I want you to be my first."

You'd think she just slapped me from the way I rear back. "Rooney, no. Not this soon. You deserve more of a buildup," I tell her. Because if she's mine, then she's going to *be* mine. I have no doubt I will be her first time *eventually*, but not today. Not like this.

Her eyes flutter open and there's hurt there. "Silas, please. I want you to make love to me."

Truthfully, I've never made love to a girl. I've only ever fucked. I want to know the difference, but what if I ruin Rooney's first time trying to figure out my own shit? I clear my throat. "Do you really want to give me that?"

She looks confused for a second and then she smiles. "There's not even a question as to if I want to, Silas."

"I don't get it," I tell her, but I lean in and brush my lips over hers because I can't deny myself of her.

"You don't have to." She lets out a sigh as my kisses leave her lips and drift down her neck. "Life's short. I've been waiting because I wanted my first time to be special—I wanted it to be with someone I love so it'll be my *only* time. You're that person for me, and I don't want to waste any of the time we have."

I start kissing my way down her gorgeous body, even if my lips are only pressing against her thin T-shirt. "I don't plan on goin' anywhere, baby. But you should know the way I see it, any second I have with you is not a waste of time because it's a second I almost pushed away because I didn't think I deserved it. I could've not had *any* time with you, and I'm so fucking grateful I do, that I'm going to honor my love for you in every way possible." I start to push up her shirt because I want her beautiful tits on display *now*. I want my hands, my mouth on them. Hell, I want my hands and my mouth everywhere on her. It's exactly what's about to fucking happen. "I'm going to make love to you, baby. I'm going to make you a damn promise that everything you're about to feel is everlasting in the best way possible."

When she shivers, it takes every ounce of control not to rip her clothes off her.

CHAPTER TWENTY-FOUR

Rooney

Is it possible for my lungs to burst? My heart to combust? My whole body just to burst into flames? If it is, then I hope I can freeze time, too. Everything I'm feeling right now is so unbelievably excruciating, yet incredible at the same time.

Silas is about to *make love to me,* which both terrifies me and excites me. All in a good way, though, because this is Silas and he's about three steps past perfect and I know he'll make this experience just as perfect.

I sit up so he can remove my shirt. His eyes flash hot and needy as his gaze lands on my breasts, almost like he's never seen them before. My cheeks heat, not because I'm naked, but because I'm envisioning how he treated them the last time he saw them.

"I swear," Silas murmurs, but doesn't finish. He doesn't need to say anything else, because there's love in his tone, along with his desire.

He leans forward and places twin kisses on both my nipples, and I don't bother holding back my breathy moan. All I want is for him to take my breasts in his mouth again and do the wonderful things he did to them before, but he doesn't. Instead, he places another kiss on my mouth that I immediately respond to. We both put everything—love, desire, hopefulness—into the kiss, so that I'm momentarily distracted. I barely notice when his hands slip beneath my shorts and slide them off, until he breaks away.

I draw in a breath as I watch his eyes travel…down…down…and then stop. I've never been this bare for anyone. I didn't really expect to be this bare for anyone, either, so I have no idea if the way I look is acceptable. Even though I know Silas loves me, fear punches me in the gut, because what if he doesn't want me after he's seen me naked? What if I'm repulsive to him in some way?

He brings a hand up to his head for the rough gesture I've grown so used to him doing. He almost looks *lost*—unsure. His gaze flickers up to my eyes and then back down. Heat unfurls where his gaze lingers.

"You're a damn treasure," he whispers in awe.

I shake my head, letting out my breath. "You are, too."

He shakes his head. "No, baby. You don't—what I'm feeling right now…"

I want to say I feel what he's feeling, but I have no way of knowing if I do. I only know what I'm feeling, which is more than just need and desire. What I feel is completeness, like I've found the rest of my life in his eyes. In him.

My fears disappear with realization. Why would I even think Silas would turn away from me in a moment like this?

He places a kiss between my legs and presses my hips back, my hands twining into his hair so tight, I have a fleeting worry I might hurt him. I lose my track of mind when his tongue flicks against me. I cry out, writhing. He pushes my hips down, holding them into place so he can explore deeper.

I say something and I'm not sure if it's his name or if

it's a prayer, but it doesn't matter. They're one and the same. His gaze meets mine, fiery and loving, maybe even pleading, but that's all I need to fall over the edge, flailing.

I don't come out of my haze until I see Silas standing in front of me at the foot of the bed. He's completely naked, his erection in his hand as he strokes in rough, jagged tugs. My breath catches and tingles shoot up from my belly, making me clutch my thighs together.

"So fucking gorgeous," he murmurs. He takes a condom off the bed—I'm not sure where it came from or how it got there, but I don't care. He uses his teeth to tear it open, hand still on his erection, and then pulls the condom out to sheath himself.

My eyes fall to his hands as he does it. I've read enough romance novels to know the girl always looks at him and wonders how he's going to fit inside of her. I always thought that was stupid—thought men and women were *made* to fit together. But now, as fear spikes, I get it. He's huge and I'm…so unexperienced.

He cages me in with his body, hot and ready at my entrance. He brushes my hair away from my face. "One last time, baby. You ready for this?"

"I am."

He grins, but drops his face in the crook of my neck. "You're shaking," he tells me.

"I'm nervous," I admit.

He lets out a shuddering sigh. "I am, too. I want this to be perfect for you, but I don't…I don't want to hurt you."

"You haven't yet," I whisper, running my hands over his buzz cut.

"You know what I mean."

"I do and you know what I mean. I love you, Silas. You own all of me, so take it. I may be nervous, but I'm ready because I don't belong to anyone else but you."

He leans back and presses a kiss to the side of my head. Then I feel him prodding at my entrance, his hand guiding him in. There's a lot of pressure and pulling, but it honestly feels like magic. But the farther in he goes, the more the stretching begins to ache and the magic begins to disappear.

He captures my mouth with his, freezing in his movements. His free hand grips my breast, pinching and tugging my nipple. Just as I cry out into his lips, he fills me to the hilt. The sharp pain makes me tense, causes tears to fill my eyes.

Silas kisses them. "That'll be the worst of it," he promises. "Are you okay?"

"It gets better?"

He chuckles and it sends a chill down my back. I feel myself tighten around him, and my hips immediately shift to find the pleasure I know is hidden just within reach.

"Fuck," he groans. "Yeah, it gets better."

He pulls out slightly, then pushes back in slowly. Oh yes, it gets better. The next time he does it, my hips rise to meet his and we both moan. The motion keeps on, like it's already ingrained in us how the other's body works, until we're both sweating and crying out.

He puts a hand between us, working me as he plunges even deeper, until I feel the snap of an orgasm. My hips buck up as my back spasms and I say his name in what sounds like a tortured whisper. He follows me over the edge with one final thrust, swelling and letting go.

When we both come down, he doesn't pull out to dispose of the condom or to clean us up. He remains inside me, flipping us so my head is against his chest. His fingers flutter down my spine as he kisses my forehead.

"Thank you for giving that to me." He's quiet for a long time until he murmurs in a voice filled with wonder and awe, "I'm your first and your only."

***

Over the course of the next day, Silas and I spend all of our time together in bed. Some of it was kissing, but a lot of it was him holding me while we talk about nonsense stuff or while we watch movies. He's more relaxed than I've ever seen him, joking easily and opening up—he even belted out a huge laugh when while we watched a movie about a man who lived in the walls of these people's house. Every once in a while, one of us would leave the confines of the little world we'd created together to check up on Mama, but we'd take up our previous position as if nothing happened. Well, usually we'd kiss for a while first—Silas is a little insatiable and, yeah, maybe I am, too—but then we'd go back to acting like a normal couple.

And that's how it felt: like we're normal. Incredibly normal.

Not to mention a couple.

I'm not sure what either of us are going to do when telling-time comes and we have to fess up. No doubt his parents and Brandon will hate me, but Silas is worth it. I'd let the world hate me if it meant getting to keep this with him. Something tells me I might just have to, what with most of the town judging him without knowing him. I'll be the first to admit what Silas did was terrible—drunk driving is irresponsible and deadly, which it proved to be. But Silas served his time and his guilt is more his punishment than any jail sentence could ever be.

Plus, Silas is actively seeking help for a disease he's never known how to control. Alcoholism is only your fault if you let it be—if you spend your whole life letting it win battle after battle against you. The second you choose to say no, to take the step toward beating it, then you've won against it, and your following battles will be just as challenging, but they won't be as dire. It's just sad Silas didn't start fighting this battle until it was too late, and his disease had cost people their lives.

He presses a kiss against my hair, almost like he knows what I'm thinking about. He doesn't, but it's still comforting. I've made it my goal today to try to enjoy Silas, rather than dwelling on my sleeping mama, who isn't really my mama anymore. Or that we're expecting Rita in about an hour so we can have the talk. She had to squeeze us in at the end of her day. Silas is planning to stay to meet with Rita along with me because he knows it's going to be hard, but I don't think he plans on leaving me afterward, either. It doesn't bother me. I want him here with me as long as I can keep him. With him here, the house that had become hell for the heart is filling up with a different kind of warmth—a good kind.

The credits on the movie we were watching start to roll and Silas gets up to take the movie out and find another one to watch. I've been letting him choose because I know he probably hasn't seen a lot of them. He's missed a lot more than I can really even begin to imagine. The world doesn't seem like it's changed much in the last few years to me, but to someone who's been cut off from it, the change is huge. Everything I take for granted is new to him. It's been fun introducing him to new things, because we're creating experiences and memories we can share together.

He tilts his head as surveys my movie collection. "You sure do have a lot of romances."

"And?"

"Nothing, just stating a fact." He glances back at me and he's smiling the smile reserves for me. I shouldn't be as selfish as I am to want it to stay only mine. "Though it does give me an idea of the standards I have to hold up to."

I grin back at them. "They're high standards."

His smile vanishes and there's no mistaking the low growl at the back of his throat. "Baby, I'll show you high standards. Over and over again and every damn time, you'll be begging for more."

My hands fist in the covers and I'm pretty sure I squeak a little bit in my speechlessness.

He shakes his head as he settles on a movie I'm too distracted to check the title of. No doubt he'll be making me pretty distracted while it's playing, too.

"This one looks good. Know what'd make it better?"

I can only imagine. "What?"

"Popcorn," he says, standing up. "Rita will be here soon, right?"

"An hour."

"Then we're good. Hey, you go pop us some up and I'll check on your mama?"

I slide out of the bed. He's still shirtless, while I've been lounging around in his shirt and a pair of sleep shorts. They keep disappearing, but I keep putting them back on. I'm not comfortable enough with myself to be undressed in front of him when we're not doing anything.

As I walk past Silas, he catches my arm, sliding his fingers down it to twine with mine. "Hey," he murmurs.

I look over at him. "Hey," I say, enchanted.

"I love you."

I can't get enough of hearing those words. I thought maybe he'd be a little bit more careful of saying them, because knowing him he probably thinks saying them will equal out to me getting hurt even more than he already expects me to. But I was wrong. He's the one who initiates those three little words and whenever I do, he's always quick to say it back. I think it's because Silas never how to love, or be loved, in any way except for the way he's known—like how you're born loving your parents, but you grow to love other people. People like me. Maybe he's just afraid to lose what we have—to lose me—so he's putting everything he has into it, which is exactly what I've been doing.

I rise up on my tiptoes and brush a kiss along the underside of his jaw. I'm new to loving someone, too. Maybe I exchanged those words with Brandon, but I didn't realize the depth of what they meant, until now. Silas taught me what it feels like to be in love and to love. I don't know how to tell him that, so when I repeat the words back, I hope he can hear it in my voice and see it in my eyes. In my blush, too.

We head in opposite ways down the hallway, me to the kitchen and him to Mama's room. I can't wipe the giddy smile from my face as I search for the popcorn bags. Yesterday, I never would've guessed Silas and I would be together. Even though it was only a day ago, it seems so far back, like Silas and I have been together forever, no matter how new it feels. Being with Silas is so comfortable and right, like we were made for each other. I wish I had known when I was a little girl how this sort of love was supposed to be. I've lived all my life watching Mama date men like they were shirts she changed every day, and I always thought her version of love was right—short and quick and interchangeable. I wish that she could've known this sort of love, because I can't imagine leaving this world without knowing it. I wish she could know how complete I feel.

I'm struggling to reach the big bowl we use for popcorn when I hear Silas yelling something.

"What?" I yell back, pulse rising. There's something in his voice…something frantic. Something terrified. I fall back on my heels, ready to take off, when I fall too hard and catch the bowl with my palm. It comes down with the ones living inside of it and crashes to the ground, glass shattering everywhere. "Oh no."

Tears rise in my eyes and my hands are shaking. Deep down, I know why Silas is yelling, I know the sound to his voice, but I'm frozen, just like I thought I would be. My chest heaves in a breath and it gets stuck, panic pouring in over top of it. Overflowing me. *Please don't let this be it…*

My body jerkily moves into the response I've had every time a situation like this happened since Mama got sick, and I grab the phone off the counter. I don't pay attention to the glass or the stinging bite of it against my feet, as I dial 9-1-1 and run down the hallway.

"911, what's your emergency?" is the immediate answer of a kind-sounding elderly male voice.

"My mama…"

I step into the room and see her. This isn't like all of those other times, where she's crying out in pain or trying to talk me down from making the call, like she always is. No, this is completely different and it makes the bile rise up in my throat. *No, I'm not ready.*

She's in the same position she was in when I checked her a little while ago, only her skin has gone from pale to ashen gray. Her eyes are open and staring lifelessly up at the ceiling and her chest…it's rising but not in labored breaths. They're quiet, imperceptible ones someone else might miss if they're not used to tracking hers. They should put hope in my heart, but it doesn't, because there's an anvil tied to my heart, pulling it down and telling me this isn't good.

"Billie!" Silas yells, shaking her, like he's trying to wake her up.

"Miss?" the man says on the phone. "Are you there?"

Silas glances up at me then and I must look lost, because he holds his hand out. "Let me," he says in a gentle but commanding voice.

Normally, I could do this on my own, but I've been through this one too many times and I know this time is the time going to break me. I let my trembling legs take me to Mama's bedside and I hand him the phone.

He says something into the receiver, his voice shaky, sounding like he's about to lose it himself, but I don't hear any of his words because I'm listening so hard for those breaths. Trying to hear Mama's voice in my head, saying something snappy at me—telling me it's too damn late for us to leave, especially because she's not wearing a bra and while that might've gone well when she was my age, there's no way she's letting a sexy paramedic see her today. I want that Mama. She seemed so sick, so close to leaving me, but she wasn't. She was still vital and alive and *weeks* away from leaving me. Everything that felt like the end then, wasn't really the end. But this…this feels like it, except it doesn't. Mama's trained me to think everything will be okay, that she'll keep on and everything will be okay, until the next time when it's not.

Somehow, my heart is telling me there won't be a next time and…I can't even wrap my head around it. What was the last thing she said to me? What was the last thing I said to her that she could hear? When was the last time I told her how much I love her and how she's my best friend? I can't even remember the sound of her voice…I can't…

"Rooney," Silas says, and his arms wrap around me. He pulls me to his chest and lays his cheek against my head. "They're on their way."

I'm so lost in my panic that I start shaking my head and muttering things even I can't decipher. No, it can't happen this way. We were supposed to have more time. The doctors said we would. We can't just lose our time—not when there's still so much more for us to share together. I need to spill to her about Silas and listen to her talk about the trashy soaps she watches during the day when she's not sleeping and I can't be without my late-night Mama cuddles. I just need her and I'm not ready to let her go. How can she be ready? Ready to let me go—to leave me?

"Shh," Silas murmurs and I realize he's crying because my hair is wet. His bare chest is glistening, too, from my tears. "You don't know what's going to happen."

I pull away and look up at him.

He draws in a breath through his nose. "She's not gone yet, Rooney. Listen."

I close my eyes and sure enough, faintly, I can hear it. I need it to be closer, louder. Silas lets me go and I crawl into bed with her the way I've always done. Here, I can hear it fine. She's still alive.

"You can't leave me yet, Mama. You've got to have the last word. I need that. Then you can…then you can go, okay? I just need to tell you I love you."

I know she won't answer, but my heart still drops when she doesn't.

I lie there until the ambulance eventually comes, while

Silas sits on the bed beside me, rubbing my back. When the EMTs do finally come, everything goes in a flash. They ask me what happened and about her history and I answer it all in quick succession because I've come to know it all, and then they're gone and Silas is ushering me into the car to follow behind them. I barely even notice he's driving, even though he doesn't have a license and he's not a fan of cars, until we get to the hospital and he's parking in the emergency parking lot, then helping me out, practically carrying me inside.

This can't be it.

Are we ever ready lose our mama?

LIZ ASHLEE

CHAPTER TWENTY-FIVE

Silas

I turn the bathroom faucet on high blast and splash icy water on my face, trying to will myself to be strong for Rooney. We've been waiting for news and as much as I hate I had to leave her, I couldn't take the waiting game anymore. I was getting agitated and ready to charge the emergency room doors. I have to be stronger, because Rooney needs someone who can calm *her* down and be someone she can lean on.

So I came to the bathroom to pull my shit together. She's been alternating between an emotional wreck and completely blank. It's killing me just as much as not knowing what's happening to Billie is. I hate seeing her cry and, in this situation, I hate watching her *not* cry. Shit, everything about this is killing me. I feel so useless when all I want to do is fix everything for her—to take all of her pain and shove it my way.

I turn off the faucet and lean back, staring at my reflection in the mirror I look like shit. My eyes are red because every time Rooney's cried, I've either cried right along with her or suppressed every damn last tear like it was my fucking job. There's also bags under my eyes, because I didn't sleep much last night because damn, it's hard to sleep with Rooney's hot-as-fuck body so close.

I'm in another EMT shirt—the same guy gave it to me again. He must think I'm incapable of dressing myself, or something. The shirt fucking pisses me off just like the last time, but for a very different reason. Not because I destroy lives, but because Rooney's mama is dying and I can't save her. If I didn't waste my life away, maybe I could've done something to help.

If we were in a avoid-the-shank-or-die situation or a how-to-throw-your-life-down-the-damn-shitter situation, I'd be gold.

I shake my head and head back out. Time to face reality—but I can't complain if it's a reality with Rooney in the picture.

I stop by the crappy coffee maker and buy us two cups. I could use the energy and I'm sure Rooney can, too. I stop by the admitting desk on the way back to Rooney and my spot.

"Anything yet?" I ask the girl manning it.

It's not Jackie, thank the fucking lord, and this one's actually pretty nice. I'm not sure she knows who I am but if she does, her co-worker could use a few tips.

"Not yet," she answers in a perky but sympathetic voice. "But I promise to tell you as soon as I know anything. Hopefully, you guys will be able to go back soon. Here, I've already made up your visitor stickers."

"Thanks." I set the coffees down and take the stickers from her. I put mine on, walk over to Rooney.

She's curled up on a two-seater chair, looking lost. I wish I knew how to find her. She sits up when I get closer and makes room for me.

"Brought you this," I say, holding out the coffee.

She looks at the cup and then up at me, and back at the coffee again. Her lips start trembling and oh man, I hate when that happens. I hate how I'm always unintentionally making her cry. Tears blur over her eyes and she catches them with the back of her hand. "I love you."

I clench my jaw and set the coffees on the end table. I take the spot beside her and pull her into my arms. She immediately buries her head in my chest, holding on to me so tight, I wonder if I'm her lifeboat or her boyfriend. Even if the thought of hurting her terrifies me, I wouldn't give this up for a minute, because at least she has somebody to be here for her. I run my hand over the back of her head and twirl her soft hair around my fingers.

"If I could take all this shit away, Rooney, I would. You having to go through this is killing me. But you have me, okay? I don't know if that means anything but it's the only way I can help right now. When she...when this is all over. You have someone." I press a kiss against her scalp. "I love you."

"That helps," she murmurs into my shirt. "I don't think I could do this without you."

She could—she's stronger than anyone I've ever met—but I won't argue with her. Instead, we sit in silence, our coffees going cold I whisper things to her I hope are meaningful, along with completely random stuff to distract her. When I sing part of "The General Specific" by Band of Horses in her ear, or what I remember of it, she laughs softly. It's the best thing I've ever heard and I'm so proud of myself, I grin. At least I've done something right today.

The emergency doors slide open and my smile vanishes. My hold on Rooney tightens because even though it's my parents and Brandon walking in, they're still an enemy threatening to break Rooney back down. Sure, maybe they're here because they mean well, but the last thing I need is for her to start crying again, and put us back where we started.

Rooney tenses even though she can't see who it is. I will my muscles to relax, because I know she's tensing because of my reaction. I went from soft and soothing to pissed off and protective.

They take the seats across from us. Brandon stares at Rooney with a look that might be pretty close to the way I look at her—*close*—and I wonder if he's realized I'm not holding her to comfort her. Or that I didn't come home last night. I couldn't care less if he knows, so long as he doesn't take it out on Rooney.

I can tell he's itching to trade spots with me. *Over my fucking dead body, bro.*

"How is she?" Mom asks. She's looking at Rooney like she wants to hold her, too. If the idea of letting Rooney go didn't make me feel sick, I might let her.

I'm not sure if Mom's talking about Rooney or Billie, so I answer about Billie. "We don't know yet. We've been waiting."

Mom's expression flickers and I know she's thinking the same thing: this isn't good. "Can I ask what happened?"

I lean my head back against the wall and try to rub out the knots in Rooney's neck and shoulders. "A lot like last time—wasn't breathing well. She wasn't..." I trail off because the word *good* will only make Rooney hurt more. My parents nod like they get it. Billie's dying—there's nothing else to say.

Dad slides forward and rubs Rooney's knee. "How are you doing, sweetheart?"

Rooney sits up, but doesn't leave my arms. "Not good," she admits.

"I don't see how you could be anything but," he says, and I love Dad more than I ever have for it. I think, along the way, I managed to isolate myself so much that even my family remained on the outside of my heart. "You know we're here for you, right? You're not alone."

"Definitely not," Mom says.

"No," Brandon adds.

Rooney's gaze snaps to his, and for a split second, I worry she'll leave me for him, she'll draw away from my arms and slip into his. But she just gives him a small, sad smile and nods. "I appreciate—"

She cuts off as the nurse walks out. Toward us. We all stand at the same time. "You can go back," the nurse says.

"How is she?" Rooney and I both ask.

The nurse swallows. "She's stable." The missing words are she's stable, but it's not a promise she'll be stable forever. It can change—will change.

Rooney nods, holding her chin up. There's my girl. Strong for her mama. "Can I see her now?"

"Yes," the nurse answers. She glances at the rest of us. "But only two at a time."

"Oh no," Mom says, "we're just here for support."

I stiffen beside Rooney as I notice Brandon's stance looks like someone who's ready to be tagged in to the game. Rooney doesn't notice. Her hand slips into mine and then she's dragging me toward the emergency doors.

CHAPTER TWENTY-SIX

Rooney

I draw in a deep breath as we go back to Mama's room. Room nine. "Tell me I can do this."

Silas doesn't even hesitate. "You can do this."

I let the breath out That was what I needed to hear—not his words, but his confidence. He squeezes my hand and we walk the rest of the way, my heart pounding with each step. She's going to die, but at least she didn't die today. I can tell her I love her and make sure I tell her everything I thought I wasn't going to have a chance to. Like how Silas sings a little off key, but has a weird bluegrass thing going for him. Or how Silas and I said our I-love-yous. I'm going to tell her I'm going to stay in our house, no matter how much it scares me to be there without her. I'm going to promise her I'll try to pass on some of her Billie-isms to my kids, so she's not really going to be gone.

I'm going to tell her everything I possibly can. Stupid things, serious things, things I'd usually be embarrassed to tell her. If the wedding taught me anything, you take what you can get however you can get it, because you might not have the chance later.

"—understand the way the DNR will work?"

My heart stops pounding, drops, and I freeze. All of my hopes and promises gone. DNR? A Do Not Attempt Resuscitation Order? We're really there? Mama's choosing to just go, if something happens? To leave without trying? From here on out, they'll only make her comfortable so she doesn't pass in pain.

"Hey, hey, hey," Silas says. He steps in front of me and cups my cheeks. He bends to look into my eyes. As always, he draws me back to where I need to be, and away from the overwhelming panic. "She has to. You don't want her to suffer."

"No. It just…" I squeeze my eyes shut. "It's happening."

"It's happening," he repeats.

I open my eyes and press a kiss against his cheek. When we make it through this, I really hope happiness finds us, because I'm not sure we'll know how to find it.

I let him lead me the rest of the way. There's a doctor in there with Mama, another handsome one of course, because Mama's lucky in that department. There's also a nurse who's staring at the monitor intently. It always worries me what they're seeing—something they don't like, or something they're unsure about. I ignore it this time because Mama's here, and this is a chance I didn't think I was going to have.

She looks infinitely better. Her cheeks have gone from an ugly gray color to a deep red and her breathing is normal. Even. Her eyes are shining in a way I haven't seen in days. She's actually here with me, not off in some place I can't see. I miss those eyes and the smile in them. Hospitals always seem to do this to her, between the medications and the cute male staff and the attentiveness…

I need to make sure I call Rita tonight. Hopefully, she's not at our house waiting on us. I'll try to find some time to get in touch with her—maybe we can send Mama straight from here to a care place. I'll probably just stay there with her, but at least I won't have to take care of her. She needs people who are trained to do it.

I also need to call Dr. Demarco, or at least make sure someone here has—

"Stop thinking, Rooney," Mom says in a weak at attempt at sounding commanding, "and sit with me."

In an instant, my eyes fill with tears and I'm at her side like I'm a child hiding from monsters. I think I am. But unlike when I was little, Mama cries with me. She takes my hand and brings it up to her lips and we say things to each other I'm pretty sure neither of us can understand, but it doesn't matter because we're saying them. We're getting in everything we need to and everything we don't.

We both know it's time to stop pretending we still have time.

CHAPTER TWENTY-SEVEN

Silas

I decide to give Rooney and her mama a break because they started talking in hushed tones, spilling secrets that should stay between them. I don't even mention I'm leaving, I just go. The second Rooney needs me, she'll call me.

Her mama seems better, but there's this ominous feeling clawing at my chest, reminding me it's all a smoke screen.

I duck outside the hospital, careful to avoid my parents, and slide down the wall to the ground. I'd kill for a smoke about now, but I'm quitting. After watching cancer eat away at Billie, I know I can never make Rooney have to go through that again.

It's step one on whatever list I'm making toward being a better person for her. There's probably a whole lot of other steps, but I have no clue how to tackle those, so I'll save those for another day. Another one of those steps is in this hospital, somewhere.

The doors slide open and I immediately know it's someone from my family. The place is unusually quiet tonight, barely anyone else here.

Dad takes the spot beside me with a heavy huff. "She okay?"

"Better," I admit.

"Good. Hate seein' either of those two hurt. They're special." Out of the corner of my eye, I see him raise an eyebrow. "Glad to see you two are together, Brandon's feelings aside. You need each other. Brandon needs…well, he'll know her when he sees her."

I only shrug. Yeah, I'm not so sure he hasn't already seen her. It's not hard to fall in love with Rooney. It's falling out of love with her that's damn near impossible. Severing all your limbs would be easier.

He looks forward again. "We send her flowers every few months. You know that?"

My jaw opens. I know who he's talking about. Exactly who he's fucking talking about. Maggie. Shit. I clutch the back of my head with my fingernails, trying to force all of this away. Why the hell is he bringing this up *now*?

"I don't give a fuck," I say through gritted teeth.

He doesn't flinch, which sparks my rage higher.

"You don't have the fucking right to go there right now."

"I have every fucking right," he growls. "We need to talk about this—we've needed to talk about this for *years* but you've fought us off any chance you've gotten. But out of everyone, I'm the one who gets you." He clenches his fists and when he releases them, a lot of his anger simmers away. "I blame myself."

My anger disappears, too. I drop my hands. "Why?"

"The addiction," he answer simply. "It's in my blood—from our side. Dates back generations, starting with Dad's grandfather. Every one of us have sworn we're gonna be different—make our lives better. We never do. All it took was simple injury playing football, and I was addicted to pain medication. Kept trading up in drugs until I met your mom and got cleaned up. Then you came along and you started showing the signs, but you were so good at hiding it. And I think I was hiding from it, too. Then the accident...I blame myself. Family blood, my conscious decisions not to make you stop, then not helping you when you needed it, not being there for you...it's all weighed on me."

I stare at him, speechless. He blames himself? "Fuck, no. All of this is on me, you got that? I chose to drink when I was still just a kid. I chose to drink again and again afterward, and let it control me. I chose to get into a fucking car when I was *drunk off my ass*. I chose to cut ties. I chose every despicable decision, up until now."

"Until Rooney," Dad corrects.

My laugh is humorless. "That's debatable."

"Other than going behind your brother's back, it's not. You love her and she loves you. You've done more for her than Brandon has, and you deserve her. We're off topic here." He turns toward me and pins me with an I-won't-take-your-shit glare. Dad only pulls that one out when he's about to say something we have to listen to. "The fact is, it's all of our faults. Yours, mine. Hell, it's even theirs."

What the fuck? "No it's not."

"Really?" He sighs and shakes his head. "You were drunk and it was your fault. But there's always more than one side. Like the fact that Vic was going twenty over the speed limit and took the turn sharp. Or how Maggie and Melanie weren't wearing their seat belts. It's called conscious decisions—it makes them responsible, too. If Vic was going the speed limit and the girls had them on, then maybe we'd be having a different conversation. They might be okay—"

I stand up and point out at the parking lot. Particularly at the car I drove to get here without a license. Another motherfucking mistake of mine, even if there wasn't any repercussions. "I was fucking drunk. It was *my* fault. Mine and mine alone."

"I'm not saying it wasn't. If all of those factors were

missing and it was just you drunk, then they'd be dead and it'd be on you. But those factors were there and they're gone. It could've easily been Vic lost control and the same result happened. But because you were drunk, all of the blame is put on you."

"Do not," I warn, "condone what I did."

"I'm not!" He stands up too, getting in my face. "I just want you to see the world isn't on your shoulders. It doesn't revolve around you and your self-hatred."

I glare at him. "Why are you bringing this up now?" *When I'm actually actively trying to be better? To move on?*

"Because I have to."

I swing my arm back and punch the wall beside him. Skin tears and blood starts oozing from my knuckles. "You have to? *You have to*? Every day I wake up and wonder why the fuck I get to live and they don't. A second doesn't go by when I'm not thinking about Maggie! How she's in there unable to live because I've taken that away from her. I think about their families and their friends and the lives they don't get to lead. I think about you guys and how I've taken and taken from you and I'm not even sure there's anything left for you to love. I marvel at how Rooney can love me, even though I'm a fucking monster who killed two—*three*—people and is constantly wishing I was the fourth but thankful I *wasn't*. I *hate* myself. But I guess that's nothin' compared to your guilt." I step closer, spit flying. All of the words are pouring out of me and I refuse to put a stop to it. "Rooney is in there and her mama is dying. *Dying*. And you want to talk about our guilt—feel sorry? No. No fucking way. This is about her— my life is about her now. I'm dry, I'm doing my damnedest to make up for the shit I've pulled, I'm trying to make her happy. There's no room for the past anymore. I'm done. Don't make me done with you, too."

He stares at me, pale. It takes him a while to regain himself. So long, I consider leaving him there. Then he nods. "I want us to go to family counseling, son."

I stare back. What the fucking hell?

"I've been waiting to hear you say that for years. I've missed my son." I shake my head in disbelief, but he holds up a hand. "I want us to move on and the only way we can do that is for us all to get help. We could all use it. I realize you're not a kid—you're an adult and can refuse this—but we need it. Rooney, too. Life's long, no matter the length, so you might as well live it fully. Loving Rooney, making the cycle stop with you, doing what's right—it's about damn time you make your life good."

He turns and starts walking toward the door. "Think about it. Talk to Rooney if you need to."

I stand there quiet for a minute. I already know what she'll say, but she won't ask me to do anything I don't want to. I might as well start making it worth it, if I belong to her and she belongs to me. "Fine. I'll do it—the counseling."

Dad just nods as he keeps walking.

"Those flowers?"

He stops. "Yeah?"

"I'd like to start helping out with that."

"Okay, son. Later."

For now, it's time to go back to my girl and start making my promises a reality.

***

I hear Rooney's musical laughter as I near her mama's room and it nearly has me doubling over. Her laugh does things to me I didn't think were humanly possible.

How much longer do I have with her laugh? We know her mama's going to pass eventually, and I'm just so damned worried this vibrant part of Rooney is going to go with Billie—at least for a short time. I have no clue how I'm going to handle her crying and seeming so broken, but I'll figure a way to bring these laughs back and make her smile, just like I'll absorb all of her tears and plaster the cracks.

I check over my knuckles, making sure there's no blood visible. I stopped by the nurses' station and asked for a bandage. They wanted to make a big deal out of it, but I just told them seeing my girlfriend's mama so sick is getting to me. As much as I hate using Billie in a lie, it's better than admitting it was either hit the wall or hit Dad—or myself. Shit, what he did back there was dangerous, and I hope he understands it.

"Silas, I see you looming out there."

Billie's voice catches me off guard. She sounds so...healthy. She sounds like I would've expected her to sound before all of this, and I don't want her to go back to the Billie I've come to know. Except that's not possible. This is just something to throw us off. A curve ball. It'll make the hurt feel like a machete to the chest.

Now is not the time to go down a rabbit hole. Rooney needs to enjoy this and I need to let her. If I'm busy worrying, she'll worry, too. I walk inside Billie's room and stop in front of her bed. "I was enjoying listenin' to you two beauties laugh."

"When did you become such a flirt? Tell me, you want a woman twice your age? Well, not twice—a little younger than *that*."

Her eyes are glowing so brightly, it makes a chuckle get stuck in my throat. I want to laugh because what she said was funny, but I need to bask in this moment more.

"I heard you and my daughter are official. You have no idea how giddy it makes me to know my daughter is in love with and loved by the man she belongs with."

My gaze finds Rooney as she stares down at her hands folded in her lap, a blush blossoming on her face. I wonder what she told Billie? Something tells me Billie doesn't like it when details are spared. My imagination runs wild with their conversation and this time, I chuckle.

When Rooney's blush deepens even further and her mama turns her head to muffle her laughs in her pillow, I cut off. Yeah, maybe my family is sitting out in the waiting room, but these two are my family, too. I love them both in different ways, but I do love Billie. I love her like she's my own mother and my friend. I wish I could have a future with both of them because I know if I did, nothing else would matter.

"And I'm glad Rooney won't be alone tonight."

"Mama!" Rooney chides in a rushed whisper.

Billie lifts a frail, IV-pricked hand up and waves her off, causing the color in her face to vanish, and she starts coughing. Rooney tenses beside her. I do the same. Billie collects herself, but all of a sudden she looks tired, back to the woman who I saw yesterday.

"I think it's time the two of you go," she says exhaustedly.

"I can stay the night—"

"No," Billie cuts in. "You go home. It'll just be a long night for you and this way you can get your sleep."

"We can stay a little longer if you want. At least until you get your room or hear some more news."

"There is no more news, Rooney. No more than we already know. When I get a room, I'll make sure someone calls you."

Rooney doesn't look convinced. At all. I rub my chin. "Billie, we can stay."

Both Rooney and Billie look up at me, eyes glistening. "You'd do that?" Rooney asks. "Stay here with us?"

I can't believe she's asking. "Yeah."

"That's kind of you, Silas," Billie says. "But the truth is, I want some sleep."

That is enough to sway Rooney. "Okay, but we'll be here tomorrow morning at nine."

"Sounds good," Billie agrees. "Tomorrow at nine."

Rooney repeats it again and then her eyes well up. Billie manages to hold her arms up, but it looks like it takes a lot out of her. Rooney doesn't give them enough time to fall. She launches—in a gentle way—into Billie's arms and kisses her. They remain there for a while before Rooney pulls back to wipe her eyes.

"I love you, Mama. I—you scared me."

Billie nods, completely serious. "I'll try not to do it again. You shouldn't have to worry, baby girl."

"I do, no matter what."

Tears fill Billie's eyes, too. "I love you, too." Rooney gives her another kiss and a hug, then backs away. Billie beckons me forward. "Do I get a hug?"

I was hoping not. The thought of hugging her scares me. She's so frail, I'm worried I might break her. I do it anyway, since it's what she wants. Her bones pop and I try not to wince as I pull away. The human body shouldn't fail a person like it is failing her.

"And you, you should know I love you, too. Thank you for taking care of her."

"Always," I tell her. "It's what I'm here for."

I take Rooney's hand in mine and squeeze it. She folds into the side of my body and lets me guide her out. Billie calls after us to turn off the light and I do, and it's not until we're walking toward the doors leading to the waiting room that Rooney lets out a breath that ends in a sob.

***

I give Rooney the keys to her car and tell her to go ahead on, I'll meet her out there in a minute. Since we're together now, I need to be more of a risk analyst. Meaning, I have to recognize mistakes before I make them. Driving was a terrible idea, but I can't see how anyone would've blamed me—driving home, though? Yeah, it won't go over well with anyone. So I have to walk back to my parents with my tail between my legs, after my yelling match with Dad. Fucking fantastic.

The three of them stand up as soon as they see us walk out, and watch Rooney as she walks away.

"Can someone drive?" I ask, point blank. There's no

use sugar-coating it.

"Sure," Dad says. His gaze flickers to my knuckles and then back up. Mom just straight-up stares at me.

When we get outside, Brandon's hand lands on my shoulder. "Can I talk to you for a second?"

A growl gains a whole hell of a lot of momentum at the back of my throat. "Rooney needs to get home and get some sleep."

"Yeah, but—" He stops and brings a hand up to grip the back of his neck.

"You two talk," Mom urges. "We'll meet you at the cars."

Brandon waits until they're out of earshot before he opens his mouth. Then he shuts it and my patience fizzles. I've never been one for patience. "Get on with it," I command.

His eyes narrow, nostrils flaring, and I see more of myself in him than I want to. "You took her from me."

I raise my eyebrows. *And?* Does he think I should say I'm sorry? That he can have her? I'm not sorry and he can't have her. There's nothing to say.

"You know, I've let you get by with a lot of shit," he says raggedly.

Sure, I've seen Brandon pissed off a few times, but not like this. He looks like me—furious, uncontrollable—and I hate it.

"But stealing *my* girl—I won't let that happen. She was mine first and she's too good for you."

"And what? You're good enough for her?" I grit my teeth together and glance to make sure no one can see us. I take a step forward and invade Brandon's space. "You're not. She's too good for anybody. If you don't see that, then you seriously fucking don't deserve her, either."

He clenches his fists at his sides, raises his chin. I may be taller, but he's got the muscle. But I've also been to prison.

"I see," he says.

"Then you should also see that I love her."

"So do I," he argues.

"Not the way I do. I can't breathe without her—she's saved me, Brandon. I'm pretty sure I've saved her, too." I step back and run my hand roughly over my face. "Where have you been? Her mama's dying and you've been where—at *school?* Shit, Brandon, I know it's important, but not important enough you can't take the *summer* off to be with your girl when she needs you."

"So what, you're saying I wanted to be away?"

"Maybe you didn't want to, but you stayed away. There was a choice and you chose wrong."

He laughs, the sound harsh. "You know how many times you've chosen wrong and gotten tons of chances? Too many to count, and the consequence was three peoples' *lives.*"

I close the space again and push my brother against the wall. Damn, this wall is getting a lot of action today. I grip the collar of his shirt. He doesn't move. Just stares at me with a hard, challenging gaze. "Throw that around all you want. I get it—you're better than me. Except right now, you're not. You're someone who thinks it's okay to throw around someone's guilt when you can't fucking understand any of it. I'm seein' my brother, who doesn't know how to appreciate somethin' wonderful when he's got it."

He pushes me away and glares. "I can't believe I thanked you for spending time with her—for being her friend when I couldn't be here—because this entire time you've been fucking her—"

In a second he's back up against the wall and my fist's pulled back. "You don't talk about her like that. You don't know shit, you got—"

"Silas." I instantly drop Brandon and turn around. Shit. Rooney's standing in the middle of the emergency roundabout. The tears are dry in her eyes, but they're red-rimmed and puffy and it makes me want to gather her in my arms again—except there's disappointment and hurt hiding in there, too. "Please stop."

"I'm sorry, baby," I say and make my way toward her to apologize.

"It's okay," she says. "I just want to go home."

I immediately relax. I'm not sure if she's disappointed or hurt by me as much as she is by Brandon. "Okay, let's go."

"For her," Brandon says, catching up to me, "I'll let this go. But not for long."

I don't blame him. Rooney shoots him a look. "You don't get to do that for me. Blame me, not Silas. I'm the one who fell in love with your brother while I was with you. But you should blame yourself, too. You didn't care, until now. Not really. You only do now because you're not perfect at something, for once.

Brandon stops and so do I. Did my girl just say that? There's the bite I love—the same bite I saw in her the day I met her. Her fire tells me that no matter what, every thing's going to be okay. Worrying about losing any side of her isn't worth my time because there'll always be another side to love.

I take a few long strides and wrap an arm around her shoulder. Then I kiss her and whisper those three words I can't seem to get enough of.

LIZ ASHLEE

CHAPTER TWENTY-EIGHT

Rooney

During the ride home, Mr. Manning funnels his nervous energy through talking. He talks about everything, and I'm pretty sure he manages to give a full synopsis of all of the books he and Mrs. Manning are reading, ticking off reasons why he did or didn't like them. Every once in a while, his gaze rises to the rearview mirror to glance back at Silas and me with worry. Silas' hand continuously does something new—holds my thigh, twines his fingers with my own, brushes my hair behind my ear. It's like he's trying to ground me from the force building inside me, which wants to scream at Mr. Manning to stop looking at me and to stop driving and to just *stop*. I want everything to stop. I need a freeze-frame to gather every single thought and fear.

We pull into the my driveway and Silas opens the door and slides out. He rounds the car and opens mine for me. He wraps his arm around my waist and kisses my temple. I sink into him. I hope he doesn't leave me. He holds me together in ways I can't do on my own.

"Are you coming over?" I ask in a whisper so his dad

241

can't hear us. I tilt my face up toward him and find he's looking down at me with both concern and confusion. "I—"

"I am," he interrupts. "Of course I am. That's what you want, right?"

I nod.

"Good." He rests his forehead against mine. "I'm not letting you be alone right now. *I* don't want to be alone. Hell, that's a lie. I can be alone. I just don't want to be without you."

"I don't, either."

He pulls back. "Can I get the keys off you, Dad?"

"Sure thing," his dad answers. He tosses the keys Silas' way and Silas catches them effortlessly with just a flick of his wrist. "See you tomorrow. Call me if you need anything."

I'm more than a little surprised he's not more…resistant to Silas and me, but I guess now is not the time. Silas leads me into my house, neither of us caring to acknowledge his mom as she pulls into their driveway with Brandon.

I don't have the heart to feel sympathy for Brandon. Me letting him go means he has the chance to really fall in love and find what Silas and I have. I can't feel sorry for him when I know only good will come of this.

When we get inside, Silas sets the car keys in the little bowl Mama and I never use. If we did, we'd still manage to misplace our keys.

His hands shake and at the clang of the metal against the ceramic, his fist clenches. It dawns on me then: he drove tonight. Sure, maybe he didn't have a license, which is something that's illegal and I might normally condone it, but he drove *for me*. He got behind the wheel even though I'm sure it terrified him in about a million different ways, worrying about somehow putting me and everyone else on the road in danger, yet he did it and he did it well.

I'm so overcome that I launch myself at him. Instead

of returning the gesture, he surprises me by lifting me into his arms, a lot like he did with Mama the first time we met, only now it's different. This feels safe and happy. Like we're a couple heading over the threshold, even though we've already passed it. All of the emotion inside of me swirls around like the most violent of hurricanes, and a giggle bubbles up. "What are you doing?"

He doesn't even try to hold back a smile. He's all teeth and crinkled, twinkling eyes—exactly what I need. "I'm going to hold my girl after a goddamn terrible day." He starts carrying me down the hallway and I grip on tight to his shirt, because while I've seen him carry Mama like she's nothing, I'm not nearly as weightless. Falling from Silas' tall height would kill my tail-bone. "How's your head?"

"My head?"

"Yeah, you said you get stress migraines. You okay?"

Can he get any more perfect? How did I ever think this man wasn't capable of being such a caring person?

"Something's been brewing, but it's getting better. Having you doesn't make it all seem so..." I let the words trail off, because how I am I supposed to say having Silas makes Mama's terminal illness not seem so devastating? It would downplay the gripping terror that seizes my gut whenever I think about everything.

Silas nods. He gets me, no matter what. "Then it's my turn to return the magic. You tired?"

I shrug. I'm worn out in every way a person can be, but I still feel like no matter how hard I try, finding sleep will be impossible. Worry and fear ebbs at your mind like that.

Silas sets me down in my room and tells me he'll take care of my bed, so I should go get changed or do whatever I need to. I quickly collect a pair of pajama shorts and a tank top, then head for my bathroom. I don't bother looking in the mirror. Actually, I avoid looking in the mirror. But I do wash my face and brush out my hair because I don't want Silas waking up and thinking he fell asleep next to a zombie version of Simba.

When I'm finished in the bathroom, I head back down the hall to my room. The lights are already out and I can see Silas lying on my bed. His side of the covers are kicked down to the bottom of the bed, revealing he's only wearing a pair of boxers, his long, muscular legs spread in front of him and linked at the ankles. He's leaning against my headboard, arms crossed behind his head.

Even in my devastated state, I'm not immune to his sex appeal. The twitching pecs and the muscles, mixed with his look of lust and love on his face, it all makes me want to crawl into bed with him and have a repeat of last night, even if I'm still sore.

Still, I know he has no intentions of anything sexual tonight, which makes me love him even more. He'll hold me and only kiss me in tender ways and by morning we'll be a mess of tangled limbs.

I crawl into bed beside him and immediately lay my cheek against his chiseled, but surprisingly comfortable, chest. I wrap my arm around him and curl fingers into his back. I'm not alone in this anymore, and having him so close is proof.

He unclasps his hands. One soothes the pounding in my temple, while the other draws shapes on my shoulder.

"I haven't slept in a real bed since I left prison," he tells me in a soft voice.

I'm not sure how to respond and I'm not sure if he wants me to. I think if he did, we wouldn't be in the dark and he would actually be able to look into my eyes. This is just about him getting his words out there.

"The beds in prison were shit. I got used to it. Embraced it. Every night I'd toss and turn, all of my wrongdoings weighing on my mind. It felt as good of a punishment as any." He pauses to gather himself before continuing on. Normally, he talks about his past with self-loathing, but now it just sounds like he's recounting a memory. Progress. "Then I got out and I knew I could come home. My parents would let me back in, but I couldn't do that to them, so I took up living on the streets. Slept in shelters or on benches. Never on a bed, though. I couldn't. It was too comfortable, too familiar, too...too much of something I couldn't let myself have. Then I met you and now I'm in a bed."

I press a kiss against his chest.

He lets out a contented sigh. "I never wanted a home until you. But you, shit, Rooney, you're it. My home. Wherever you are, it's where I'm supposed to be. That can't ever be broken. The foundation ain't gonna crack and the walls aren't going to cave in. The mattress ain't gonna turn brown. I'm here for you no matter what. I'm done leaving. You can count on me, okay? You'll *always* have me."

I didn't realize how much I needed to hear his words until now. Tears prick at my eyes and I hold my breath, counting to ten to stuff it all back inside. Once I reach ten, it all pops right out. The tears, the sob, the breath. I tell him how much I love him and hug him tighter, while he hugs me even tighter. I tell him he's my home, too, my bed is his bed, my heart is heart, and he's my world.

CHAPTER TWENTY-NINE

Silas

My first thought is, shit, I've got to take a piss.

I slept better than I've ever slept in my entire life, even though most of it was spent with me awake. It was on purpose, though—goddamn it if I was willingly going to fall asleep and lose the view of Rooney wrapped up in my arms, her head on my arm and her forehead tucked against my chest.

When she let out a soft sigh, completely lost to sleep, and mumbled something that without a doubt sounded like my name, I knew this was it. She's what I want. *This* is what I want for the rest of my life. There'll have to be a real ring, her last name switched for mine, lots of fucking, sex, and lovemaking. The idea of forever doesn't even seem nearly long enough for me and her. How could I have ever tried to deny myself of her? Or acted so sorely toward her? Fuck, if I could go back in time.

I've been trying to remain as still as possible, only moving when she did, afraid the slightest thing might take this from us. I must've dozed off, because I quickly realize my need to piss might have been my first thought, but that wasn't what woke me up. Not a goddamn chance.

The place where Rooney was is empty, her sweet smell hanging around as a reminder of what once was. *Don't freak the fuck out,* I warn myself, because the morning light is sneaking in between her blinds and for all I know, she could be up. She could be taking a piss herself or checking in on Billie or just doing something non-threatening to what we have.

Then a shrill noise breaks through and I know the truth. Everything's about to break apart. Chaos slicing through peace.

Wrong again. *That* was what woke me up.

I throw the covers off my body and trip out of bed with a filthy curse. The phone cuts off mid-ring and I hear Rooney groggily say, "Hello."

Holy hell, Rooney, wait. Just wait for me, baby. Don't let them tell you...

She sobs.

It's an awful, wretched noise, mirroring the noise happening inside my chest as it cracks wide open. I run down the hall to her, heart beating in my ears. I come to a halt when I see her. She's on the floor, legs pulled to her chest and her face buried in her arms and knees. The phone is lying beside her. The back cover that holds the batteries in is inches from it, where she must've dropped the phone and broken it.

I don't have to ask what the call was about. I already know.

I breathe her name and walk toward her slowly, my mind racing as I try to distinguish what's the best maneuver. She looks up at me, tears flooding her eyes, with a look so helpless and in pain, that all of the air rushes from me like I've fallen flat on my back and had the wind knocked out of me.

She swallows and says, "She's gone." Then a sob bubbles back up and she crumples back into her previous position.

She's gone.

Billie's gone.

I didn't know her long, but if I'm being honest, it feels a little like I've lost my own mom. My *mama*, as Rooney prefers to call her. Because Billie is not only a supporter and friend of mine, but she is—was, *fuck*—the mother of the girl I love. Chances are, she would've been in my life forever, just like Rooney. She would've eventually become my mother-in-law, the grandmother to my children, the woman I knew best *not* to piss off, or else my balls would be pinned to the wall.

It hurts so fucking bad and all I want to do is drink it away because once again, why the fucking hell is my goddamn life worth saving when people as good as Billie are given a terminal illness? Are given death? I'm the one who deserves death—up until a couple of months ago, no one would've known if I went missing. My parents didn't even know I was homeless. Sure, they would've mourned, but they have each other. They have Brandon. They have a whole community that would probably gather hands and sing like those damn Whos when the Grinch died. I have no doubt they would've come out of the woodwork to express their apologies, while secretly thanking the lord for my death. But Billie doesn't deserve this. She was a good woman, mother, friend, everything. And through her death, the one perfect human being on this earth, with the most beautiful soul I've ever encountered, will be alone.

No, she'll have you, you dumbass.

She will have me. So long as I give her me. So long as I put the right foot forward, man up, and give her what she needs. My grief, my pain, is nothing compared to Rooney's. The only way to alleviate what I'm feeling is to get her through this. I'm here to do what she did for me, which is to save her.

I drop down beside her and pull her into my lap. She comes willingly. I wrap my arms around her and hold her as tight as I can against my chest, hoping to absorb her sobs and her pain. I know I won't, but I hope she'll at least know she's not alone.

Even if I'm a fucking selfish prick for stealing her away from the safety of a relationship with Brandon, if I wouldn't have done that, she'd be alone right now. I have no doubt she would've sent him home and he would've done what she wanted. If she tried to make me go home, I would've fought tooth and nail to stay with her because it's not about what she wants, it's about what she needs.

And the truth is, selfish prick or not, she needs me. She loves me and I love her and I'm tired of telling myself I'm not enough. Life's too short for that shit.

Poor Billie.

There's a hole now. It's so tangible I can almost feel it. It's visible, too. It's the hole in our lives Billie used to fill. We won't get to see her flirty attitude or her love for Rooney. I won't get to hear the two of them laugh together or hear Billie tease Rooney. I won't get to see her sparkling, mischievous eyes, but they'll stay imprinted in my memory until the day I die. It all will.

How does a person just be there one second and the next they're gone? Missing? Absent? Dead. The hole in my life, though, doesn't even fucking compare to the one in Rooney's.

I don't know what else to do but kiss the top of her head and hold her tighter.

All of a sudden, she stills. She says something muffled, then she's pushing at my chest with strength which has to be coming from the adrenaline of her grief.

I let her go only slightly, afraid she'll hurt herself the way she's acting. "What's wrong, baby?"

She keeps pushing and a small, disgruntled screech come from her. She thrashes and I know my hold on her has to hurt, but I don't know what she's doing.

"Let go of me!" she wails.

"Rooney, shit," I grumble. I grip her tighter and give her a little shake. "What's wrong? Talk to me, baby."

Rooney stops and meets my gaze with desperation. "She's alone, Silas. She's alone—she shouldn't be alone. We have to go—"

"We will." One hand maintains its steel grip on her because she shouldn't be doing anything right now. The last thing I need is her jumping into a car and trying to get to her mama. The other, I bring up to her cheek and brush away her tears. "But you don't want to go to her like this. It'll only make it worse."

She squeezes her eyes shut. "I have to see her."

"I know you do." I loosen my grip, seeing some of her fierce need to run to her mama is disappearing. The tears aren't slowing up, though. I suspect they won't for a long time. "You're my priority, Rooney. I'm not going to let you go in there like this and have you break you apart. You need some time to accept this before we go in there, or else it'll be too much."

She nods and falls back into my chest. Thank God. I rub small circles on her back and say, "Now, I'm gonna call my parents and get them over here with us. Then I'm going to put out a call to the hospital and find out the steps we need to take."

"Don't let me go," she begs in a soft voice.

"I never will," I promise her. "I'll keep you in my arms as long as you need."

CHAPTER THIRTY

Rooney

Mama looked beautiful.

I made sure she was put in her favorite dress—a navy blue and white polka dot dress that came to her knees with an A-line cut. She always pulled it out for special occasions. She called it her hot-damn dress because it not only made her feel gorgeous, but it also made the over-thirty crowd wag their tongue at her. I figured if people were going to be looking at her, she'd want to wear this dress. I even gave the funeral home her favorite sandals, even though they said shoes weren't necessary. I didn't want her feet to be cold. They did her hair and makeup perfectly, too.

She didn't look like the sick mama who will forever haunt my memory until I can separate her from my happy, funny, *alive* mama. She just looked like she was fast asleep after having a long, exciting night out, or a lunch date that wore her out.

As much as I want that to be the case, I'm almost glad it isn't. Sometimes I feel so guilty for feeling relieved, my gut clenches tight and I understand why Silas can be so angry and unforgiving with himself. But the fact is, Mama was sick and in pain and wishing was never going to make her better. The only way she was ever going to get better was to slip away. Her only way of finding peace was passing away and leaving me. It was natural and inevitable, even though it was heartbreaking.

Silas' hand slips into mine and squeezes as all the people who came for Mama's funeral leave for their cars. I was honestly surprised at how many people came to the funeral. I didn't think we were here long enough before Mama got sick for us to form ties. I was wrong.

Rita was here with her family, but I was surprised Dr. Demarco was, too. He gave me a hug and said in a quiet voice that he knew my mama had a crush on him, and had circumstances been different, he thought they would've made a great couple; his eyes were red and scratchy. The ladies and the man at the pharmacy came—because I'm sure they remember me from the zillions of times I burst into tears on them when I saw the cost of Mama's medicine. All of the people from our street came, the people Mama charmed when she went on a barhop when we first got here, an old man Mama once made laugh in the market after his wife had just passed, a young girl who had just lost her own mama and wanted to console me...the list went on and on and it was amazing, because although I knew virtually none of those people, it was the first time I felt like I belonged.

Everyone also seemed to accept Silas, even though he's a pariah to this town. There was something close to approval in some of their eyes as they watched him hold me close and whisper kind, encouraging words in my ears. I could see it, too, when he walked me up and stood with me while I spoke about Mama in front of everyone.

Whenever it felt like my lungs started to fail to work or my eyes started to flood with tears, Silas would sense it and his fingers would casually caress the small of my back while he distracted both me and the crowd from the emotions swirling inside. He'd say something about Mama to make everyone laugh. I knew that there was a reason why I was so drawn to loving him.

Mrs. Manning squeezes the hand of someone who I vaguely recognize and then she, Mr. Manning, and Brandon make their way over to us. I can see Brandon's still mad, but I can tell he's sad, too. He wants to be here for me, but he's not sure how. I hope he knows that I want him to be here for me, too, and vice versa.

"How're you doing?" she asks with a sympathetic, motherly smile I need.

I can't answer her so I just shake my head.

"I know it's not the same—you're so young—but when I lost Mom…it takes a while. Give it time," she tells me. "I promise it'll get better. Not easier, just better."

"I hope so," I say.

"It will," Mr. Manning says confidently.

Mrs. Manning looks affectionately at her husband and then back at Silas and me. He's practically been a part of me all day, which I'm completely okay with. "Are you going to come over to our house and…"

Her words trail off as Silas starts shaking his head. "I'm beat and I'm sure she is, too. I think maybe we'll just go home and sit around."

That sounds absolutely wonderful and I can't help nodding in agreement. I don't think I can pretend to be okay for another second, and he senses it. I doubt he can pretend, either. We've spent a lot of the last few days, when we haven't been planning Mama's funeral, just lying around in each other's arms, napping and talking and sharing secrets. We're creating a world together and I won't give it up. Ever.

"I don't blame you," she says and starts for our car, still parked in the lineup from our drive here. Mr. Manning drove us all here, which was mighty awkward with Silas, Brandon, and me all crammed in the back seat. There was no way I was going to drive today, and Silas definitely couldn't. We didn't have much of a choice, but I was honestly happy for it. They've become a huge part of my life—they're my family.

Mr. Manning follows after her, but Brandon stays in place. His gaze flickers between Silas and me. I know he's not going to start in—he's actually a lot calmer than he was in the hospital parking lot and I hope this will continue forward—but I just can't help wondering what he's going to do. He brings a hand up to the back of his neck and my chest squeezes because he reminds me so much of Silas, and I wonder if either of them can see the resemblance.

All of a sudden, he takes a step forward and Silas overreacts by pulling me into his side like we're magnets. It doesn't hurt, it feels good like it always does when Silas holds me. But it does shock the living daylights out of me.

Brandon holds up his hands. "Just want to give her a hug, man. Not gonna steal her back." He drops his hands and hangs his head, almost saying to the ground, "I still love her, you know. Maybe not in the same way as you, but I *do* love her."

"It's okay, Silas." I step away from Silas, despite his steel grip. "I could use a hug."

Silas growls but doesn't stop it, bless his heart. Brandon closes the space between us and, very hesitantly, wraps his arms around me. I place my cheek against his chest and the situation's genericness overwhelms me. It's nice, but not *nice*. He squeezes me tight and draws a breath in. "I'm so fucking sorry."

I nod against his chest. *Me, too.*

"You'll get through this," he assures me.

I know I will and it's because of the man about to Hulk out in the middle of a cemetery, next to a hearse. I pull away from Brandon. I can tell he hasn't reached the same resolution about our relationship as I have, so I figure that's our only hug for a while. This one might've been too much as it is. Too long, at least.

Silas quickly claims me by wrapping an arm over my shoulders to lead me over to the car.

We slide in, Silas in the middle, because...well. He takes my hand and I lean my head on his shoulder. Mr. Manning starts the ignition and ice-cold fear and panic settle in. My hand reaches to grab the already locked door handle.

Silas, still freaked out, but somewhat used to this after the last few days, leans in as close to me as he can. He uses his free hand to turn my head to look at him. I'm sure I have wild eyes. I feel wild on the inside. Because we're going home. God, we're going home.

And Mama's not

"Hey, baby, what're you doin'?" he asks in a cautious voice.

I pull my lip in between my teeth and try to ignore Mr. Manning, Mrs. Manning, and Brandon's worried stares. "She's going to be lonely. Cold."

Silas stares at me and then blinks, fighting back tears. It's not the first time I've caught him on the verge of crying. Seeing how much he cares—how big his heart is—makes the world seem less claustrophobic and less like it's falling apart. He runs a thumb over my cheekbone.

"Remember how you asked me if I believed in heaven?"

I nod.

"Well, I know I said I believed in hell, so therefore I have to believe in heaven, and that's still the truth. But I believe in heaven for a new reason: you. If we were just animals put on this Earth for the reason of living without a particular existence, then I wouldn't. But the fact that I'm so fucking in love with you that love doesn't even describe what I feel for you, tells me we're not. There's gotta be some higher force giving me the ability to love so deeply and to want things I never thought I could have. And I know, without a doubt your mama is up there, warmed up by her own love and seeing every single face she's ever made smile and every person she's affected. She's watching you and she's waiting for you for when the time's right. She's not alone, Rooney. She's not cold. Her body might be, but she's not. She's still with you." I brush my lips against hers. "Heart, head, memories, everywhere."

I draw in a breath, his gaze so intense and loving, willing me to see his point. I hear his mom sniffling and his dad murmuring things to her and I can see Brandon clearly watching the two of us closely, but none of that matters. All that matters is Silas.

"Step Three: made a decision to turn our will and our lives over to the care of God."

He lets out a breath as if the one I just took in was his. "Exactly."

CHAPTER THIRTY-ONE

Rooney

Five Years Later

"I'm starting to get worried," Silas calls through the door.

"I'm fine," I answer. I pull my legs to my chest and rest my chin on my knees. My back is up against the rim of the bathtub. "There's no need to be worried. I'm just taking a bath."

"Babe, the door's *locked*. You never the lock the door." A pause, then the door rattles. I can image him leaning his forehead against the door or flattening his palm against it. "We both know even when something is completely, horribly wrong, you don't lock the damn door and sure as hell don't lock me out. Besides, I haven't heard any water run."

"That's because I haven't started *taking* my bath yet."

"It's been a half hour."

"Oh." I don't really have a good excuse and it means I'm going to stand up, open the door, and face him.

"If you don't come out here or start talkin', then I'm finding my way in there. You really want a broken bathroom door in our house?" His voice starts to rise and for the millionth time, and I'm surprised he was ever cold, compressed, composed. I don't even remember that version of him and whenever he gets this way, I forget how I ever handled it. I loved that Silas, but I love *my* Silas even more. The one who tickled me senseless the other day, or gets passionate when talking about the people he's sponsoring at the rehab center, or cried with me at Mama's grave this afternoon.

"Today's Mother's Day," he finally says. "You don't need to hide away from me on a day like this."

It's been five years since Mama passed. The first holidays—everywhere from Mother's Day to Christmas to Pie Day—were horrendous. For most of those days I cried. It didn't matter if I was in our bed at home or if I was spending the day at the Mannings', I was crying. Inconsolable, heart-wrenching, unbelievably ugly sobs Silas didn't leave me alone with.

The first year was the hardest and the second year was just as terrible, but it felt watered-down. In the space where I wasn't feeling devastated, I was able to fill in those good memories of Mama. The space got bigger the third year, then the fourth, and then this year. I still haven't gotten used to a life without Mama and I don't think I ever will, but it's not why I'm crying.

Silas knocks lightly against the door. "Baby…"

I let out a sigh. I don't know what I'm so afraid of. I love Silas and he loves me. He immediately moved in with me after Mama's death, although it was more unspoken. Gradually, his things found a home in my house and suddenly everything was ours. Our kitchen. Our garden. Our bed. *Our everything.*

Our engagement was just as unspoken, something I'm actually pretty glad for. After being proposed to in a fancy restaurant—even if it was a failed attempt—I didn't want anything fancy. One night, about six months after Mama's death, I woke up with a terrible tightness in my chest and I couldn't breathe and it felt like I'd just lost her all over again, the day before. Silas woke up immediately and he held me while I cried. Eventually, we started talking back and forth or just lying there in silence, staring at each other, but we were up all night. It felt like that in itself was a proposal of eternity.

When I woke up the next morning, there was a rose on Silas' pillow beside me, looped through a sparkling ring. Beneath it was a piece of paper with the "Twelve Steps of Loving and Being Addicted to Rooney Oliver" and in smaller print, "(Hopefully you'll say yes and be *Rooney Manning*)."

Of course, I said yes.

We got married four months later. We rented a little beach house and the two of us and his parents stayed there, then we got married on the beach. A real, ordained pastor married us and it was special in a different way than the one with Mama, because this one was official. This one made our future together real and concrete. And when I closed my eyes as we faced his parents, I could picture Mama there with me. Smiling, clapping her hands, tears in her eyes. More so, I could feel her in the wind. In the way the sand felt between my toes. In the fact that Silas had found his way to me when I needed him most, and *stayed.*

Even Brandon came, though he still wasn't too comfortable around us. When he met his special girl, the discomfort faded away real quick. I think he understood exactly why we didn't work out and he was probably happy about it, too.

I stand up on my wobbly knees and go to the door. I turn the lock and I'm half surprised Silas doesn't open the door for me. When I pull it open, though, I can see he's about three seconds away from desperate measures. He's the picture of false composure, all stiff and questioning.

He takes in my face. I haven't been crying and I'm sure it shocks him the most. Still, I know I'm probably pale—my cheeks feel like they're drained of blood. If he could hear my heart, he'd know it's not for lack of circulation.

His hands cup my cheeks and I can see the fear in his eyes. The worry. "Did I do something wrong? Are you hurt—what happened…"

I place my hands over his. "It's okay, I promise. I'm fine, you're fine. *We're* fine." I bite my lip because I'm not completely sure how I'm going to tell him what I need to. Well, I guess I'll have to *tell* him tell him, because dropping hints won't work if the "we're fine" was good enough.

Before I can continue, his gaze flickers over my shoulders and to the little sticks I have lined on the bathtub rim. All little plus signs. All positive.

"What are they?" His brow furrows and he takes a step away from me, a step closer to the tests.

I had a few inclinations maybe I was pregnant, so I went to the drugstore this morning and picked up the tests before we did our Mother's Day visits. Nothing abnormal—I was just about two weeks late, my stomach felt swollen, and I was having some nausea. Maybe I was hoping, too.

As happy as I was, I didn't—still don't—know how Silas would react. The subject of kids has been brought up before, but we haven't been actively trying. This is completely accidental, not that we haven't been having a lot of sex. We have been. I just knew I had to be careful because Silas still freaks easily about his past. There are still points where I can see he—although he's lighter—still hates himself. And I know he's terrified whatever it is in him that he finds so disgusting, along with his addictive personality, will pass down to his kids.

Maybe it will, but it also might not. Even if love wasn't enough to keep him away from going down a dark path, it was enough to take him off of it. And we've both got so, so much love to offer our baby.

"We're having a baby, Silas." My hands automatically go to my stomach. How strange is it to have a tiny life from growing inside of me? Half Silas and half me? It's marvelous.

He keeps staring at the pregnancy tests and then he glances over me, his gaze immediately going to my belly. Then my face. I try to smile warmly, but my lips quiver.

"You're afraid?" he asks slowly.

I can't look into his eyes, so I look down at the tile floor. "Yes."

"Why?"

"Because I don't want to disappoint you."

I feel, rather than see, him step closer. The pull between us is still so strong, after all of these years. He grips my waist and bends his knees to look into my eyes. "You can never disappoint me. Sure, maybe you thinking you need to lock yourself away because you're afraid of how I react is a little alarming, but I love you and I'll love this baby."

My eyes widen and my heart fills with love. Here I didn't think it was possible to love him any more.

He chuckles. "Don't look so surprised. That baby is as much yours as it is mine and that's not something I can *not* be happy about. When I met you, kissed you, made love to you, proposed to you, married you, *everything*, I intended for us to be a family and have a family."

I don't know what else to do but throw my arms around his neck and bury my face deep in his chest. "I love you."

"I love you, too." He kisses my neck, just below my ear. "And I love our little Billie or Billy."

I pull away. "You want to name our baby after Mama?"

He nods as if he's surprised I'm on the same level. "Yeah."

I bury my face in him again. I whisper words of love and he whispers them back and I realize Silas has been running all of his life, but maybe it's not away from something. Maybe it's toward something—me, us, this baby. Maybe he's made as many wrong choices as he has good, but it's all led him here and those good choices will soon outweigh the good. The thing is, life's just more than choices and Steps.

It's about living.

ACKNOWLEDGEMENTS

I've always said that my dream is to create a special space for my readers, as so many other authors have done for me. Because of Melissa Keir and Inkspell publishing, I'm working toward that dream; I'm indescribably thankful and proud of the opportunity they have given me. I'm also very thankful to my professors and classmates at Northern Kentucky University who molded me into the writer and woman I am today. However, I don't think I would've made it without a few close friends: Megan Collins, Chelsea Parman, Megan Parsons, and Brittany Smart. They each encouraged me throughout varying stages of this process and gave me the courage I needed to send *Step Toward You* out into the real world. Lastly, I would like to thank my mom and dad for creating the foundation for my firm belief in love's existence. Their marriage, my friendship with them, and our family were the sources of my inspiration.

Beyond this, I would also like to acknowledge the strength of anyone who has experienced tragedy of any kind—whether it has happened to them or happened around them—and has come out on the other side. You make me believe in happy-endings not only in fiction, but in real life.

ABOUT THE AUTHOR

Liz Ashlee is a romance novelist who recently graduated from Northern Kentucky University with her B.A. in English and B.S. in Library Informatics. She has been published in *Loch Norse Magazine* and *The Pentangle*, and has won the Miller Award for Outstanding Fiction Writing. She currently lives in Independence, Kentucky, with her family and dog-daughter, Hero.

Facebook: https://www.facebook.com/LizAshleeAuthor/
Twitter: https://twitter.com/LizAshleeAuthor
Instagram:
https://www.instagram.com/LizAshleeAuthor/?hl=en
Blog: http://liz-ashlee.com/

CHECK OUT...ANOTHER STORY BY LIZ ASHLEE

BROOKE MOSS, LIZ ASHLEE, CLARA WINTER,
TAMMY MANNERSLY, SARAH VANCE-TOMPKINS,
KITSY CLARE, MARK LOVE, MELISSA KAY CLARKE

Beaches, boyfriends and danger...summer is certainly hot! Grab a hold tight as these eight authors wow you with stories from sweet to sizzling! After all, every day can have some summer fun!

Breaking Girl Code by Brooke Moss

Aubrey is having the perfect evening out, with the perfect guy, on a perfect summer night The problem is... Preston's not her date. His real date is her B.F.F., and she's passed out in the backseat.

Wishing on Water by Liz Ashlee

After watching everyone's else's lives hit huge milestones, all Hope wants is to escape to her boring, unchanging, single life. So, where's the one logical place to escape to? *A retirement home.*

Art with a Pulse by Clara Winter

Artist Alice finds herself rescuing a seal on the sands of Laguna Beach with screenwriter Elijah. Can Alice put her past behind her and give Elijah the chance he deserves?

A Natural Passion by Tammy Mannersly

How will marine biologist, Dylan O'Day, solve the illegal poaching problem threatening the ecosystem he loves and protects when the gorgeous, new intern, Kyra Shine, is occupying his every thought?

You Had Me at Aloha by Sarah Vance Tompkins

Social media guru Vivienne Parker's dream trip to Hawaii turns into a nightmare when her roommate in the luxurious surf shack is the hot Olympic athlete who just got her fired.

More Than Puppy Love by Kitsy Clare

Fireworks spark when Arianna, a city girl with an elite pet portrait business is in a wreck and asks Dave a country auto mechanic for help, but can these two beagle owners from different worlds see eye to eye?

Stealing Haven by Mark Love

Sand, sun, romance and a mystery to solve. Sounds like a perfect vacation for Jamie.

Harmony in the Key of Murder by Melissa Kay Clarke

Summer in the South can mean a different type of heat when a newly appointed investigator and a mechanical genius cross paths leading to murder and love.

AVAILABLE IN EBOOK AND PRINT AT ALL MAJOR RETAILERS.